AN EVIL MIND
A Suspense Novel

AN EVIL MIND

How do you stop a serial killer who can escape from any prison?

On December 11, fifteen-year-old Helen Hinton is brutally murdered in an abandoned house. Her killer, Edward Phillips, is caught and sentenced to death. Helen's blood was on Edward's clothes and shoes, the murder weapon has his fingerprints on it.

Edward claims he's innocent. He's telling the truth.

Two months after Edward Phillips is transferred to death row, a murder similar to Helen's occurs in another city. The victim is eighteen-year-old Laura Sumner.

On an October morning, Mark Hinton, Helen's father, visits Edward in prison to talk about Laura Sumner's case. Edward tells him that he knows who really killed Helen.

What he doesn't tell Mark is that the real killer is the most dangerous criminal on the planet.

TIM KIZER

AN EVIL MIND

Also by Tim Kizer

The Girl Who Didn't Die
The Vanished
Spellbound
Mania
The Mindbender
Days of Vengeance

Copyright 2016 Tim Kizer

All rights reserved.

This book contains material protected under International and Federal Copyright Laws and Treaties. Any unauthorized reprint or use of this material is prohibited. No part of this book may be reproduced or transmitted in any form or by any means, electronic or mechanical, including photocopying, recording, or by any information storage and retrieval system without express written permission from the author/publisher.

Published in the United States of America.

CONTENTS

An Evil Mind 1
A sample chapter from The Vanished. . 291

AN EVIL MIND

AN EVIL MIND

TIM KIZER

Chapter 1

1

She had a tender face with a small pimple on her left cheek. Her lipstick was a mess; he had smeared it when he pressed a chloroform-soaked rag against her mouth and nose forty minutes ago. Her blue puffer jacket was open, revealing a white T-shirt that read: "They Hate Us Cause They Ain't Us."

"What's your name, sweetheart?" he asked.

"Helen."

The girl's eyes were bulging with terror.

"How old are you?"

"Fifteen."

"If you scream, I'll kill you."

Helen lay on the floor with trash strewn around her, and he was hunkered down beside her, his elbows on his knees. Lit only by a lantern, the room was dim. The cold breath of the winter night flowed into the house through a broken window in the kitchen.

The girl couldn't put up much resistance as her wrists were bound behind her back with rope.

"Are you going to rape me?" Helen whimpered.

He liked the girl's straightforwardness. And he found it amusing that Helen thought she could get an honest answer. Grinning, he said, "Yes. Yes, I am. I'll be very gentle, I promise."

It was a lie; this was not about sex. He lied to put the girl at ease. (He would love to have sex with Helen, but it was not why he had brought her here.)

"Please don't kill me," the girl pleaded. "I won't tell anyone, I swear."

The girl was breathing rapidly, tears running down her thin cheeks, her face scrunched up, her upper lip wet with snot.

"You won't tell anyone?"

"No, I won't."

"Good."

AN EVIL MIND

He pulled Helen's T-shirt up to her neck and pressed his hand against the girl's chest. He could feel Helen's heart hammering wildly under his fingers.

Helen wasn't flat-chested, but her tits were too small for his taste.

"Don't be scared. Everything will be all right."

"Don't kill me, please."

"Have you ever done anything with a boy?"

"No."

He slid his hand into her panties and rubbed her pubes. Her crotch was smooth.

"You shave down there," he said.

His penis was as hard as a rock. The urge to fuck Helen grew stronger by the second.

It would only take a few minutes.

No, he couldn't have sex with her. He didn't have a condom with him. You should never rape without a condom unless you want the police to have your DNA.

He reached behind him and picked up the knife from the floor.

"Please don't kill me," Helen whined. When she shifted her eyes to the knife, she had seen the barbwire tattoo that circled the man's wrist.

He slipped the blade under the front strap of Helen's bra and cut it in two.

"I'm not going to kill you."

The girl seemed to breathe a sigh of relief.

He raised the knife and plunged it into the girl's left breast, piercing the heart. When he pulled out the blade, two drops of blood splattered on Helen's face. He looked at the wound in Helen's chest for a moment and then stabbed the girl in the right breast.

He shivered with excitement. The young bitch was dead.

I did it again, and I didn't falter.

He sank the blade into the girl's abdomen, just below the sternum, and ripped it open. He stopped cutting when the knife reached Helen's groin.

After he yanked the knife out of Helen's belly, he saw that a thin stream of water had trickled out from under the girl's thigh. His eyes fell on the large dark stain on the crotch of the girl's pants, and he realized that Helen had peed herself.

He stood up, placed the knife in a plastic bag, and picked up the lantern from the floor.

"They hate us cause they ain't us," he muttered under his breath as he walked to the car.

Chapter 2

1

The visiting room was cold. Mark Hinton felt that he would be able to see his breath if the temperature dropped just one degree.

He lifted the receiver off the hook, wiped it on his suit coat, and put it to his ear. Then he propped his elbows on the metal counter.

"Did you read my letter?" Edward Phillips asked.

Phillips was dressed in a white sleeveless uniform, which had the letters DR printed on its back. The fluorescent lights gave his skin a greenish-gray cast. His shoulders hunched, his face haggard, with dark circles under his eyes, Phillips looked broken and hopeless, which made Mark feel satisfied, even gleeful. It was great that his daughter's killer was miserable. Murderers didn't deserve to be happy; they deserved to suffer the same fate as their victims had.

The thing that angered Mark the most was that it was going to be a long time before the appeal process was completed and Edward Phillips was executed—probably over ten years.

"Yes," Mark said.

"I was afraid you wouldn't come."

"Why did you kill my daughter?"

"I didn't kill your daughter."

"Was she alive when you cut open her stomach?"

"I didn't kill her."

"Did you cut open her stomach before or after you stabbed her in the heart?"

"Mark, I didn't kill your daughter. I swear."

Mark pictured himself pulling a gun from the holster and shooting Phillips in the forehead. He had been fantasizing about killing Phillips every day since Phillips was charged with Helen's murder. Sometimes he imagined himself strangling the bastard with his bare hands, sometimes beating him to death with a baseball bat, and sometimes disemboweling him.

If he was ever going to shoot Edward Phillips, it would not take place here. Although Mark was a cop (he was a detective with the Robbery Unit of the Dallas Police Department), he was not allowed to bring a firearm into the visiting room.

"Yes, you did."

"Do you know how many death row inmates have been exonerated in the last forty years? One hundred and fifty."

"They were exonerated because they were innocent. You are not innocent."

"Let's talk about Laura Sumner."

"Okay."

Mark had received a letter from Phillips a week ago. He recognized the sender's name as soon as he saw it, and his first impulse was to throw the letter away without reading it. Then he changed his mind and, wondering if Phillips wrote to ask forgiveness for killing Helen, opened the envelope. The letter read:

"Dear Mark,

I have important information about the murder of your daughter, Helen. Six weeks ago, a woman by the name of Laura Sumner was murdered in Austin. She was killed the same way as your daughter. I think it would be a good idea for you to talk to your colleagues in Austin about this case. Why? I'll tell you why: the man who killed Helen killed Laura Sumner.

Please verify that what I told you about Laura Sumner is true. You can't take my word for it, can you? After you talk to your colleagues in Austin, come see me. I know who killed Laura Sumner. You can find me at the Allan B. Polunsky Unit in Livingston, Texas. My inmate ID number is 01999593.

Regards,
Edward Phillips."

AN EVIL MIND

The next day Mark logged into the Austin Police Department's crime database and searched for homicide cases in which the victim's name was Laura Sumner (he limited the search to cases opened after July 31).

There was one match. The victim was eighteen years old at the time of her death. She had been killed on August 23; the time of death was estimated to be between eight p.m. and midnight. The police believed the murder had taken place in the abandoned house on Felix Avenue where Laura Sumner's body had been discovered. Helen had been murdered in an abandoned house, too.

Mark's arms broke out in gooseflesh as he looked at the pictures of Laura's body. There were two stab wounds on the young woman's chest: one in the right breast and one in the left. Her abdomen had been cut open from the sternum to the groin.

What Edward Phillips had said was true: Laura Sumner had been killed the same way as Helen.

An image rose in his mind of Helen's dead body lying on a morgue slab, and his heart twisted with pain.

Mark scanned the autopsy report and saw that no evidence of sexual assault had been found. Helen's postmortem examination had revealed no evidence of rape, either.

Laura Sumner's case was still open. The police had no suspects.

"Did you talk to Austin cops about the Sumner case?" Phillips asked.

"No. I looked through the case file."

"Good. Did you verify that Laura was killed the same way as your daughter?"

"Yes."

"Do you agree that Laura was killed by the man who murdered your daughter?"

"I know who killed Helen—you."

Phillips shook his head. "How well do you sleep, Mark?"

"Why do you care?"

"Do you have nightmares?"

Mark nodded.

Although it had been ten months since Helen's murder, Mark still had nightmares. They were vivid, terrifying, and hard to wake up from. He had thought they would stop after Edward Phillips was sentenced to death, but he had been wrong.

His wife, Joan, still had nightmares, too.

"Do you see your daughter in your dreams?"

"Yes."

Phillips leaned forward and said, "I wouldn't be able to sleep at night if I knew that the man who killed my daughter was walking free."

"The man who killed my daughter is on death row."

"I can't expect you to believe me. But what I want you to do is ask yourself: what if Ed Phillips is telling the truth? What if the real killer is out there enjoying life?"

"You are the real killer."

"I swear on my mother's life that I did not kill your daughter."

If Edward Phillips was executed in ten years, he would have lived twenty-seven years longer than Helen. That was unfair.

Mark glanced at his watch. "Is there anything else you want to tell me?"

"I know who killed Laura Sumner."

"Who is it?"

"I'll give you the name after you admit that there's a chance Laura Sumner was killed by the man who murdered your daughter."

"All right. I think there's a chance Laura Sumner was killed by the man who murdered Helen. Now give me the name."

"His name's Sam Curtis. We shared a cell for a month in the county jail last winter."

"How do you know he killed Laura Sumner?"

"Sam told me he killed your daughter, and we know that Laura and Helen were killed by the same person."

"We don't know that."

"Okay. They were probably killed by the same person."

"I don't believe you."

"You don't believe Sam Curtis told me he killed Helen?"

"Would you believe that if you were me?"

"I wouldn't dismiss that out of hand, that's for sure."

Phillips must be lying, but what did he have to gain? It was the appellate court that he needed to convince of his innocence not the victim's father.

"Why didn't you tell the prosecutor that Curtis confessed to killing Helen?"

"Because no one would have believed me. You don't believe me."

"What am I supposed to do with this information?"

"I'm sure Sam will kill again. You could follow him and catch him in the act."

"Suppose I catch him in the act. How does that help you? Do you think he'll confess to killing Helen?"

"No."

"Then what's in this for you?"

"I want Sam Curtis to pay for his crimes." Phillips paused. "Please don't confront him or tell the police about him. If he finds out the cops are onto him, he'll disappear and change his identity."

"When did Curtis tell you that he killed Helen?"

"The day he was released from jail."

"Did he know you were accused of killing my daughter?"

"No."

Mark tilted his head to one side and saw a handprint on the glass that separated him from Phillips. He pictured an inmate pressing his palm against the window and his visitor aligning her hand with his on the other side.

"You know why Curtis told me that he murdered Helen?" Phillips said.

"Why?"

"He trusted me. And I can prove it."

"How?"

"He told me that he robbed a convenience store in Garland in April of last year. The name of the store was Eddie's Mini Mart. Sam hid the gun he'd used in the robbery in the air vent in his master bedroom. He said it was a nine-millimeter Heckler & Koch."

"What do you want me to do?"

"Get the gun and see if it was used in that robbery. Sam said he fired his gun at the ceiling to scare the store clerk. Your guys must have extracted the bullet."

Inside every pistol barrel there were spiral grooves (also known as rifling) that gave the bullet a spin, which increased its accuracy. The marks left by the rifling (ballistics examiners called them "striations") allowed a bullet to be traced to the gun it had been shot from because each barrel had a unique set of grooves.

Would the jury find Curtis guilty of robbery if the pistol was the only evidence against him? Mark supposed it was going to depend on the skill of his lawyer.

"You think he'll let me search the air vent in his bedroom?"

"You can do it when he's not home."

"You want me to break into his place?"

"If you get caught, you can say you heard screams inside."

"Do you want him to go to prison for robbing that convenience store?"

"No. I told you about this robbery to prove that Sam trusted me, that he shared his secrets with me."

There was a desperate, imploring look in Phillips's deep-set gray eyes, and for a moment it seemed as if he was going to tear up.

"All right. Let me think about it."

"Can I ask you for a favor?"

"What do you want?"

"Can you give me your cellphone number?"

"Are you going to call me?"

"Is it okay if I call you? I'll do it only when I have something important to tell you, I promise."

"Okay, you can call."

Mark told Phillips his cellphone number and then, at Phillips's request, repeated it twice.

"Is it okay if I write you letters?" Phillips asked. "I'm allowed to make only one phone call every ninety days."

"Okay, you can write me letters."

2

On the way home Mark thought about the things Helen had not done and would never be able to do because of Edward Phillips. His daughter would never graduate high school, go to college, drive her own car, or get married and have kids.

When Mark learned of Helen's murder, the life had gone out of him, and he had not felt happy since. Many people drowned their sorrows in booze. Mark didn't enjoy alcohol, so he couldn't use it to ease the pain caused by Helen's death.

He parked in front of his house, took out his wallet, and pulled Helen's photo from it. As he looked at the picture, sorrow squeezed his heart with its thorny hand.

They shouldn't have given Helen so much freedom. If Helen had had an eight p.m. curfew, she wouldn't have been murdered by Edward Phillips.

Mark got out of the car and went into the house. The delicious smell of baked chicken permeated the air, making Mark remember that he hadn't eaten since this morning.

Joan sat on the couch in the living room, watching something on her laptop. Her eyes were red and puffy, as if she had been crying.

"What are you watching?" Mark sat down next to her.

On the screen, Helen, dressed in shorts and a T-shirt, was guzzling milk from a bottle. Her friend Dennis, clad only in shorts, was standing a few feet from her, doing the same thing.

Joan was watching a video of Helen and Dennis competing to see who could drink a gallon of milk the fastest without vomiting. Helen had filmed the video, which was forty-two minutes long, in August of last year in their backyard. Neither Helen nor Dennis had managed to finish their bottles, and both of them had puked.

Helen had posted the video on the Internet the day she had made it, and Joan had found it two days after her death.

Mark had watched the milk video at least fifty times, and Joan probably at least twice that many.

He felt tears well in his eyes, and he blinked them back.

"Why did this happen to us?" Joan sniffled.

Mark wrapped his arms around Joan and kissed her on the cheek.

"Are you hungry?" Joan asked.

"A little."

In the kitchen, Mark put two pieces of chicken and some rice on a plate and sat down at the table. When he began to eat, Joan asked, "Where have you been?"

"Livingston."

"Where is it?"

"About two hundred miles from Dallas. I went there to see Edward Phillips."

"Why?"

"I got a letter from him last week. He said he had something important to tell me."

"You never told me he sent you a letter."

"I didn't think it was important."

AN EVIL MIND

"So what did he tell you?"

"He said that he's innocent and that he knows who killed Helen."

"When are they going to execute this son of a bitch?"

They were silent for half a minute, and then Joan said, "Phillips said he knows who killed Helen. Did he tell you who it was?"

"Last August, a young woman was killed in Austin in the same manner as Helen. Phillips said she was murdered by the guy who killed Helen."

"Does he know his name?"

"No."

"What's that woman's name?"

"Laura Sumner."

Joan stood up, put a tea bag in a cup, filled the cup with hot water from the kettle, and said, "He's lying. I'm sure of it."

Mark nodded.

"I hate him so much," Joan said.

They both thanked God that their daughter's killer had been caught so quickly.

The police had gotten their first lead just hours after they arrived at the crime scene: there was a fingerprint on Helen's belt buckle that didn't belong to her. They ran the print through the database and found that it belonged to Edward Phillips. Phillips's fingerprints were in the system because he had been arrested for driving while intoxicated two years before (Phillips must be really pissed about that arrest).

Phillips was arrested at home at seven p.m. the day after Helen's murder.

The police discovered three small blood stains on Phillips's Levi's jeans and traces of blood on the soles of his Timberland boots. DNA tests revealed that the blood belonged to Helen. They searched Phillips's house for the murder weapon and didn't find it.

Phillips had no drugs in his system on the day of Helen's murder, so it wasn't mind-altering substances that made him kill her. The police suggested two possible motives for the murder. According to one theory, Phillips killed Helen to cover up a rape he'd been unable to complete. According to the other, he was a psychopath who enjoyed killing.

3

Joan was staring at the TV remote as if it were the most interesting thing in the world.

"We should have bought her a Taser," Joan said, running her thumb along the side of the TV remote.

"Who?"

Helen used to say that when she put batteries in the remote, she felt as if she were loading a shotgun.

"Helen. If she'd had a Taser, she'd still be alive. She would have tased Phillips and run away."

If Helen had been home with the flu that day, she would still be alive, Mark thought.

Mark took Joan's hand and squeezed it lightly. Sighing heavily, Joan put the remote on the coffee table.

The more Mark thought about what Edward Phillips had said, the more convinced he became that he should look into his claims. He would have dismissed Phillips's assertions if there had been a videotape of him killing Helen, but there was no such tape, and therefore it was possible Phillips was telling the truth.

Who had murdered Laura Sumner?

Was it a copycat? Helen's murder had not been a high-profile case and not many people had followed it, so the likelihood of it being imitated was quite low. On the other hand, all it took was one lunatic with an itch to kill. The lunatic would have had no problem finding out how Helen had been killed because it had been described in detail in the newspapers.

They say that the simplest answer is usually the correct one. In this case, the simplest theory was that there was no connection between Laura Sumner's and Helen's murders. For some reason Mark felt that this theory was wrong.

Could Laura Sumner have been killed by the bastard that had murdered Helen? Mark supposed it was conceivable.

He had hated Edward Phillips for so long that he found it very hard to believe anything the man said. However, he was willing to listen to Phillips and to investigate his claims. Call it curiosity.

How did Phillips know what the killer had done to Laura Sumner? Had it been reported in the newspapers?

Mark opened his laptop, typed "Laura Sumner stabbed in the chest cut open stomach" into the search box, and pressed the Enter button. The top search result was a story on the website of NBC's Austin affiliate, which mentioned that Laura Sumner had two stab wounds in her chest and that her abdomen had been cut open.

That night, before going to bed, Mark put a screwdriver in his jacket pocket: he was going to use it to remove the vent cover screws at Sam Curtis's place tomorrow.

He didn't fall asleep until three in the morning, and he knew exactly what kept him awake: when Phillips received his sentence, Mark had regained a semblance of emotional balance, and now it was gone.

Chapter 3

1

On Monday, October 9, Mark called Glenn Baxley, the Assistant Warden of the Dallas County Jail, and asked him to confirm that Sam Curtis and Edward Phillips had shared a cell for a month last winter. Baxley said he would call back within an hour.

After talking to the assistant warden, Mark ran the address of Eddie's Mini Mart through the system and found that the convenience store had been robbed on April tenth of last year. The perpetrator had made off with nine hundred and ninety dollars. The case was still unsolved.

The robber had worn a ski mask and carried a pistol. He had fired a shot at the ceiling of the store, and the bullet had been recovered. Mark was pleased to see that the images of the bullet's rifling marks had been added to the ballistics database.

He spent the next half hour studying the incident report for the armed robbery of the McDonald's restaurant on Grand Avenue and Meadow Street that had occurred last night. When he was finished with the report, he began searching for information on Sam Curtis.

Sam Curtis was thirty, two years younger than Edward Phillips. He had been booked into the Dallas County Jail for drunk driving and resisting arrest on December 16 of last year, five days after Helen's murder. He was released on bail on January 13 of this year. At the end of January, Curtis accepted a plea bargain and was sentenced to time served.

Curtis's bail had been only three thousand dollars. A bondsman's fee for posting it would have been about three hundred bucks. Why had it taken Curtis almost a month to come up with the money?

At the time of his arrest last December Curtis resided at 4540 Spring Lane, Dallas. Mark punched Sam Curtis's driver's

AN EVIL MIND

license number into the Department of Motor Vehicles' database and scanned the information that appeared on the screen.

Curtis didn't live at 4540 Spring Lane, Dallas anymore. Last February he changed his address to 2111 Walnut Avenue, Arlington. Mark ran Curtis's old address through the database and found that Tyler and Rhona Stelter currently resided there.

The only vehicle registered to Curtis was a four-year-old Mazda 6.

Mark's plan was to go to the Stelters' house later today, after he interviewed the employees of the McDonald's on Grand Avenue.

If the Stelters refused to cooperate, he would not request a search warrant.

Could this be a trap?

He doubted it was a trap, but he would watch his back anyway.

The chances were small that the gun was still in the air vent: people usually didn't leave their firearms behind when they moved.

The Assistant Warden of the Dallas County Jail called at nine-thirty. He told Mark that Curtis and Phillips had shared a cell from December 17 to January 12.

2

The house at 4540 Spring Lane was a one-story bungalow with an attached garage. A gray Honda Accord sat in the driveway. As Mark climbed the porch, he heard a TV murmuring inside. He unsnapped the clasp on his holster. He needed only two seconds to draw his gun and fire a round.

Strangely, part of him wanted the Stelters to refuse to let him in.

He pushed the doorbell button. The chimes rang cheerfully. A dark-haired man in a wife-beater and shorts opened the door. Mark held up his badge and said, "I'm

Detective Mark Hinton with the Dallas Police Department. Can I come in?"

"What is this about?"

"The previous tenants left something important in this house, and I came to retrieve it."

The man stepped back. "Please come in."

Mark went inside. In the living room, the man grabbed a remote from the coffee table and muted the TV. "What did they leave?"

"You'll see. What's your name?"

"Tyler."

"Tyler Stelter?"

"Yes."

Tyler was not carrying a gun: there were no bulges in his pockets or wife-beater.

"Where's the master bedroom?"

"Let me show you." Tyler led Mark to the master bedroom, which adjoined the kitchen.

"Do you know who lived here before you?" Mark asked, looking around the room.

"No," Tyler replied. "Did they leave something valuable?"

"When did you move here?"

"Last March."

Mark patted his pants pocket to see if the screwdriver he had brought with him was there. Then he took out a pair of latex gloves and slipped them on. Tyler Stelter stood by the dresser with his arms folded across his chest, silently watching him. Pointing to the air vent, which was located above the door, Mark asked, "Have you ever removed this vent cover?"

"No."

"Do you mind if I remove it?"

"No, I don't."

"Can you bring me a chair, please?"

"Sure." Tyler walked out of the room. When he came back, he carried a wooden dining chair. He stood in the doorway and asked, "Here?"

Mark nodded, and Tyler put the chair down.

"Thank you." Mark climbed onto the chair.

"Did the people who lived here before us put that thing in there?"

Mark peered through the grille, and saw only blackness.

"Yes."

Mark pulled out the screwdriver and undid the cover screws. He put the screws and the screwdriver in his shirt pocket, removed the cover, and looked inside the vent.

There was a pistol in the duct. Covered with dust, it lay about five inches from the edge of the vent hole. Mark picked up the gun with two fingers and took it out of the duct.

It was a nine-millimeter Heckler & Koch USP. Its serial number had been filed off.

Mark was surprised by how excited he was to see the gun. Edward Phillips's story had checked out: Sam Curtis had indeed told Phillips where he had hidden his Heckler & Koch. Phillips's credibility had just grown a little.

The question now was, had this pistol been used in the Eddie's Mini Mart robbery?

If he dropped the gun off at the crime lab today, he would have the answer tomorrow.

"It's a gun," Tyler said.

Mark stepped off the chair, laid the vent cover on the floor, and placed the pistol in a plastic bag.

Why hadn't Curtis come to get his gun back? It was eight months since he had moved.

Maybe he had kicked the bucket shortly after he moved.

"Are those people criminals?" Tyler asked.

"They're suspects." Mark stripped off the gloves and shoved them in his jacket pocket.

"What are they suspected of?"

"Robbery. This is confidential information, so don't share it with anyone."

"What if they come here to get their gun?"

"Don't let them in."

"What if they break in?"

"Call the police."

Tyler frowned. "Have they ever killed anyone?"

"No."

"Do you think we should move?"

Mark shook his head. Tyler still looked worried.

"If they come to you, call me." Mark handed Tyler his card.

He and Rhona are probably going to move, he thought.

"Can you put the cover back in place?" Mark pointed at the vent.

"Yes."

"Thank you." Mark took the screws from his shirt pocket and gave them to Tyler.

3

On the drive to Dallas PD headquarters Mark came up with a new theory.

Maybe Edward Phillips had gotten one of his friends to kill someone the same way he had murdered Helen. Maybe that friend had helped him kill Helen. It could be his folks that Phillips had gotten to imitate Helen's murder: most parents would do anything for their children, and Mark figured some of them would take an innocent life.

After dusting Sam Curtis's gun, Mark found two full fingerprints on the grip and one on the barrel. He lifted the prints and then went to the Crime Scene Response Section, where he asked the specialist to run the prints through the system. The specialist's name was Lydia Afonso. She had a sweet face and wore her hair in a ponytail.

"It's urgent," Mark said.

"It's always urgent," Lydia replied.

Ten minutes later, she gave Mark a report, which said that all three fingerprints belonged to Sam Curtis.

The fingerprints proved that the Heckler & Koch hadn't been planted in the vent by Sam Curtis's enemies.

When Mark got back to his desk, he wiped the pistol clean with a paper towel and sealed it in an evidence bag. Then he called assistant wardens of the Allan B. Polunsky Unit and the Dallas County Jail and asked them to send Edward Phillips's visitor logs. Both assistant wardens promised to provide the information tomorrow.

4

Mark arrived at the crime lab at ten minutes past nine. The building was quiet. As Mark filled out the laboratory submission form, a wave of doubt washed over him.

Was it wise to let the convicted killer of his daughter influence him? Had he betrayed Helen by thinking that Phillips might be innocent?

In his mind's eye Mark saw Helen looking down at him from heaven, shaking her head disapprovingly.

Phillips is pulling the wool over my eyes.

Or maybe not.

If it turned out that Sam Curtis's gun had not been used in the Eddie's Mini Mart robbery, he would stop the investigation.

When Mark handed him the submission form and the pistol, the clerk, a bald black man in his thirties, said, "Want to hear a joke?"

"Sure."

"What's the difference between boogers and spinach?"

"What?"

"You can't get your kids to eat spinach." The clerk's face broke into a broad grin.

A moment later, Mark burst out laughing.

"It's a funny joke," he said.

"My son told it to me. He's ten."

I had a daughter. She was murdered when she was fifteen, Mark said in his head.

If this conversation had taken place in the first three months after Helen's death, he would have said that out loud: back then he had told anyone who would listen about what had happened to his daughter. He hadn't done it to get sympathy — he didn't care for sympathy. He had thought that talking about his tragedy eased his pain.

After leaving the crime lab, Mark went to Sam Curtis's house to see if he was still alive. Luckily, he did not have to stake out Curtis's place: Curtis's Mazda 6 was sitting in the driveway when Mark arrived there.

Sam Curtis was still alive, so it was possible that he had murdered Laura Sumner.

AN EVIL MIND

Chapter 4

1

The next morning Mark wrote Carlos Aguero, the lead detective on the Laura Sumner case, an email saying that he would like to discuss the Sumner case with him. Mark asked the detective to call him at his convenience.

As he typed the message, an idea occurred to him. If Sam Curtis was Laura Sumner's killer, he might have used his credit card in Austin to pay for a hotel room, gas, or food. He needed to look at Curtis's credit card transactions that had taken place last August. After he emailed Aguero, Mark requested a search warrant for Sam Curtis's credit and bank card records for the last two months. In his request he stated that Sam Curtis was a person of interest in the investigation of the pharmacy robbery that had occurred on September 20.

From nine to ten-thirty Mark interrogated Rory Hargadon, who had robbed a pizza shop in Dallas yesterday. Hargadon had been arrested shortly after fleeing the crime scene. Mark's efforts were successful: Hargadon confessed to the robbery.

When he checked his email after the interrogation, he found messages from the Allan B. Polunsky Unit and the Dallas County Jail containing Edward Phillips's visitor logs.

Mark started with the visitor log from the county jail. Four people had visited Phillips while he was in the Dallas County Sheriff's custody: Jeff Phillips (his father), Emily Phillips (his mother), Leonard Barlow (his attorney), and Christopher Novak (Mark had no idea who it was). The email from the county jail said that recordings of the visits had been deleted.

Besides Mark, the only person who had come to see Phillips in the Allan B. Polunsky Unit was Leonard Barlow.

The idea that it was Phillips's lawyer who had murdered Laura Sumner, or hired someone to do it, was so far-fetched that Mark discarded it right away.

Christopher Novak had visited Phillips twice: on December 20 and January 24. He was probably Phillips's close friend: people usually didn't visit their casual acquaintances in jail. And he might be loyal enough to kill for Phillips.

Maybe Novak was Phillips's accomplice in Helen's murder.

Mark logged into the DMV database and looked up Novak's record. Novak was twenty-nine years old and lived in Irving. He had no rap sheet.

He should talk to Novak about the conversations he had had with Edward Phillips in the county jail.

Jeff Phillips had visited his son four times; his last visit was on January 6. Emily Phillips had visited her son two times; her last visit was on December 27.

Edward Phillips's parents hadn't visited him since January 6. Why?

Had they passed away?

Had they disowned him for murdering a child?

Would he have visited Edward Phillips in prison if he were in Jeff and Emily Phillips's shoes?

He probably would. Parents were supposed to love their children no matter what, right?

After studying the visitor logs, Mark did some research on Phillips's parents.

Edward Phillips's father was fifty-six and resided in Carrollton. Phillips's mother was fifty-five and lived with Jeff Phillips in Carrollton. Apparently, Jeff and Emily Phillips were still married.

Emily Phillips had no criminal record. Jeff Phillips had been charged with assault twenty-nine years ago, but the case had been dismissed. He hadn't been charged with a crime ever since. Evidently, Jeff Phillips was capable of physical violence.

Men in their mid-fifties were typically strong enough to overpower an eighteen-year-old girl. Mark wasn't sure if the same was true for women.

Two months after Helen's death Mark had learned that Jeff Phillips was a professor of sociology at the University of Texas at Dallas. Mark checked the faculty list on the university's website and saw that Jeff still taught at the UT (which meant he was still alive).

Mark had never inquired about Emily Phillips's occupation.

2

As Mark prepared an application for a search warrant for Christopher Novak's credit and bank card records, his phone rang. It was Peter Franken from the crime lab.

"I've just finished testing the Heckler & Koch you gave us," Franken said. "The test bullets match the bullet from the robbery of Eddie's Mini Mart in Garland, which took place on April tenth of last year."

The test bullets matched the bullet recovered from Eddie's Mini Mart. This meant that Sam Curtis's pistol had really been used in that robbery.

"Thank you, Peter. Was the mini mart robbery the only hit?"

"Yes, it was."

There was no doubt now that Sam Curtis had told Edward Phillips he had robbed Eddie's Mini Mart. And the evidence supported the conclusion that Curtis had committed that robbery.

Why had Curtis told Phillips about the Eddie's Mini Mart robbery?

Perhaps because he was a blowhard.

Why had he told Phillips where he had hidden the gun?

Perhaps because he was stupid.

He might have been stupid enough to confess to his cellmate that he had murdered a fifteen-year-old girl.

It was important to keep in mind that so far he had seen no evidence that Sam Curtis had killed Helen or Laura Sumner. And...

Mark's thoughts were interrupted by his cellphone. It was an unknown number. He tapped the Answer button.

"Hello."

"This is Edward Phillips. How are you doing, Mark?"

Mark leaned back in his chair and said, "I'm fine. Why are you calling?"

"I just wanted to ask if you got the gun from Sam's house."

"Yes, I have the gun."

"Did you meet Sam?"

"No. He doesn't live in that house anymore."

"Did you do a ballistics test?"

"Yes. That gun was used in the Eddie's Mini Mart robbery."

"Did you find Sam's fingerprints on it?"

"Yes, we did."

"I knew he was telling the truth."

"You said Curtis trusted you. Why did he trust you?"

"I don't know. Maybe I look trustworthy."

Mark shifted his eyes to his computer monitor, which had gone into screensaver mode and was now displaying a digital clock bouncing around the screen. The time was 1:29 p.m.

"Let's say I believe you. What do you suggest I do?"

"He's going to kill again, and you should catch him in the act."

"I'll have to follow him every day, won't I?"

"I guess so."

Was Phillips serious?

"I have a job, you know," Mark said.

"You can do it after work. I think he prefers to kill at night."

"Why do you think so?"

"Helen was killed at night, wasn't she?"

Phillips had a point. A serial killer was likely to stick to a method that had worked in the past. Laura Sumner had been murdered at night, too.

"Okay, I'll think about it."

"If you catch him in the act, don't kill him. You have to take him alive."

Mark knew why Phillips didn't want Sam Curtis to die: he hoped Curtis would confess to killing Helen.

"Sure. Is that all?"

"Yes."

"Goodbye."

"Goodbye, Mark."

I should have asked him about the fingerprint and the blood stains, Mark thought when he hung up.

If he had asked Phillips how his fingerprint had gotten on Helen's belt buckle and Helen's blood on his pants and boots, what would Phillips's answer have been?

Phillips might have said that he had found Helen's body after the killer had left.

Suppose it was true. Why hadn't he called the police?

Perhaps he had been afraid he would become a suspect.

Why hadn't he told the detectives he had found Helen's body when he was interrogated?

Because they wouldn't have believed him.

He should talk to Phillips's attorney, Leonard Barlow. He needed someone to convince him that Phillips might be innocent, and who could do it better than his lawyer?

Did he want Phillips to be innocent?

No, I just want to get to the truth. I want to know who killed Helen.

If you want to get to the truth, you need to talk to the prosecutor and the detectives who handled the Phillips case, too.

That was fine by him.

Leonard Barlow's office was a fifteen-minute drive from Dallas PD headquarters. Mark called him and made an appointment for tomorrow morning. He did not tell the lawyer it was about Edward Phillips.

3

At half past four Mark picked up Sam Curtis's pistol at the crime lab. When he was halfway to police headquarters, his phone rang. It was Detective Aguero.

"You asked me to call you," Aguero said.

"How are you doing, Detective? I really appreciate you calling me." Mark put on his blinker and began to pull over.

"Are you busy?"

"No."

Mark brought the car to a stop and turned off the engine.

"You said you wanted to discuss the Sumner case."

"Yes. I have a few questions I want to ask you."

"Ok, shoot."

"Do you have any suspects?"

"No."

"Are there any persons of interest?"

"There was one, Laura's ex-boyfriend, but we cleared him."

"Did you find any fingerprints or DNA evidence?"

"No, we didn't."

"Did you interview a man named Sam Curtis?"

"No."

"Has his name ever come up?"

"No. Why are you interested in this case, Mark?"

Mark looked out his window and watched a fuel truck pass by. He could barely hear the traffic.

"Have you heard of Helen Hinton?"

"No."

"She's my daughter. She was murdered the same way as Laura Sumner."

"I'm sorry about your daughter. When was she killed?"

"Last December. They found the killer."

"Is he in custody?"

"Yes. He's in prison awaiting execution."

"Do you think there's a connection between these murders?"

"I don't know. Maybe."

There was a silence on the line. Then Aguero said, "I'm going to look into this. I'll let you know if I find something."

"Okay. Thank you."

Chapter 5

1

"Did you murder Helen Hinton?" Jeff asked.

"No," Sam replied.

"I know you killed her. I have proof. We found your DNA on her body."

"It's impossible. I didn't kill anyone."

"If you confess, the DA will take the death penalty off the table. Do you want to live, Sam?"

"You got the wrong guy. I didn't kill Helen Hinton."

"Will you take a lie detector test?"

"No."

"Why?"

Sam thought for a long moment and said, "I don't know to say. What should I say?"

"Tell them you think that lie detector tests are unreliable."

"Got it."

Five minutes later Sam saw what looked like a human figure far down the road. A rush of excitement filled him, the kind a hunter felt when he found his prey.

"I think I see a hitchhiker." Sam pointed down the highway.

Jeff leaned forward between the front seats and said, "Yeah, it does look like a hitchhiker."

"Let's pick him up."

People rarely hitchhiked these days, so they had to seize this opportunity.

"Why?" Jeff asked.

Sam explained, and Jeff nodded agreement.

When they were about fifty feet from the hitchhiker, Sam pulled over to the side of the road and honked the horn.

"Don't put him to sleep right away," he said to Jeff. "Wait five, ten minutes."

AN EVIL MIND

"Okay."

The hitchhiker was a man; he wore jeans and a fleece jacket, and had no bags. As he approached the car, Sam rolled down his window.

"Where are you headed, bro?" Sam asked the man, smiling.

"Rockwall."

The hitchhiker was in his twenties and had a stubbly face and short dark hair.

"We can take you there. It's right on our way."

"Awesome! Thanks a lot." The man's lips drew back in a wide grin. He opened the front passenger door and got in the Ford Explorer.

"What's your name?" Sam asked, pressing the gas pedal.

"Edgar."

"I'm Sam. And this is Jeff. He's my uncle."

Edgar turned to Jeff and said, "Nice to meet you, Jeff."

"Nice to meet you." Jeff shook Edgar's hand.

Seeing that the hitchhiker hadn't fastened his seat belt, Sam said, "Buckle up, bro."

This suggestion was supposed to make Edgar believe he was dealing with decent, caring people, and lull his vigilance.

"Right." Edgar snapped his seat belt into place. "Where are you going?"

"Richardson."

"You live in Richardson?"

"Yeah. Do you live in Rockwall?"

"No. A buddy of mine lives there."

"Where do you live?"

"Waco. Have you ever been there?"

"Yes, a couple of times."

"Did you like it there?"

"It's a nice place."

Edgar nodded. "Do you smoke?"

"No."

"I saw fishing rods on the roof. Did you go fishing today?"

"Yeah. We went to Lake Tawakoni."

"Cool. Did you catch anything?"

"Yes, we did. But we released all the fish we caught."

When they got back to Carrollton, they would have to wipe off everything Edgar had touched in the Explorer to erase his fingerprints, and then vacuum the car and clean the front passenger seat with a lint roller to remove all the hairs that might have fallen from Edgar's head.

Jeff pulled a flannel rag and a bottle of chloroform from his pocket.

"Do you like fishing?" Sam asked.

"Yes, I do," Edgar said.

Jeff opened the bottle and soaked the rag with chloroform.

"Want to hear a—"

Before Edgar could finish, Jeff clapped the rag over his face. His screams muffled by Jeff's hand, Edgar struggled for a few seconds and then passed out. Jeff dropped the rag on the floor and took two ampoules of chlorpromazine and a syringe with a needle on it out of the bag. Chlorpromazine, also known as Thorazine, was a powerful sedative, which was widely used in mental hospitals to subdue out-of-control patients. Jeff drew the drug from both ampoules into the syringe, then pulled up Edgar's left sleeve and injected the tranquilizer into his arm. They needed to sedate Edgar because chloroform wore off within just a few minutes after the person stopped inhaling the fumes, and Jeff didn't want to spend the entire trip giving chloroform to Edgar. The dose Edgar received was going to put him into a stupor for at least an hour.

"Get his phone," Sam said.

Jeff extracted the cellphone from Edgar's jeans pocket, removed its battery, and put it in the duffel bag.

AN EVIL MIND

2

Sam tapped the brakes, turned off the worn blacktop onto a dirt road, and then pressed the gas pedal. They were headed for the secluded spot about a mile south of Kitsee Inlet of Lake Tawakoni they had found three weeks ago. It was located in a wooded area and was a good place to bury a body. There were two shovels in the trunk of the Explorer, which they'd taken with them specifically to dig graves.

The road was rough and bumpy and was only wide enough for one car. Sam felt as though he were on one of those coin-operated mechanical horses.

"Let's do it here." Sam pulled off the road onto the grass, stopped the car, and switched off the headlights. To Edgar, he said, "Hey, buddy. Are you okay?" He poked the man in the chest.

His eyes half-closed, Edgar turned his face to Sam and grunted quietly.

"Give him another dose, just in case," Sam said to Jeff.

He looked at the road to make sure there was enough room for another vehicle to pass, pulled the key from the ignition, and got out of the car. The air was filled with the smell of earth and leaves. It was silent except for the whisper of a breeze blowing through the trees. Sam stood for a moment, peering into the moonlit woods, then went around to the back of the SUV, opened the liftgate, and took out the shovels. When he reached the front passenger door, Jeff was putting the syringe back in the bag. Sam leaned the shovels against the fender and opened the door.

"Are you done?" he asked.

"Yeah." Jeff climbed out of the Explorer.

"How much did you give him?"

"A hundred milligrams."

Away from the light pollution of the city, the stars were amazingly bright and sharp. Staring at the sky, Sam wished he lived on a ranch in the country.

Someday I will, he thought.

Jeff reached into the bag and produced two pairs of latex gloves, one of which he gave to Sam.

"You want to get a drink after this?" Jeff asked as they put on the gloves.

"Sure."

Sam grabbed a flashlight from the glove box, switched it on, and fished his keys out of his jeans pocket. Shining the flashlight at the small compass attached to the keychain, he took his bearings.

The road ran from east to west. This information would help them find their way back to the car after they buried Edgar.

"Which way are we going?" Jeff slung the duffel bag over his shoulder.

"This way." Sam pointed south. "I'll carry him, and you'll carry the shovels."

He pocketed the keys and the flashlight.

"Let's go, buddy." Sam unfastened Edgar's seatbelt, grasped him under the arms, and pulled him out of the car. The hitchhiker wasn't fat; Sam estimated he weighed about one hundred and sixty pounds. The smell of sweat emanating from Edgar's body made him think of his high school locker room. He remembered stealing glances at other guys' penises to see how big they were.

"Is he heavy?" Jeff asked.

"No." With Jeff's help, Sam hoisted Edgar onto his back.

Twigs crackling underfoot, the toes of Edgar's sneakers scraping the ground, he entered the woods. The hitchhiker's body was limp; he made no effort to hold onto Sam.

For a moment Sam wondered if Edgar was just pretending to be out of it.

If he tries to strangle me, Jeff will whack him with a shovel.

If Edgar scratched him, he would have to cut off his fingers so the police wouldn't get his DNA from his skin under Edgar's fingernails.

AN EVIL MIND

Carrying the shovels on his shoulders, Jeff ambled beside Sam.

"Do you want to do it, or should I?" Sam said.

Sam believed Jeff would understand that by "do it" he meant "kill Edgar" — and he was right.

"You do it," Jeff replied.

It was easy to walk as the terrain was level and there were no mounds or hollows. After about fifty yards, Sam's back began to complain.

I should go to the gym more often, Sam thought.

He had read that gorillas could lift ten times their own weight. It would be nice if humans were that strong, wouldn't it?

When they were a hundred yards from the road, Sam stopped and said, "This is far enough." He laid Edgar on his back on the ground and wiped sweat from his forehead with his sleeve.

"Should we dig the grave before or after?" Jeff asked as he tied Edgar's legs.

"Before," Sam said, flexing his fingers, which had become numb from holding Edgar's arms.

He picked up a shovel and then turned toward the road, thinking he had heard a car. He saw no headlights.

"What is it?" Jeff asked.

"Nothing."

It took them forty five minutes to dig the grave, which was about two feet deep. No cars passed by during that time. Edgar lay quietly on the ground and did not attempt to get up or crawl away.

Sam knelt down, unbuttoned Edgar's shirt, and bared his chest and stomach. Edgar raised his head slightly and mumbled something unintelligible.

"Relax, man." Sam patted him on the cheek. "Everything's fine."

He emptied Edgar's pockets and handed the contents to Jeff: he wanted to make it harder for the police to identify the body.

"Knife," he said.

Jeff took a knife out of the bag and gave it to Sam.

Sam ran a hand over Edgar's hairy chest, mentally marking where he was going to stab him, raised the knife, and gripped it tightly. A guttural sound escaped Edgar; his right hand rose, and a moment later fell down. His heart pounding with excitement, Sam drove the knife into Edgar's left breast, pulled it out, and plunged it into his right breast. Edgar slapped his hands to his chest and let out a throaty groan; a shudder shook his body.

Sam drew a deep breath and began to cut Edgar's abdomen open.

As soon as he got back to Arlington, he would throw the clothes he was wearing now in a Dumpster.

When Sam withdrew the blade from Edgar's stomach, Jeff took out a Ziploc bag and gave it to him.

"Good job," Jeff said.

"Thank you." Sam wiped the knife on Edgar's jeans and placed it in the Ziploc bag.

Before they began to fill the grave, they made sure they hadn't dropped their keys and wallets.

3

Sam volunteered to carry both shovels to the car. When they reached the road, Sam found that their Explorer was nowhere in sight. This did not worry him as they couldn't be too far from the car. He pulled out his car keys and pressed the unlock button on the fob. There was no beeping.

"You go there," Sam pointed west, "and I'll go there." He pointed east.

"Okay."

AN EVIL MIND

The trees rustled in the wind that carried the smell of algae. Sam walked about fifty feet and pushed the unlock button again. A chirping sound broke the silence, and the Explorer's parking lights flashed twice ahead of him.

"It's here!" he shouted to Jeff.

Jeff turned around and trotted toward him. When Sam got to the car, he put the shovels in the trunk and climbed behind the wheel. It felt good to sit down and relax.

"Are you tired?" he asked Jeff, who had gotten in the Explorer as he closed the liftgate.

"No. What about you?"

"A little."

Jeff gasped and said, "Oh my God, I lost my phone."

Sam turned his face to him. "Where?"

"Just kidding." Jeff grinned.

As they drove through Garland, Jeff put the battery back in Edgar's phone. Twenty minutes later, they tossed Edgar's cell in a storm drain in a residential area near Interstate 635. When the police examined Edgar's cellphone records, they would conclude that he had made it to Dallas.

Chapter 6

1

Leonard Barlow was a blond-haired man in his late thirties with a round face and nearly invisible eyebrows. When Mark entered his office, the lawyer gave him a welcoming smile, then stood up and shook his hand.

To Barlow's right on the desk was a coffee mug, which read: "Lawyer. Someone who writes a 10,000 word document and calls it a "brief."" The crystal clock that stood next to the penholder sparkled in the sunlight streaming in through the open blinds. Hanging on the wall behind the lawyer was a framed diploma from the Emory University.

"What can I do for you, Mark?" Barlow said.

"I want to talk to you about one of your clients."

Was he supposed to despise Barlow for defending Phillips?

The guy was just doing his job.

So what? The Nazi concentration camp guards were just doing their jobs, too.

"Are you a journalist?"

"No. You represented the man who killed my daughter."

Barlow shifted in his chair. "What's his name?"

"Edward Phillips. He was sentenced to death last July."

Barlow nodded. "Yes, he was. I'm sorry about your daughter. Her name was Helen, wasn't it?"

"Yes. I have a question for you. Do you think Phillips killed my daughter?"

"Why do you ask me? I'm his lawyer, remember?"

"The trial is over. You don't have to defend him anymore."

"Mister Phillips maintains his innocence. I believe he's innocent."

"But you're not completely sure, are you?"

AN EVIL MIND

Barlow looked at him for a long moment and then said, "I'm his lawyer. I take him at his word."

"Do you have any proof that he didn't kill Helen?"

"I don't want to sound rude, but what's the point of this conversation?"

"I think Edward Phillips might be innocent. I was hoping you had some proof that he didn't kill my daughter."

"Here's my answer. No one saw Edward Phillips kill Helen, no one saw him near the crime scene. The murder weapon was never found. This is not an open-and-shut case."

"Did Phillips say he had an alibi?"

"No. He said he was home alone that night."

"Did he explain how his fingerprint got on Helen's belt buckle?"

"No, he didn't. But the fingerprint doesn't prove he killed her."

"What did he say about Helen's blood on his clothes?"

"He doesn't know how it got there."

"Do you have any idea how it might have gotten there?"

"Edward might have bumped into your daughter when she had a nosebleed a few hours before the murder. And maybe that's how his fingerprint got on her belt buckle. Truth is stranger than fiction, they say."

"I know you're bound by the attorney-client privilege, but I really need to know the truth. Did Phillips actually tell you he didn't know how Helen's blood got on his clothes and how his fingerprint got on her belt buckle?"

Barlow took a sip from his mug and said, "What you're trying to find out is if Edward confessed to me that he'd killed Helen. Here's my answer. Edward did not make such a confession, and that's the truth."

"Has Phillips ever mentioned the name Sam Curtis to you?"

"No." Barlow looked away for a moment.

People often broke eye contact when they lied. Did Barlow glance away because he was lying?

"What's your gut feeling, Leonard? Is Phillips guilty?"

"Why do you care what I think? I could be wrong, you know. The only person who knows whether Ed Phillips is guilty or not is Ed Phillips." Barlow looked at the clock on his desk.

"I talked to him a few days ago. In prison."

"You visited Ed in prison?"

"Yes."

"Why?"

"He asked me to come."

Barlow picked up a pen and began to roll it between his fingers. "What did you talk about?"

"He tried to convince me he was innocent."

"That's odd. It's not you that he needs to convince of his innocence."

"I agree."

"What arguments did he present?"

"He told me about Laura Sumner. Has he ever mentioned Laura Sumner to you?"

"What did he tell you about her?"

"He said Laura and my daughter were killed by the same person."

"I told Ed about Laura Sumner. He asked me to find a murder similar to your daughter's, and I found the Sumner case."

"Did you tell this theory to the police?"

"What theory?"

"That Helen and Laura were murdered by the same person?"

"No, I didn't."

"Why?"

"Because I don't think that's the case."

If Laura Sumner had been killed before the end of Edward Phillips's trial, Barlow would surely have mentioned her murder to the jury and the Dallas police to create reasonable doubt.

"Have you contacted the detectives handling the Sumner case?" Barlow asked.

"Yes."

"Did you tell them about your daughter's murder?"

"Yes."

"Do they have any leads?"

"No, they don't."

"I'm going to keep an eye on the Sumner case. I hope they catch the killer soon. And I'll be very happy if he confesses to killing Helen." Barlow put the pen on the desk. "Why did you come here, Mark? To be honest, this is a very odd conversation."

"As I said, I thought you had some proof that Phillips didn't kill my daughter."

"I'm sorry I disappointed you. Why do you think Ed Phillips might be innocent?"

"If we assume that my daughter and Helen Sumner were killed by the same person, then Phillips must be innocent."

"That's true." Barlow nodded. "You asked me what my gut feeling was. Ed doesn't strike me as a murderer. He's not an angel, he's far from perfect, but I don't think he killed your daughter."

"Are you handling his appeal?"

"Yes. By the way, what did Ed tell you about Sam Curtis?"

"It doesn't matter."

Barlow wouldn't have asked this question if he hadn't heard Sam Curtis's name before today, would he?

Mark stood up. "Thanks for answering my questions, Leonard. I'll let you get back to work."

2

An hour later Mark called Assistant District Attorney Frank Backus, the lead prosecutor in the Edward Phillips case, and asked for a meeting. Backus agreed to meet him next Monday.

When Mark checked his inbox at four-twenty, he saw he had a message from the bank that had issued Sam Curtis's Visa credit card. The email contained a list of Curtis's credit card transactions from last August. Mark ran his eye down the list and found that Curtis had made a purchase at a gas station in Austin at 4:17 p.m. on August 23. It was the only transaction that had taken place that day. No transactions had occurred on August 24.

Sam Curtis had been in Austin the day Laura Sumner had been killed.

Edward Phillips's credibility got another boost, and a big one at that.

At five o'clock, Mark received a list of Sam Curtis's August checking account transactions. Curtis hadn't used his bank card on August 23 or 24, so he remained a viable suspect.

The information provided by the issuer of Curtis's MasterCard credit card, which came half an hour later, did not clear Curtis, either: no charges had been made on the card on August 23 or 24.

When he closed his email, Mark realized he was pleased there was evidence that Sam Curtis might have murdered Laura Sumner. Perhaps it was force of habit: police detectives liked it when the tips they received proved accurate.

He decided to follow Sam Curtis for a few hours this Saturday. For some reason, he had a hunch it wouldn't be a waste of time.

AN EVIL MIND

Chapter 7

1

On Thursday morning, Mark received transaction records for three of Christopher Novak's credit cards and one of his debit cards. There were three transactions that had taken place on August 23: the first one at a Chinese restaurant in Dallas at 5:24 p.m., the second one at a gas station in Irving at 6:04 p.m., and the third one at a grocery store in Irving at 9:11 p.m. Only one transaction had occurred on August 24: at a coffee shop in Dallas at 12:05 p.m.

Austin was about two hundred miles from Irving, so Novak could have gotten there before midnight if he had set out shortly after 9:11 p.m.

At half past four, Mark received a call from Detective Isaac Kearns of the Garland Police Department, who was the lead detective on the Eddie's Mini Mart case.

"I heard you found a gun used in one of my robberies," Isaac said.

"Are you talking about the Eddie's Mini Mart case?"

"Yes."

"Yes, I did find the gun. I'm sorry I forgot to tell you about it. I'll send it to you today."

"No problem. Where did you find it?"

"I got it from one of my CIs."

"Is he the one who robbed the place?"

"No."

"Does he know who did it?"

"No, he doesn't. He said he found the gun in an alley in Mesquite."

"Were there any prints on the gun?"

"Only my CI's."

2

When Mark's shift was over, he headed for Christopher Novak's place. Novak lived in a low-rise apartment complex called Stonewood Apartments. Mark parked about a hundred yards down the street from Novak's building. The courtyard gate was locked, and Mark asked the young boy who was playing in the courtyard to open it. The boy obeyed his request.

Novak's apartment was on the second floor. As Mark climbed the staircase, he unsnapped the safety strap on his holster. About ten seconds after he rang the bell, a man dressed in a T-shirt and underpants opened the door. He had long wavy hair that reached his shoulders. Mark recognized him. It was Christopher Novak.

He seemed like a harmless fellow.

"What do you want?" Novak asked.

A faint smell of marijuana wafted out of the apartment.

"Good evening. Are you Christopher Novak?"

"Yes."

Mark flashed his badge and said, "I'm Detective Hinton. I need to ask you a few questions."

"About what?"

"Your friend Edward Phillips."

Novak hesitated, then said, "Just a second." He closed the door. When Novak returned, he wore sweatpants. He let Mark in, and they went into the living room.

The room was a little messy: various articles of clothing were strewn on the chairs, a few pairs of socks lay scattered on the floor by the couch, an empty pizza box, two crumpled paper bags, and five empty beer bottles stood on the coffee table.

"How close are you with Edward Phillips?" Mark asked when he sat down.

"He... He was a friend. I'm not really close with him right now."

"Why?"

"Because he's in prison."

AN EVIL MIND

"How close were you with Edward before he went to prison?"

"As I said, he was a friend."

"Was he your best friend?"

"I wouldn't say so." Novak scratched his shoulder.

"How long have you known Edward?"

"About ten years."

"Do you keep in touch with him?"

"No."

"Do you know why he's in prison?"

"Yes. He killed someone."

"You visited him in the county jail on December twentieth. What did you talk about?"

"I asked him how he was doing. He said, "Not too good.""

"What else did he say?"

"He said he was innocent."

"Do you think he's innocent?"

Novak shrugged. "I don't know. I kinda want to believe that he didn't do it."

"You visited him again on January twenty-fourth. What did you talk about that day?"

"Ed said that he didn't want to talk and told me to go home. He asked me not to visit him anymore."

"Did he explain why he didn't want you to visit him?"

"He said he was depressed."

"Has Edward called you since January?"

"No."

"Did you follow his trial?"

"Not really."

"Do you know how he killed the victim?"

"He stabbed her to death with a knife."

"Did Edward tell you that?"

"No. I read it on the Internet."

"What did Edward tell you about the murder he was convicted of?"

"Only that he didn't do it."

"Did he ask you to help him with an alibi?"

"No."

"When was the last time Edward called you from jail?"

"It was in December. I don't remember the exact date."

"Did he trust you?"

"I guess so."

"Why didn't you visit Edward after the trial?"

"Because he asked me not to visit him."

Novak looked longingly at the muted TV.

"Where were you on the night of August twenty-third?"

"I don't remember. It was so long ago."

"Did you visit Austin in August?"

Novak shook his head. "No, I didn't. What day of the week was August twenty-third?"

"Wednesday."

Novak grabbed his cellphone from the coffee table and tapped on its screen. "I think I know where I was on that day." He scrolled down the screen and said, "I was in Waco visiting my cousin."

Waco was one hundred miles from Austin.

"When did you go home?"

"The next morning."

"I need your cousin's name, phone number, and address."

After giving Mark the requested information, Novak said, "What are you investigating?"

"I can't tell you that. Can I have your cell number?"

Novak told Mark his number, and he wrote it down.

"Did Edward ask you to help him prove his innocence?" Mark asked.

"No."

"Did he ask you to kill anyone?"

"What?" Novak raised his eyebrows. "Kill?"

Mark nodded.

"No. He never asked me to kill anyone."

"I'm going to listen to recordings of your conversations with Edward, and if it turns out that you lied to me, you'll be charged with obstruction of justice. It's a serious offense. You could go to jail for a year. So let me ask you again: Did Edward ask you to kill anyone?"

"No, he didn't. I swear."

4

Later that day, Mark called Novak's cousin, whose name was Randy Polansky. Randy said that Novak had been in Waco from eleven p.m. on August 23 to nine a.m. on August 24.

He thought about talking to Jeff Phillips on Friday but decided it could wait until next week.

On Friday, Mark contacted Edward Phillips's last cellphone company and found out that Phillips had never received any text messages or calls from Sam Curtis, which meant that they hadn't known each other before becoming cellmates.

Chapter 8

1

When Mark woke up on Saturday morning, he found he still wanted to follow Sam Curtis. He figured five hours would be enough.

At three o'clock, he went into the kitchen and made four ham sandwiches (he intended to eat them in the car during the surveillance). He put the sandwiches in a plastic bag, then opened the refrigerator, grabbed a quarter-full bottle of orange juice, and emptied it into two glasses. He was going to use the bottle, which had a wide mouth, as a receptacle for his urine.

When he opened the pantry door, Joan came into the room, saw the sandwiches, and asked, "Going somewhere?"

"I'm going on a stakeout."

"Did they call you again?"

"Yes." Mark placed his hands on Joan's waist and kissed her. "And you know I can't say no."

Joan didn't need to know he was going to tail Sam Curtis.

"What time are you coming home?"

"Before midnight."

Joan picked up a glass of juice and sat down at the table. "Have you talked to Phillips since last Saturday?"

"Yes. He called me last Tuesday." Mark took six bottles of water from the pantry and put them in a duffel bag.

"What did he say?"

"He asked me about Laura Sumner's murder." Mark drank some juice from the other glass.

"By the way, have they caught her killer yet?"

"No."

"You talked to the detectives?"

"Yes, I did."

"I read about this girl on the Internet. It seems she really was murdered the same way as Helen."

Why did she search for information about Laura Sumner's murder? Didn't she say Phillips was lying?

"Was anyone else killed this way?" Joan asked.

"I don't know."

"What if..." Joan paused. "Text me when you're done with your stakeout."

"Okay."

He left the house at four o'clock. Curtis's car was nowhere in sight when Mark arrived at his place.

It could be in the garage.

There were no lights in the windows visible from Mark's vantage point.

Maybe Curtis had already left to hunt for another victim.

Let's hope he hasn't.

He should have bought one of those GPS tracking devices that you could attach to a car. It would have made his job so much easier.

To prevent Curtis from spotting him, Mark moved to the back seat.

2

Mark checked his watch. It was six o'clock. So far no one had gone into or come out of Sam Curtis's house. The windows were still dark.

It shouldn't be very hard to pick the lock on his front door, Mark thought as he looked at Curtis's porch.

I could search his house for evidence—secretly, of course.

What kind of evidence could he hope to find there? The knife used to murder Laura Sumner (or his daughter)? Mark was willing to bet Curtis had gotten rid of the knife shortly after the murder.

At 6:26 p.m. Sam Curtis's Mazda 6 pulled up in front of the house. The driver, a slender man about six feet tall, got out of the car and started walking toward the driveway. It was Sam Curtis. His hair was longer than in his mug shot.

Mark scanned the rear window, the trunk, and the rear bumper of Curtis's Mazda, looking for something that made the car unique. The only distinctive feature he could see was the sticker on the right side of the bumper, which read: "I Was An Honor Student. I Don't Know What Happened." The sticker was white and would be highly visible against the gray bumper when night fell.

Fifteen minutes after Curtis came home, Mark took a ham sandwich out of the duffel bag and began to eat it. By the time he finished the sandwich, the sun had gone down.

Assuming Curtis was the killer, where would he go to look for his next victim?

Austin was about two hundred miles from Arlington. There were two other major cities that were two hundred miles from Arlington: Houston and Oklahoma City.

At a quarter to eight, Curtis's front door opened, and Curtis came out of the house. He was carrying a plastic bag. Accompanied by a beeping sound, the Mazda's parking lights blinked twice. When Curtis got in the Mazda, Mark slipped out of the car through the right door, then climbed behind the wheel and started the engine. As he buckled his seat belt, Curtis drove off. After a few seconds, Mark pulled away from the curb and headed down the street.

Curtis turned north when he got to Fielder Road, one of the main streets of the neighborhood.

The shortest route from Curtis's place to Houston was via Interstate 45, and to Oklahoma City via Interstate 35. Depending on the traffic, it would take Curtis thirty to forty-five minutes to reach either of the highways.

When Curtis entered I-30 eastbound, Mark began to doubt he was going to Oklahoma City. Five minutes later Curtis turned north onto Highway 161, and it became clear that he was not headed for Houston.

Curtis stayed on Highway 161 for five miles and exited at Conflans Road in Irving. After two miles, he turned right at

Story Road. Less than a minute later, he pulled off the street and into the parking lot of Pistons Bar and Grill.

Mark checked the clock. It was 8:04 p.m.

Curtis parked at the edge of the lot, stepped out of the Mazda, adjusted his crotch, and then walked into the bar.

Curtis wasn't looking for another victim here—assuming he specialized in teenage females, of course.

Perhaps he'd go hunting after leaving the bar. Chances were that he'd stay within the Dallas-Fort Worth metropolitan area this time.

Soon Mark became curious about what Curtis was doing, and he went into the bar. Inside, the air was cool and smelled of beer and fried food. A rock song was playing, which he didn't recognize. Mark scanned the room, found Curtis—he sat alone at a table in the back—and then walked over to the counter.

"What can I get you?" the bartender asked.

"I'll have a Guinness," Mark said.

While the bartender was filling his glass, Mark looked toward the billiard tables, then at Curtis.

He should have a friendly chat with Curtis. In bars you could talk to strangers without being taken for a kook. He could learn a lot about Curtis if they became friends.

Considering that there were empty booths and tables in the bar, would Curtis find it suspicious if he sat down at his table?

He could say he didn't like to drink alone. A lot of people didn't like to drink alone.

Curtis was sipping his drink with an impassive look on his face. His cheeks were covered with stubble, his brown hair was fashionably tousled. Pointing at the chair opposite Curtis, Mark said, "Is this seat taken?" He smiled.

Curtis gave him a vacant look and said, "No."

"Great." Mark put his glass on the table and sat down. "I hate drinking alone." He smiled again.

Curtis nodded silently.

"I'm Michael." Mark held out his hand. When Curtis shook it, his right jacket sleeve slid up, revealing a barbwire tattoo circling his wrist. "Do you come here often?"

"Once a week."

"This seems like a fun place. What are you drinking?"

"Scotch."

Curtis checked his watch, and as he did, Mark noticed a chain tattoo on his left forefinger.

"I like Scotch," Mark said. "Do you shoot pool?"

"Yeah." Curtis stared at Mark for a moment and then looked away.

"Wanna play?"

"Let me think about it."

Mark drank some beer and then said, "Did you see the Cowboys game last week?"

"No. I don't watch football."

Mark wasn't getting a serial killer vibe from Curtis, but then again many serial killers looked normal.

"Do you watch baseball?" Mark asked.

"No. I'm not into sports. You know what pisses me off? These guys are paid millions of dollars for running around a field. That's not fair. Do you think it's fair?"

"No, it's not."

"And these morons don't appreciate their money. Almost all of them eventually go broke."

"Yeah."

"Easy come, easy go."

"Right. Remember Mike Tyson? The guy blew three hundred million dollars."

"Yeah. That's crazy. Boxing is the most useless sport, if you ask me."

Curtis raised his hand and waved to someone. Pretending to be nonchalant, Mark didn't turn to see who it was. A few moments later, a lean man in his fifties sat down at their

AN EVIL MIND

table. He wore a fleece jacket and jeans, his hair was mostly gray, as was his neatly trimmed beard.

The man glanced at Mark and asked Curtis, "When did you get here?"

"Twenty minutes ago," Curtis said.

The man motioned the waitress over and ordered a Budweiser and french fries.

Curtis's friend's face seemed familiar. As he sipped from his glass, Mark remembered where he had seen it: the man looked exactly like Jeff Phillips, Edward Phillips's father.

Was it Jeff Phillips?

"Hi, I'm Michael," Mark said, offering his hand to Curtis's friend.

"Jeff." The man clasped his hand briefly.

So it was Jeff Phillips.

Why was Edward Phillips's father hanging out with Sam Curtis?

"What do you do for a living, Mike?" Curtis asked.

"I'm a real estate agent," Mark said.

"A real estate agent? It's a nice gig. What kind of houses do you sell?"

"All kinds."

"Have you sold any mansions?" Jeff asked.

Mark nodded. "Are you looking to buy one?"

Jeff laughed and said, "No. Do you know any billionaires?"

"No. Why?"

"I'm looking for an investor. I have a great green energy idea."

"What is it?"

"Sorry, it's a secret."

The waitress brought Jeff's beer and french fries, and Jeff said to her, "Thank you, darling."

"Are you guys related?" Mark asked.

"No, we're just buddies."

"Do you play poker?"

"Yes, about once a month. Do you live nearby?"

"I live about ten minutes from here."

Would it look suspicious if he asked Jeff if he could join his poker group?

It might seem so to Jeff.

It wouldn't look suspicious if he brought it up the next time they met because he would be considered an acquaintance then.

"Is he good at poker?" Mark asked Curtis, pointing at Jeff.

"He's all right," Curtis said.

Jeff glanced toward the billiard tables and said to Curtis, "Let's shoot some pool."

"Okay."

Jeff and Sam grabbed their glasses and made their way to the billiard tables.

If they wanted him to play with them, they would have invited him, wouldn't they?

Mark watched the two men play for a couple of minutes and then moved to another table, which was about twenty feet from the entrance. Feeling hungry, he ordered a cheeseburger.

Had Edward Phillips told his father to spy on Curtis? Of course he had. The chances of this being a coincidence were microscopic.

What was Jeff Phillips's plan? Did he want to arrest Sam Curtis while he was trying to kill his next victim?

Or was Jeff going to capture Curtis and torture him until he agreed to confess to the police that he had murdered Helen?

By the way, the idea of torturing Sam Curtis until he confessed to killing Helen seemed worth considering. He might try it if all else failed.

3

AN EVIL MIND

Jeff and Sam played pool for forty minutes before they went back to the table. Mark chose to observe them from a distance and didn't join them.

It was twenty past ten when Jeff and Sam exited Pistons Bar and Grill. Mark followed the pair outside, waited at the entrance until Jeff got to his car, a black Cadillac CTS, and then walked by the Cadillac to look at its license plate. When he slipped behind the wheel of his Impala, he saw that Curtis had already backed out of his parking space. Keeping an eye on Curtis's car, Mark started the engine and shifted into reverse. Curtis pulled out onto Story Road, heading south. By the time Mark turned onto the street, Curtis's Mazda was approaching the intersection, its right blinker flashing. Mark stepped on the gas.

After rounding the corner, Mark found Curtis's car and then looked in the rear-view mirror to see if Jeff was following Curtis. There were no Cadillac CTSs behind him. Evidently, Sam and Jeff went their separate ways.

After two and a half miles, Curtis got on Highway 161 southbound, and Mark wondered if he was headed home. Mark hoped Curtis would try to kill someone tonight: it would be nice to catch him in the act and solve the mystery once and for all, wouldn't it?

At 10:41 p.m. Curtis pulled into his driveway. Brightly illuminated by the headlights, the garage door began to roll up.

He was putting the car in the garage, which meant that he wasn't going anywhere else tonight.

As Curtis drove into the garage, Mark decided to continue the surveillance for another hour, just in case.

If Jeff captured Curtis tonight, he wouldn't intervene. He might even join him.

Mark took out his cellphone, opened the notes app, and wrote down Jeff's license plate number.

The lights went on in Curtis's house.

Maybe Curtis was going to kill someone tonight but changed his mind because he noticed he was being tailed?

Usually people drove around the block or turned a few corners to make sure they were being followed, and Curtis had done neither of those things.

Perhaps he didn't need confirmation.

Mark checked his messages and saw a new text from Joan asking if the stakeout was over yet. He texted back saying he'd be home around 12:30 a.m.

In the following hour and a quarter Curtis didn't go outside and no one came to visit him. The lights were still on in his house when Mark went home at midnight.

The next morning, Mark ran Jeff's license plate and found that it was actually registered to Jeff Phillips.

Chapter 9

1

"Thanks for meeting me, Frank." Mark took out his notebook.

"No problem," Frank Backus replied. "How have you been doing? It's been almost a year since…"

"It's been hard. Thanks for asking."

The assistant district attorney was of medium build and had a lean, tanned face. His small office was cluttered with boxes and files.

Mark had known Backus since long before Edward Phillips's trial; they had first met eleven years ago, when Backus was working on a case investigated by Mark.

"You said you wanted to talk about the Phillips case," Backus said.

"Yes. I have a couple of questions about it."

"Okay, go ahead."

Mark opened his notebook to the page with the questions he was going to ask Backus, and said, "Besides Edward Phillips, were there any other suspects?"

"As far as I know, Phillips was the only suspect."

"Any persons of interest?"

"No, there were no persons of interest."

"Did Phillips take a lie detector test?"

"Yes."

"Did he pass it?"

"What does it matter?"

"I'm just curious."

"Yes, he passed it."

The fact that Phillips had passed the polygraph exam didn't mean that he was innocent. There were a number of ways to beat the test.

Then why had he asked this question?

The truth was, Phillips passing the test added credibility to his story.

"Can I see the test report?" Mark said.

"What do you need it for?"

"I want to know what questions were asked."

Backus looked at him for a long time and said, "All right. I'll send it to you."

"Did you offer Phillips a plea deal?"

"Yes. We offered him a life sentence with the possibility of parole."

Under the circumstances, it had been a good deal for Phillips. He could have been out in thirty years.

"Why do you think he didn't take the deal?"

"I suppose he overestimated his chances."

"Was there any evidence you were unable to present at the trial?"

"No. We presented all the evidence we wanted to present."

"Did he say anything incriminating on the phone while he was in the county jail?"

"No."

"Did he say anything incriminating to his visitors?"

"No, he didn't."

"Did you keep the recordings of his conversations?"

"No."

"Did he tell you he knew who had really killed Helen?"

Backus shook his head. "No."

Mark closed his notebook and said, "Just between you and me, is it possible that Edward Phillips is innocent?"

"Do you doubt that Phillips is the killer?"

"No. Well, I just want to be sure that you got the right guy."

"We got the right guy, Mark."

"But you can't be completely sure, can you?"

"Why?"

"It wasn't an open-and-shut case."

"So you're not sure Phillips is guilty?"

"Is it possible that he's innocent?"

Backus thought for a moment and then said, "Anything's possible, you know. It's possible that the sun will explode tomorrow." He leaned forward. "I understand your doubts, Mark. The system isn't perfect, mistakes happen, but I assure you Phillips is guilty. Helen's blood was on his clothes. How do you think it got there? Phillips gave us no explanation."

He bumped into Helen when she had a nosebleed.

It wasn't really an implausible idea, was it?

"What makes you think Phillips might be innocent?" Backus went on. "Did his parents talk to you?"

"No. It just came to me one day."

"You said it wasn't an open-and-shut case. Would you have felt better if Phillips had been acquitted?"

Mark shook his head.

2

Had Edward Phillips rejected the plea deal because he was innocent?

Maybe he had been persuaded to reject the deal by Leonard Barlow.

Mark called Barlow's office and left a message with his secretary asking him to call back.

As he looked at the calendar on his desk, it occurred to him that Saturday might have been the wrong day to follow Sam Curtis. Laura Sumner had been murdered on a Wednesday, so the logical thing to do was to tail Curtis on a Wednesday.

He didn't feel like following Curtis this Wednesday. He might do it on Wednesday of next week.

He kept thinking about the results of Edward Phillips's lie detector test. It was a big deal that Phillips had passed the test, no two ways about it.

Leonard Barlow called Mark at half past one. Mark asked him why Phillips had refused to take the plea deal, and he replied, "Because he's innocent."

"Did you advise him to take it?"

"I told him that he should seriously consider it."

"Did you tell Phillips the prosecution had a weak case?"

"No. Can you meet me at my house tonight? There's something I want to tell you about the Phillips case."

"Sure. What's your address?"

Barlow gave Mark his address. "What time should I expect you?"

"Around eight. By the way, you should have mentioned that Phillips had passed a lie detector test."

"I thought you knew."

3

Mark pulled to the curb and checked the dashboard clock before killing the engine. It was 7:38 p.m.

He was hungry, and now he wished he had stopped by a fast-food restaurant.

What was Barlow going to tell him? For some reason, Mark thought it would be something unfavorable to Edward Phillips.

A blond woman in her early thirties opened Barlow's front door.

"Hi," Mark said. "I'm here to see Leonard."

"He's not home yet," the woman said.

Mark held up his police badge. "I'm Detective Mark Hinton with the Dallas PD. Leonard asked me to meet him at his house."

The woman stepped back and said, "Please come in. He should be home any minute now."

Mark thanked her and went inside. In the living room, he asked the woman what her name was.

"Alice," she replied. "I'm Leonard's wife. Would you like something to drink?"

"Yes."

"We have soda, water, and iced tea."

"Iced tea."

When Alice came back with a bottle of iced tea, Mark asked, "How long have you been married?"

"Six years."

"Do you have children?"

"No, not yet." Nodding at the TV, where Shark Tank investors were grilling a young female entrepreneur, she asked, "Do you watch this show?"

"Sometimes. My wife likes it."

Mark was silent for a few minutes, and then said, "What time does Leonard usually come home?"

"Around six." She glanced at the wall clock. "He's probably with a client. I can call him, if you want."

"Let's wait ten minutes."

Barlow didn't answer the phone when Alice called him ten minutes later. Alice sent Barlow a message informing him that Mark was at his house, and then said, "It must be something urgent. I'm sorry."

"It's all right."

Mark left Barlow's place at twenty minutes past eight. He wasn't mad at the lawyer for wasting his time as he believed that circumstances beyond Barlow's control had prevented him from telling Mark he would be late. Alice promised to ask her husband to call him as soon as he came home.

Mark didn't hear from Leonard Barlow that night.

Chapter 10

1

"See you tomorrow, Leonard," Sharon said from the doorway.

Leonard looked at his secretary and replied, "See you tomorrow." Then he continued reading the police incident report lying on the desk in front of him.

He called it a day at five-twenty. As he rode the elevator down, Leonard thought about Mark Hinton. He was going to meet Hinton in less than three hours. Was he doing the right thing by telling Edward Phillips's secret to him?

But was it a secret? Edward had never asked him to keep quiet about this.

The doors slid open, Leonard stepped out of the elevator and went outside through the back entrance.

The parking lot was silent except for the clatter of Leonard's shoes. A gust of cool wind blew the fallen leaves across his path and ruffled his hair. He parked in the corner farthest from the building to get additional exercise. He had lost six pounds in the last four months, and he suspected that he had burned at least one of them by walking to and from his car.

When Leonard was twenty feet from his Lexus, he took out his car keys and unlocked the doors.

How would Hinton react to Edward's story?

He'd probably laugh. And he'd call Edward crazy.

Leonard opened the driver's door, put his briefcase on the passenger seat, and got behind the wheel. There was a knock on his window, and a male voice said, "Excuse me, Leonard, can I talk to you?"

The voice belonged to a young long-haired man in sunglasses and a baseball cap. Leonard rolled his window down and asked, "Do I know you?"

The man put his right hand in his jacket pocket. "I need to show you something."

AN EVIL MIND

"What—"

Before Leonard could finish, the man stabbed him in the heart with the knife he had taken from his pocket. Leonard let out a groan and started to reach for the knife, his blue eyes bulging. The man pulled out the blade and severed Leonard's carotid artery. The lawyer exhaled his last breath, and then his hands fell into his lap and his head dropped. The man wiped the knife on Leonard's suit jacket, put it in his pocket, and walked away.

Leonard's body sat in the car for two hours before it was discovered.

2

At ten o'clock on Tuesday morning, Mark called Leonard Barlow's office, but no one answered the phone. He tried the lawyer's cellphone and got voice mail.

When Mark was about to leave work, he dialed Barlow's home number. Alice picked up the phone.

"This is Mark Hinton," Mark said. "We met last night. Can I talk to Leonard?"

"Leo…"

Mark heard Alice crying.

"Leo's dead," Alice wailed. "He was murdered last night."

Shocked, Mark was silent for a moment. Then he said, "I'm very sorry."

On Wednesday morning Mark read the initial police report in the Leonard Barlow murder case to find out what had happened to the lawyer. He learned that Barlow had been murdered in his car in the parking lot of the building where his office was. The killer had stabbed him in the chest and cut his neck open.

The killer hadn't taken the lawyer's wallet or briefcase, so it wasn't a robbery.

Was Barlow's murder spontaneous or planned?

Barlow might have been killed by a madman or by a hot-tempered stranger he had offended in the parking lot, but Mark was inclined to believe that this murder was premeditated.

The killer hadn't bothered to make it look like a robbery. Perhaps he had wanted to flee the crime scene as soon as possible.

Had Leonard Barlow been killed because of what he knew about the Phillips case? It was not a baseless speculation: the lawyer had been murdered when he was about to share some information about the case. There was no such thing as coincidence, as the cops liked to say.

Maybe Barlow had found proof that Sam Curtis had killed Helen, and Curtis had wasted him to prevent him from talking to the police? Barlow had said that Phillips had never mentioned Sam Curtis to him, but that must have been a lie.

This theory was bolstered by the fact that Barlow had been killed with a knife, like Helen.

3

When Mark came home, Joan handed him a letter from Edward Phillips. It read: "Dear Mark, I hope this finds you well. I'm writing to ask if you have followed Sam yet. If you have, please tell me when and for how long.

Did you see anything strange?

Are you going to follow him again? You need to follow him every day. There's no other way to catch him in the act.

Are you going to visit me again?

I look forward to hearing from you.

Regards,
Ed Phillips."

"What does it say?" Joan asked.

Mark gave her the letter. She read it, and said, "Who's Sam?"

"Phillips claims this Sam guy killed Helen."

AN EVIL MIND

"I see."

Mark wrote a letter back to Phillips, which read: "Hello, Edward. I followed Sam on October 14, from six p.m. to midnight. I saw nothing strange. I might follow him again. I'll visit you this Saturday."

Mark thought of asking Phillips about Helen's blood on his clothes and his fingerprint on Helen's belt buckle, then decided to talk about it in person, wanting to watch Phillips's face and body language and try to determine if he was telling the truth.

Lying in bed that night, Mark thought about Phillips's request to follow Sam Curtis every day. He would have gladly granted Phillips's wish, but only if he was sure that Curtis was Helen's killer.

Was there a less time-consuming way to get to the truth?

In Mark's opinion, the most effective alternative was to capture and question Curtis, using torture if necessary. Seizing Curtis wouldn't be a problem; Mark could do it alone if he had to.

Where was he going to interrogate Curtis?

If Curtis lived by himself, he could do it in Curtis's house. If Curtis had a roommate, Mark could use his parents' house at Lake Ray Hubbard.

There was one problem, however: Curtis might give a false confession just to make the torture stop.

Mark quickly found a solution. If Curtis confessed, he would ask him how he had killed Helen and where he had left the body.

Chapter 11

1

His conversation with Mark Hinton gave Detective Carlos Aguero a lot of food for thought. He saw two possibilities. Possibility number one: Edward Phillips had a partner, who had participated in killing Helen Hinton, and it was that partner who had murdered Laura Sumner. Possibility number two: there was no direct link between the two murders.

It was not uncommon for serial killers to work in teams. The Los Angeles Hillside Strangler, who had raped and killed ten women in the late 1970s, was actually two people, Kenneth Bianchi and Angelo Buono. The infamous Henry Lee Lucas, who had been convicted of eleven murders, had had a partner by the name of Otis Toole. Between 1984 and 1999 nineteen people had been murdered by a serial killer duo nicknamed Speed Freak Killers, which consisted of Loren Herzog and Wesley Shermantine (they had gotten their moniker because they were methamphetamine junkies).

On October 13, Aguero went to Livingston to have a chat with Edward Phillips. He had no expectations for this meeting: that was the easiest way to avoid disappointment.

The way things stood, the likelihood of Laura Sumner's murder being solved was low. They had no witnesses, no murder weapon, no fingerprints, no hairs, no skin under the victim's fingernails, nothing. There had been no activity on the case for over a month, and it felt great to finally do some work on it.

Aguero's plan was simple. He was going to offer Edward Phillips a deal: if Phillips helped them catch Laura Sumner's killer, they would get the governor to commute his death sentence to life in prison. His only concern was that Phillips would make something up and send them on a wild-goose chase.

2

The room was as ascetic as the other prison interview rooms Aguero had been in: bare walls, a metal table bolted to the floor, and four chairs, also bolted to the floor.

"Good morning." Aguero shook hands with the guard and sat across from Edward Phillips, whose eyes had been fixed on him from the moment he entered. The chair was cold, as was the table.

Aguero nodded to the guard, and he left the room.

"I'm Detective Carlos Aguero. I'm with the Austin Police Department." Aguero opened his briefcase and took out a file folder and a digital voice recorder.

"What can I do for you?"

Phillips's hands were cuffed and chained to his waist belt, and his legs were shackled to the table. He looked serene, but Aguero was willing to bet it was just a façade.

Aguero pressed the Record button on the recorder and said, "I'd like to inform you that this conversation is being recorded."

"Okay."

"Please state your name."

"Edward Phillips."

"Can you tell me why you're in this prison?"

"I was convicted of murder."

"You were sentenced to death, weren't you?"

Phillips nodded. "Yes."

"Would you like your death sentence to be commuted to life imprisonment with the possibility of parole?"

"That would be nice, I guess."

"We could help you with that."

"What do I have to do?"

Aguero opened the file folder, found a photo of Helen Hinton's body, and put it on the table. "Do you recognize her?"

The picture, which had been taken at the crime scene, showed Helen lying on her back with her T-shirt pulled up to her neck, and you could see all the wounds inflicted by the killer. Phillips looked at the photo for a long moment and said, "Is it Helen Hinton?"

"Yes, that's Helen Hinton. You stabbed her twice in the chest and cut open her stomach."

Phillips shook his head. "I didn't kill Helen Hinton. I'm innocent."

"All right. I understand. I didn't come here to get you to confess." Aguero pulled a crime scene photo of Laura Sumner's body from the folder and placed it beside Helen's picture. "This is Laura Sumner. She was murdered in Austin last August. As you can see, there are two stab wounds in her chest, and her abdomen was cut open."

"Yes, I can see that."

"Her wounds are similar to those on Helen Hinton's body."

"Yes, they are."

"Do you know why?"

"No."

"Do you have any information about the murder of Laura Sumner?"

"No, I don't."

"Do you have any idea who might have killed her?"

"No."

Aguero leaned forward and said, "Edward, if you help us catch Laura Sumner's killer, we'll get the governor to commute your death sentence."

"Can you get him to pardon me?"

Phillips was bargaining. That was a good sign.

"I don't know. I'll have to discuss that with my boss. Do we have a deal?"

"I wish I could help you, but I have no idea who might have killed this woman."

AN EVIL MIND

Phillips moved his legs, and the chain connecting his ankle shackles jingled softly.

"I think I know what your concern is," Aguero said. "You're afraid Laura's killer will tell us something that you want to keep secret."

"What are you talking about?"

"For example, he might say that you and he killed a bunch of people together."

"I've never killed anyone."

"If you help us catch this guy, nothing he says will be used against you. You'll be granted immunity for all crimes exposed by him. It's a great deal, Edward. This is the best chance you'll ever have to save your life. You don't seriously think your appeal will succeed, do you?"

"I'd be lying if I said I did. It's a good deal, I agree. But the thing is, I don't know who killed Laura Sumner. I'm sorry, Detective." Phillips smiled apologetically.

"You know what? I think you *are* innocent. I believe the person who killed Helen Hinton also killed Laura Sumner. That's why the wounds on their bodies match. And I think you know who that person is. You were with him when he murdered Helen. You did not participate, you just watched. Am I right?"

"I don't know who killed these girls."

"I'm trying to help you, Edward. You'll never have an opportunity like this again. Do you understand that?"

"Yes, I do. If I knew who killed Helen Hinton, I would have told you."

"How did Helen's blood get on your clothes? How did your fingerprint end up on her belt buckle?"

"I was framed."

"You were there when Helen was murdered."

"No, I wasn't."

Aguero pressed the Stop button on the voice recorder, took out his business card, and said, "All right. If you change your mind, call me." He got up from the table and put his card in Phillips's hand.

Aguero's intuition told him Edward Phillips was lying. He could think of only one plausible reason why Phillips would withhold information: Laura Sumner had been killed by someone Phillips cared about, someone whose life he valued more than his own. It could be a close relative or a lover.

Thinking that Edward Phillips might want to warn his partner, Aguero asked the assistant warden to keep him informed of every phone call made by Edward Phillips and every letter written by him.

On Monday, October 16, Aguero called Leonard Barlow and told him about the deal he had offered to Edward Phillips. The lawyer promised to talk to Phillips about the deal as soon as he could. Four hours after their conversation Barlow was murdered.

On October 18, Aguero sent all police and sheriff's departments in Texas letters asking them to contact him if they had unsolved cases similar to Laura Sumner's. Then he searched through all cases investigated by the Austin PD Homicide Unit in the last two years, and found none similar to Laura's.

AN EVIL MIND

Chapter 12

1

On Thursday, October 19, Mark received the report on Edward Phillips's polygraph exam. Phillips had taken the test on January 26. The following relevant questions had been asked:

"Do you know who killed Helen Hinton?" (Phillips answered, "No." The examiner concluded it was a lie.)

"Did you kill Helen Hinton?" (Phillips answered, "No." The examiner concluded it was a truthful response.)

"Were you present when Helen Hinton was murdered?" (Phillips answered, "No." The examiner concluded it was a truthful response.)

The polygraph test results supported Phillips's claim that he knew who had murdered Helen.

After reading the report, Mark called the Allan B. Polunsky Unit and scheduled a visit with Edward Phillips.

2

At half past five on Friday, as Mark drove to Dallas PD headquarters from Greenland Hills, where he had interviewed the victims of a home invasion that had taken place last night, his phone rang. It was Detective Aguero. Mark answered the phone and put it on speaker.

"Hi, Mark. This is Detective Aguero," Aguero said.

"How are you doing, Detective?"

"Not bad. I visited Edward Phillips in prison a week ago. I assume you know who he is."

"What did you talk about?"

"We talked about Laura Sumner. I asked if he knew who might have killed her, and he said that he didn't. I can send you a recording of our conversation, if you want."

"Thank you, Carlos. Yes, please send it to me."

"I'll do it today."

"Did you mention that it was me who told you about Laura?"

"No."

"Did you offer him anything for information?"

"I offered him a very good deal. I promised that we'd get his death sentence commuted if he helped us catch Laura's killer."

Should he tell Aguero about Sam Curtis? The police had the resources to monitor Curtis twenty-four/seven. He could warn Aguero that Curtis would disappear if he found out that the cops were onto him.

The Austin Police Department might screw up and scare Curtis off. Besides, it could be several months before Curtis killed again, and Mark doubted that Aguero would be allowed to keep him under surveillance for that long.

"Do you think he's telling the truth?" Mark said.

"I believe he's hiding something."

"Are you going to try to get him to talk?"

"No. I'm going to talk to his parents. They might know something useful."

"I believe Phillips's father might be involved in Laura's murder."

"This thought crossed my mind, too. I have a theory. Do you want to hear it?"

"Yes."

"I think Phillips had a partner, who helped him kill your daughter. And this partner killed Laura Sumner. Maybe Helen wasn't their first victim."

"When do you plan to talk to Phillips's parents?"

"Next week."

"Thanks for the call, Carlos. Please keep me posted."

"Sure."

After terminating the call, Mark realized he had never checked to see if Jeff Phillips had used any of his credit cards in Austin on August 23 or 24. When he got to police headquarters,

AN EVIL MIND

he requested a search warrant for information on all of Jeff Phillips's credit card and bank card transactions that had taken place last August. While Mark was preparing the warrant application, he received the audio file of Detective Aguero's conversation with Edward Phillips. He copied the file to a flash drive to listen to it later at home.

3

Mark came home at a quarter to eight. Joan had cooked a shepherd's pie for dinner, which was one of his favorite dishes. While Mark was eating, the landline phone rang. Joan muted the TV and picked up the receiver.

"Hello," she said.

"Hello, can I talk to Joan Hinton?" said a man's voice. The voice sounded artificial, robotic.

"This is Joan."

He's using a voice changer, she thought.

Honest people didn't need a voice changer. A vague uneasiness crept into Joan's mind.

"My name is Chuck. I have something important to tell you."

"I'm listening."

She looked at the caller ID. The area code was 214. It was a Dallas number.

"It's about your daughter, Helen. She was murdered last year, wasn't she?"

A dull pain gripped Joan's heart when she heard Helen's name.

"Yes, she was," she said.

"I found the knife."

"What knife?"

"The knife Helen was killed with. I think it's that knife. I want you to have it."

"Where did you find it?"

"Not far from the place where your daughter was murdered. I found it before the police got there."

"Why didn't you give the knife to the police?"

"I was afraid they'd think I was involved."

"Why do you want me to have it?"

"I'm giving it to you so you'll turn it over to the police. I think the killer might have left his fingerprints on it." He paused, then added, "I didn't clean the knife. It's in the same condition as when I found it. Please put on gloves before you touch it."

"When do you want to meet?"

"I'll mail it to you."

Why had he waited over ten months to come forward?

"Do you know my address?"

"Yes, I do."

He told Joan her address and asked if that was the correct address.

"Yes," Joan replied. "All right, mail it."

"I'll do it tomorrow morning. I'm very sorry about your daughter, Joan."

"Where did you get my number?"

"I found it online. I'm sorry if I scared you."

"Your voice sounds odd."

"I changed it because I want to stay anonymous. Do you have any more questions?"

"No."

"Goodbye, then."

"Goodbye." Joan hung up.

She stood by the phone for a few moments, then went to the dining room.

"Did someone call?" asked Mark, who was finishing his meal.

"Yes. Some guy named Chuck. He said he has the knife Helen was killed with. He said he's going to send it to me." Joan sat across the table from her husband.

Mark set down his fork. "Did he tell you his last name?"

"No."

"Where did he get that knife?"

"He found it near the place where Helen was killed. He said he didn't clean it. He wants me to give it to the police."

"Did he witness the murder?"

"I didn't ask him about it." Joan pushed a strand of hair from her forehead. "He used a voice changer."

"What else did he say?"

"Nothing. Do you think he's some kind of lunatic?"

"You think he's a lunatic?"

"Why did he keep the knife? Normal people don't do that."

"Sometimes normal people do strange things."

That was true.

Chuck could be one of those murder memorabilia collectors she had read about on the Internet.

4

Before listening to the recording of Detective Aguero's conversation with Edward Phillips, Mark did a reverse lookup of the number Chuck had called from on the Internet and found that it belonged to a pay phone.

This could be a hoax, Mark thought as he opened the audio file sent by Aguero.

Fortunately, it would be very easy to determine if it was a hoax: the real murder weapon should have traces of Helen's blood on it.

He would test the blood from the knife at a private DNA lab. And he would dust the knife for fingerprints himself so there could be no tampering.

Would the police reopen Helen's case if the fingerprints on the knife didn't belong to Edward Phillips?

They would certainly interview the person who had left the prints (if they managed to find him). If the guy confessed to Helen's murder, he would go to prison, but if he said that he had found the knife in the street, picked it up and then dropped it (or told another story that didn't involve murder), the police would have to let him go unless they proved that the fingerprints belonged to the killer.

How do you prove that the fingerprints got on the knife during the murder?

I'll think about it when I receive the knife.

What was he going to do if the person who had left the prints escaped conviction only because there was no proof that the prints belonged to the killer? He would kill the guy. Yes, he would take the law into his own hands.

I'll make him confess to Helen's murder before I kill him.

Would Chuck wipe away his fingerprints before mailing the knife? Mark was sure that he would. Anyone with half a brain would have done that. Hopefully, he wouldn't wipe away all of the killer's prints along with his.

If there was no match in the system for the prints on the knife, they might never find out the identity of Helen's killer and that bastard would go unpunished.

The thought of Helen's murderer roaming free and having fun made Mark's stomach turn over.

What if the fingerprints turned out to belong to Edward Phillips?

He would be pissed at Phillips for wasting his time, and he would do his best to make sure that Phillips was executed.

When the recording of Aguero's conversation with Phillips ended, Mark went to the living room and said to Joan, "When you receive the knife, don't touch it. I don't want you to mess up the fingerprints."

"Okay." Joan took his hand. "If they find Phillips's fingerprints on the knife, his appeal will fail for sure, right?"

"I think so, yes." Mark nodded.

"If the fingerprints belong to someone else, will they reopen the case?"

"I'll make sure that they reopen it."

AN EVIL MIND

Chapter 13

1

Phillips looked as dejected as he had two weeks ago. This time it gave Mark no pleasure.

"I'm glad to see you, Mark." Phillips tried to smile but managed only a grimace.

"You haven't had many visitors, have you?" Mark said.

"It's my birthday today. Did you know that?"

"No. Don't tell the others."

"Why?"

"They'll beat the shit out of you."

"Thanks for the heads-up."

Staring at Phillips, Mark remembered that when he was a child, he had been very nervous every time he blew out his birthday candles: he had feared he would fail to blow them out in one breath and thus would prevent his wish from coming true. He had stopped believing in birthday wishes at the age of fifteen—but he kept making them nonetheless, just in case.

"Why did your parents stop visiting you?"

"I don't know. You should ask them."

"Do you keep in touch with them?"

Phillips shook his head.

"Why?" Mark asked.

"I guess we have nothing to talk about." Phillips's face remained emotionless; there was not a hint of sadness in it. He didn't seem to miss his parents at all.

"Did you get my letter?"

"No."

"I followed Sam last Saturday from six p.m. to midnight. I saw nothing strange."

"Thank you, Mark. I really appreciate it. Did Curtis see you following him?"

"No."

"Are you going to follow him again?"

"Maybe next week."

"Thank you. You need to follow him every day. The only way to stop Sam is catch him in the act, and to do that, you need to follow him every day."

"I understand that."

"He might kill someone tonight."

"I'll follow him tonight if I have time."

"Have there been any new cases similar to your daughter's?"

"I don't know. I'll look into it. Have you heard what happened to your lawyer?"

"No. What happened to him?"

"He's been murdered."

Phillips's eyes widened in surprise. Frowning, he asked, "Are you talking about Leonard?"

"Yes."

"When?"

"Last Monday."

"How was he killed?"

"He was stabbed in the chest and his neck was cut open. He was in his car in the parking lot of his office building when it happened."

Phillips put the phone on the counter and dropped his head to his chest. He was silent for a long time, then he picked up the receiver and said hoarsely, "Do they know who killed him?"

There were tears in the corners of his eyes. It wasn't the first time Mark had seen Phillips cry. He had wept when the jury returned its guilty verdict and when the judge sentenced him to death.

"No. Who do you think did it?"

"I have no idea."

"Just before he was killed, Leonard asked me to meet him. He said he wanted to tell me something about your case. Could his murder have anything to do with your case?"

"I don't know." Phillips wiped his eyes. "He was a good man. This is just terrible. Terrible."

"I'm very sorry."

"He was a good man." Phillips clenched his free hand into a fist.

"Did you tell Barlow about Sam Curtis?"

"Yes."

"And what did he do about it?"

"Nothing. He said it was too expensive to hire a private detective to follow Curtis."

"Did you ask him not to tell the police about Curtis?"

"Yes, I did."

"I could help you find a new attorney. I know some good lawyers."

"I can't afford a private lawyer."

"What about your mother?"

"My parents hate me. I already told you that."

"You said your father hated you."

"My mother hates me, too."

"Who paid Barlow?"

"My parents paid Leonard some money when they hired him, but then they said they couldn't afford to pay him anymore. Leonard agreed to keep working on my case, for free."

The odds of Phillips winning the appeal had been slim when Barlow represented him, but they would be infinitesimal with a public defender.

Phillips must be in a very bad mood now.

"Detective Aguero told me he talked to you," Mark said.

"Yes, we talked."

"He asked you to help him catch Laura Sumner's killer, and you said you didn't know who killed her."

"Yes, that's what I said."

"You didn't tell him about Sam Curtis. Why?"

"You know why. As soon as Sam finds out he's under suspicion, he'll skip town, and the police will never find him."

"Why would he skip town if there's no evidence that he killed Laura Sumner?"

"Because he doesn't like to take chances."

Mark opened his mouth to say that Curtis couldn't hide forever, but then he thought: the police are not going to look for Curtis because there's no evidence linking him to Laura Sumner's or Helen's murder. Edward Phillips's claim that Curtis had confessed to killing Helen would be disregarded: he was convicted of Helen's murder and therefore had every reason to lie.

"Did you tell Aguero about Sam?" Phillips asked.

"No, I didn't."

"Was it you who told him about Helen?"

"Yes."

"Did you tell him that Helen and Laura were killed by the same person?"

"I told him these murders could be connected."

Phillips said nothing.

"Did Curtis tell you why it took him four weeks to post bail?" Mark asked.

"He said he didn't have enough money."

"What about his family?"

"His parents refused to help him because they wanted to teach him a lesson."

"What about his friends?"

"He said that both of his best friends were in prison for selling weed." Phillips switched the phone to his other ear. "Do you believe me, Mark? Do you believe what I said about Curtis?"

"I haven't made up my mind yet. I know that you passed a lie detector test."

"Yes, I did. I wouldn't have passed it if I was Helen's killer."

"I'd have an easier time believing you if you explained how Helen's blood got on your shoes and jeans."

"I don't know how it got there. Maybe someone sprinkled your daughter's blood on my clothes to frame me."

The pitch and tone of Phillips's voice remained unchanged. Mark searched Phillips's face for any sign that he was lying, and saw none.

"Who?"

"I don't know. Cops, maybe. Sometimes cops plant evidence."

"What about your fingerprint on Helen's belt buckle? How did it get there?"

"I don't know."

"Cops didn't put it there, that's for sure."

Phillips said nothing.

"Maybe you found my daughter's body after she was killed?"

"No, I didn't."

"You have to come up with an explanation if you want me to believe you."

"I'll try."

"Did Curtis tell you why he killed my daughter?"

"No."

"I checked Curtis's credit card records. He used his credit card at a gas station in Austin on the day of Laura Sumner's murder."

"You see. He did it. He killed Laura Sumner. And he'll kill again. Please follow him every day, I'm begging you."

Mark hesitated, then said, "Did you ask one of your friends to imitate Helen's murder?"

Phillips raised his eyebrows slightly. "What do you mean?"

"I have a suspicion that Laura Sumner was killed by one of your friends at your request."

It felt good to let Phillips know that Detective Mark Hinton was a hard man to deceive.

Phillips's lips curved in a small smile. "I see. You think I'm some kind of mastermind. Do I look like a mastermind?"

"Did you ask one of your friends to imitate Helen's murder?"

Phillips shook his head. "No, I didn't."

He seemed to be telling the truth.

"Sam Curtis killed Laura Sumner, and I didn't ask him to do it," Phillips said. "Sam Curtis killed your daughter. Please believe me, Mark."

"By the way, I saw your father drinking with Curtis in a bar last Saturday."

"Are you sure it was my father?"

"Yes."

Phillips thought for a moment, then said, "Have you talked to Sam?"

"No, I haven't."

"If Sam finds out he's under suspicion, he'll disappear and you'll never find him. You need to remember that."

"I remember it."

"Have you talked to my dad?"

"No. Is your father friends with Sam Curtis?"

"Did they look like they were friends?"

"Yes. They spent two hours together."

"Then I guess they are friends."

"Did you tell your father about Curtis's confession?"

"Yes. I told him not to confront Sam."

"Did he believe you?"

"No, he didn't."

His own father didn't believe him, and I still think he might be telling the truth.

"Did you ask your father to become friends with Curtis?"

"No, I didn't."

"I don't believe you."

"Why would I lie?"

Mark had no answer.

"Why did your father become friends with Curtis?"

Maybe it was Sam Curtis who had initiated the friendship?

Mark could think of no reason for Curtis to do it. If he were Curtis, he would have stayed away from Edward Phillips's family.

"I don't know. I haven't talked to him since January."

"Did you ask your father to spy on Curtis?"

"No."

"I think your father became friends with Curtis to spy on him."

"You may be right. Are you going to talk to him?"

"I might."

"Don't do it."

"Why?"

"Because my dad hates me."

"Why does he hate you?"

"I dishonored my family."

"I see. All right, I won't talk to your father."

Maybe Jeff Phillips had become Sam Curtis's friend to manipulate him into imitating Helen's murder? He might even have helped Curtis kill Laura Sumner.

"Do you think Sam Curtis had a motive to kill your lawyer?"

Phillips nodded. "Yes."

"What is it?"

"He wants my appeal to fail."

"That's a weak motive."

"I agree."

On the other hand, if Curtis is a murderous psycho, he doesn't need a good reason to kill, does he?

"When are you going to visit me again?" Phillips asked.

"I don't know."

"I really enjoy talking to you, Mark."

"I could ask your parents to visit you."

"Don't do it. I don't want to see them. They won't come anyway."

Mark hesitated, then said, "Last night my wife got a call from someone named Chuck. He said he had the knife used to kill my daughter, and he promised to send it to us. If I find Sam's fingerprints on that knife, I'll start following him every day."

After a silence, Phillips said, "Do you know where that Chuck guy lives?"

"No."

"Do you know his phone number?"

"He called from a pay phone."

"It's probably a prank."

"We'll see."

Mark was inclined to believe that Chuck was not playing a prank. What was the fun in lying to the mother of a slain girl about the murder weapon?

"I hope you find Sam's fingerprints on that knife." There was no enthusiasm in Phillips's voice. "If you catch Sam in the act, don't kill him."

"Okay."

"Do you want to find out why my dad made friends with Sam?"

"Yes, I do."

"Read the text messages they've sent each other."

It was a good idea. He might give it a try.

"Why don't you just ask your father?"

"He doesn't want to talk to me."

"Maybe he changed his mind about you. Aren't you curious why he made friends with Sam?"

"No, I'm not."

"What if Sam kills your father?"

"Why would he do that?"

"For fun."

"He's not going to kill my father."

AN EVIL MIND

Perhaps Phillips didn't care if Sam Curtis killed his dad.

Chapter 14

1

Sam squatted down and peered at the video receiver that sat on the bottom shelf of the TV stand next to the cable box. The tiny ball of paper Sam had placed on the device was exactly where it had been when he left the house; that meant no one had tampered with the receiver.

Sam sat down in a chair and switched on the monitor.

There were surveillance cameras in the living room and bedrooms, which were hidden in wall clocks. Sam had bought them shortly after he was released from the Dallas County Jail in January. It was not burglars that he wanted to catch on video. It was cops and FBI agents. He feared that one day the cops or the Feds would sneak into his house to look for evidence or install eavesdropping devices. His fear was not baseless.

The cameras were motion- and body-heat-activated, so it didn't take him long to review the security footage. The receiver had a battery backup which allowed it to operate for up to ten hours without external power supply.

Sam checked the footage religiously every day. So far not one burglar or law enforcement agent had broken into his house.

Monitoring his abode was not the only thing Sam did to detect the activities of the police and the FBI that were directed at him. Every night he put his car in the garage and swept it for GPS tracking devices. So far he hadn't found any trackers on his vehicle.

There had been no intruders today.

Sam switched off the monitor and said, "We're good."

Jeff Phillips grinned. "Excellent."

Jeff had hidden surveillance cameras in his house, too, and, like Sam, he regularly checked his car for GPS trackers.

Sam grabbed the remote and turned on the TV.

"Looks like we got away with it," he said.

AN EVIL MIND

He was talking about the murder of Leonard Barlow. It had been five days since he had killed the lawyer, and no one from the Dallas Police Department had paid him a visit yet.

Sam wasn't worried: there was no connection between him and Barlow, and therefore he wasn't going to get on the cops' radar.

"I hope you're right," Jeff said.

Sam went to the kitchen, got two bottles of beer from the refrigerator, and returned to the living room. He gave Jeff a bottle and said, "I talked to Leticia today. They have a woman with Stage Four ovarian cancer. Her son is worth at least a hundred million."

"What's his name?"

"Gordon Stryker."

"Never heard of him."

"Me neither."

"Do you have his contact information?"

"Yes. Leticia gave me his number."

"When are you going to call him?"

"As soon as we get an office. I called the company that runs that building by Parkland Hospital, and they said they still had space available."

"How much do they want?"

"A dollar thirty per square foot."

"Not bad. Let's take it."

"Okay. I'll go to their office on Monday."

"Five hundred square feet. That's all we need."

"I know."

"Use the fake ID."

"I know."

Tapping his foot on the floor, Jeff said, "How long has it been since we did that girl in Austin?"

"Two months. We have plenty of time."

Chapter 15

1

At one o'clock on Monday afternoon, as he was leaving Dallas PD headquarters, Mark ran into Robert Blanco, the lead detective on the Edward Phillips case. They had known each other since Blanco joined the Homicide Unit four years ago, but they weren't friends. Before coming to work at the Dallas PD Homicide Unit, Blanco had been a homicide detective with the San Antonio PD. He was married and had a six-year-old daughter.

"Do you have a minute?" Mark said after shaking Blanco's hand. "There's something I want to talk to you about."

"Is it going to take more than a minute?" Blanco asked.

"Yes. Fifteen minutes tops."

Blanco glanced at his watch and said, "I'm on my way to Hugo's. Let's talk there."

Hugo's was a Mexican restaurant about a mile from the Dallas Police Department. Mark had lunch there once every two weeks.

"Okay," Mark replied.

They arrived at the restaurant at the same time. Blanco ordered a grilled steak fajita and a Coke, and Mark three chicken enchiladas and lemonade.

"How are you?" Blanco said, looking at Mark solemnly. His shaved head gleamed in the lamplight.

"I'm fine," Mark said.

"How's Joan?"

"She's okay. How's your family?"

"They're fine. So what do you want to talk about?"

"The Phillips case."

Blanco nodded. "Okay, I'm all ears."

"Was Edward Phillips the only suspect in the case?"

"Yes, he was."

"Was there any evidence that he had an accomplice?"

AN EVIL MIND

"No. Have you heard what happened to his lawyer?"

"Yes, I have. Poor guy."

The waitress came back and set down their drinks.

"Did the name Christopher Novak ever come up during the investigation?" Mark asked.

Blanco thought for a long moment, then shook his head. "I don't think it did. Who is he?"

"A friend of Phillips's. Did the name Sam Curtis ever come up?"

If he asked Blanco whether he had planted evidence in the Edward Phillips case, he would probably get really mad. He might even throw the soda in his face. Mark doubted Blanco would punch him in the face, though.

"No, it didn't. Do you think Phillips had an accomplice?"

"I believe that he might. Did you talk to his parents?"

"Yes, I did."

"What are they like?"

"They seem to be nice people."

To his neighbors John Wayne Gacy had seemed to be a nice guy, too.

"Did either of them strike you as violent or psychotic?"

"No."

The waitress set their plates on the table, and Blanco thanked her.

Mark took a bite of his enchilada and then said, "When you looked for the murder weapon, did you search Phillips's parents' house?"

"No."

"Did you ever consider the possibility that his father was involved?"

"Involved how?"

"His father might have helped him kill Helen."

"No, we never considered this possibility."

Mark hesitated, and then said, "Did you do everything by the book in the Phillips case?"

"What do you mean?"

"You didn't have to bend the rules to prove that Phillips was guilty, did you?"

"No, of course not."

"I talked to Edward Phillips two weeks ago. He said he didn't kill Helen."

"That's what they all say."

"So there's no chance he's innocent?"

Blanco shook his head. "He did it. Trust me, Mark."

"But he passed a lie detector test."

"So what? All it tells me is that he learned how to beat a lie detector."

"He said he was framed."

"And who framed him?"

"Police."

Blanco laughed. "How original."

"Is it possible that Helen's blood was planted on his clothes?"

"Who could have done it? I know it wasn't me." Blanco smiled. "Maybe the CIA did it?"

"I'm not saying you had anything to do with it."

"Let me ask you, Mark. Have you ever framed anyone? Have you ever bent the rules?"

"I'm sorry, Rob. I didn't mean to offend you."

"It's all right." Blanco took a sip from his glass. "For a second I thought you believed that son of a bitch. Why did you talk to him in the first place?"

"I don't care about Phillips. I just want to be sure Helen's killer isn't still out there enjoying life."

Blanco speared a piece of steak with his fork and said, "You know, it's entirely possible that Phillips had an accomplice. But unless Phillips gives him up, we'll never find out who it is."

Mark nodded. "Can you do me a favor?"

"Sure."

"Can you give me a copy of Helen's DNA profile?"

"What do you need it for?"

"I just want to have it."

"All right. I'll send it to you."

"Thank you."

Blanco kept his word and emailed Helen's DNA profile to Mark shortly after five o'clock.

2

At three p.m., Mark went to Thomas Shaw, a homicide squad supervisor, and asked him if there had been any unsolved stabbing murders in the last two months. Shaw said they had two cases: Albert Estes, a forty-eight-year-old homeless man, who was killed on September 5, and Elvira Herrera, a thirty-six-year-old woman, who was killed on October 12. Albert Estes had been stabbed in the leg and Elvira Herrera in the stomach.

Mark was relieved to learn that there had been no cases similar to Helen's in Dallas since Edward Phillips had first told him about Sam Curtis.

A few minutes later he sent Detective Aguero an email asking if there had been any cases similar to Laura Sumner's in Austin since Laura's murder. Aguero emailed back saying that none of the murders that had occurred in Austin this year resembled Laura Sumner's.

At four-thirty Mark received a list of Jeff Phillips's Visa transactions. He opened the document and scrolled down until he saw the date "08/23." On August 23, at 6:07 p.m., Jeff Phillips had made an $18.56 purchase at a Burger King in Austin. The next transaction had taken place on August 25.

At Burger King, two people could eat for eighteen dollars. Jeff had either had a traveling companion or been very hungry.

Staring at the computer screen, Mark leaned back in his chair.

The fact that Jeff Phillips had been in Austin on August 23 supported the theory that he had killed Laura Sumner.

Sam Curtis was in Austin on August 23, too. Maybe they went there together.

Why would Jeff Phillips go to Austin with Curtis?

To make sure that Curtis killed his victim the same way his son had killed Helen.

He could try to find out if Jeff and Curtis had gone to Austin together by reading the text messages they had sent each other on August 23 and 24.

There was a third possibility, which was consistent with Edward Phillips's story. Maybe Jeff had followed Curtis to Austin to see what he was up to.

Why didn't Jeff stop Curtis from killing Laura Sumner?

Perhaps Jeff had lost Curtis before he attacked Laura.

After writing a report on an interview he had conducted today, Mark prepared an application for a search warrant for Sam Curtis's text messages from August 22 to 24.

When Mark got home, he spent an hour searching the Internet for new cases in which the victim had been killed the same way as Helen. All he managed to find was the case of Walter Kindred, who had been murdered in Newton, Massachusetts, in October of last year. Kindred's murder had been solved, so Sam Curtis had nothing to do with it.

AN EVIL MIND

Chapter 16

1

As the door closed behind him, Mark looked toward the corner where Detective Nelson Coogan's cubicle was. Coogan, the lead detective on the Barlow case, was at his desk, talking on the phone. Approaching Coogan's cubicle, Mark waved to him, and he waved back. The detective's fingers were so hairy that from a distance it seemed as though they were smeared with soot.

Two minutes later Coogan hung up the phone, then swiveled in his chair to face Mark and said, "What's up?"

"Leonard Barlow's murder is your case, isn't it?"

"Yes, it is."

"Do you have a suspect yet?"

"No, we don't."

"Did the killer leave any fingerprints?"

"No. The fingerprints we found belong to Barlow and his wife. Why do you ask?"

"I knew him. Not well, though."

"He was Edward Phillips's lawyer."

"Yes, he was. Were there any witnesses?"

"No witnesses. And the part of the parking lot where Barlow was killed wasn't covered by surveillance cameras. It's a tough case. His family announced a fifty thousand dollar reward, but so far no one has come forward."

"Did you find a murder weapon?"

"No."

Phillips said that Sam Curtis would disappear if he was confronted about Helen's murder. Would he disappear if the police questioned him in connection with Leonard Barlow's murder? Mark had no idea.

He would ask Phillips about it.

"Why do you think he was killed?"

"It could be a robbery gone wrong. Or a carjacking. He had a very nice car. It might have been premeditated."

"Did he have any enemies?"

"His wife says he had no enemies and he never received any threats. But she could be wrong. We started reading his emails yesterday; we might find something useful there. By the way, do you know anything that can help us?"

"No, I don't."

Suppose Sam Curtis was Barlow's killer. How would the police prove that he had murdered the lawyer if there were no witnesses and no physical evidence?

"Have you met Barlow's wife?"

"Yes."

"Do you think she could be involved?"

"I doubt it. Did she take a polygraph test?"

"No. I'm going to ask her to take it this week. Do you think Barlow was cheating on his wife?"

Mark shrugged. "I have no idea." He held out his hand. "I'll leave you alone now." They shook hands. "Let me know when you make an arrest."

"Sure, man."

2

At five-fifteen, Mark received a text message from Joan saying that the knife sent by Chuck had arrived. The message also said that Joan hadn't touched the knife.

As he pocketed his phone, Mark thought about his parents' house at Lake Ray Hubbard. He wasn't going to spy on the person whose prints were on the knife and try to catch him committing murder. He would torture this bastard until he confessed to killing Helen. And then he would kill him.

When Mark came home, Joan was in the living room reading a book.

"Hi, honey," Mark said.

"Hi."

"Where's the knife?"

"In the study." Joan put the book on the coffee table and rose from the couch.

"Did Chuck call today?"

"No."

When they went into the study, Joan pointed at the yellow bubble mailer on the desk and said, "It's in the envelope."

Mark took a pair of latex gloves from the bottom desk drawer, slipped them on, and looked inside the mailer. Joan stood beside him, watching. He could smell her perfume; it was Paloma Picasso, her favorite fragrance. There was a plastic zipper bag in the envelope, which contained a kitchen knife with a black handle. He got the bag out, opened it, and pulled out the knife.

There were brown stains on both sides of the blade. The thought that it might be his daughter's blood turned Mark's stomach.

"Is it blood?" Joan asked.

"It could be blood."

Mark stared at the knife as if hypnotized.

This knife might be the knife that had pierced Helen's heart. The knife that had cut open her stomach.

His arms broke out in gooseflesh.

Mark measured the blade with a ruler and found that it was six inches long. The deepest wound in Helen's body was six inches deep.

It's not a hoax. This is the knife used to kill Helen.

From the top drawer, he retrieved a DNA collection swab, which he had brought from work two days ago. He dampened the swab with tap water, then rubbed it over one of the larger stains on the blade and placed it in a storage envelope.

"Are you taking the swab to a lab tomorrow?" Joan laid a hand on his shoulder.

"Yes."

"When will the results be ready?"

"Thursday."

Joan watched him for a few more seconds and then walked out of the room.

Mark put the knife in a plastic evidence bag and then examined the bubble mailer. The sender's name was Chuck Smith, and the sender's address was 1094 Lakeland Drive, Dallas, TX 75218. Mark entered the address into Google Maps and discovered that it was bogus. That did not surprise him at all. The name was probably bogus, too. Both the sender's and the recipient's names and both of their addresses were printed, not handwritten.

"Chuck" had taken all the usual precautions to protect his anonymity. And he might even have made sure to leave no fingerprints on the mailer and the plastic bag the knife had been in.

Mark picked up the knife and studied it for about three minutes before admitting to himself that he had no idea how to prove that the fingerprints—assuming there were any—had gotten on the knife during Helen's murder.

As they sat in the living room watching TV, Joan asked him if he was going to turn the knife over to the police.

"I haven't made up my mind yet," Mark said.

"Are you going to dust it for prints yourself?"

"Yes."

"Don't give it to the police if the fingerprints don't belong to Phillips. I think it will be impossible to get a conviction."

Their eyes met.

"We have to take care of this ourselves," Joan said.

They sat in silence for a moment, then Mark said, "Do you want me to kill him?"

"Yes. And I'll help you."

Mark nodded. "Okay, I'll do it."

He felt a surge of adrenaline. He couldn't wait to beat Helen's killer to death, to see terror in his eyes, to hear him scream in pain.

Chapter 17

1

"They discovered a cure for cancer a long time ago, but they don't want us to know about it. You know why?"

The guy's name was Tony. He was young, no older than thirty. He had come to Beacon Cancer Center with his father, who had Stage II prostate cancer.

"Why?" Sam asked.

"It's more profitable to treat cancer than to cure it," Tony said. "That's how Big Pharma operates. All they care about is money."

"I've heard this theory. I believe it's wrong."

"Why?"

"Steve Jobs died. He had cancer."

"You mean the Apple guy?"

Sam nodded.

Tony thought for a long moment and then said, "You may be right, man."

Although Sam didn't believe Big Pharma was hiding the cure for cancer, he was sure that the people running pharmaceutical companies were corrupt enough to hide the cure when it was discovered.

Two days ago, on October 23, Sam had signed a lease for a five-hundred-square-foot office, which was available for immediate occupancy. Yesterday, he and Jeff had gone to an Office Depot store and bought furniture, computers and other equipment for their office. Two guys Sam had found on craigslist (their names were Kevin and Omar) assembled the furniture and set up the equipment. While Kevin and Omar were unpacking the computers, Sam received a call from Leticia, a nurse at Beacon Cancer Center that had agreed to provide him with information about patients for a fee. She told him that Charlotte Stryker, Gordon Stryker's mother, was scheduled for chemotherapy on October 25. Sam decided to catch Gordon

Stryker at the cancer center and try to talk to him about his proposal. If Charlotte came to the center without her son, he was going to call Stryker and make an appointment.

At nine-fifty, an old woman and a middle-aged man entered the waiting room. The man was Gordon Stryker; Sam recognized him from his picture he had seen on the website of his company, Alliance Group. Sam figured the old woman was Charlotte Stryker. They sat down across from Sam. Stryker whispered something to his mother and grabbed a magazine from the table.

Sam was glad that Stryker had come to the cancer center with his mother: it meant that the guy loved his mom very much and would pay a lot of money to save her life.

Five minutes later, a nurse took Charlotte to the infusion room. Sam waited half a minute, then got up and sat next to Gordon Stryker.

"Excuse me, is your name Gordon Stryker?" Sam asked.

Stryker looked at him and said, "Yes, it is. And you are?"

"My name is Jake Ford."

"Do I know you from somewhere?" Stryker closed the magazine and dropped it on the table.

"I can help your mother, Mister Stryker."

"What do you mean?"

"She has cancer, doesn't she?"

"Yes, she does."

"I can make it go away."

Stryker's round face became serious. "Do you know what kind of cancer my mother has?"

"Let's talk in the hallway."

"Okay."

They stood up and went out into the hallway.

"My mother has Stage Four ovarian cancer," Stryker said. "How are you going to make it go away?"

"We've developed a procedure that can permanently cure Stage Four ovarian cancer."

"Is it a surgical procedure?"

"No. It doesn't involve surgery, drugs, or radiation. It's an experimental, highly effective procedure."

Stryker adjusted his glasses. "Do you work for Beacon Cancer Center?"

"No. I work for New Horizons."

"Is it a cancer center?"

"No. It's a technology company. This is a totally risk-free offer, Mister Stryker. If we don't deliver, you don't pay."

"How much does this procedure cost?"

"It's not cheap. Ten million dollars."

Stryker raised an eyebrow. "Ten million?"

"Yes. Your mother's cancer will be gone for good. She'll be completely healthy. Healthy and happy. I believe it's worth much more than ten million."

"Do I have to pay anything upfront?"

There seemed to be genuine interest in Stryker's voice.

"No, you don't."

"If the procedure fails, I pay nothing?"

"That's right."

"How does this procedure work?"

"We replace malignant cells with healthy ones."

"Is it risky?"

"No, it's totally safe. And it has an exceptionally high success rate. You don't have to decide right now. Here's my number. Feel free to call me anytime." Sam gave Stryker his business card. The card had his alias, the name of his fake company, and a phone number, which belonged to one of his disposable cellphones. "When does your mother's chemotherapy treatment end?"

"Next February."

"Has she had surgery?"

"Yes."

"What's the prognosis?"

"Not very good. How many people have undergone this procedure?"

"Ten. And all of them were cured. How old is your mother?"

"Seventy-two."

"Would you like her to live twenty-five more years?"

"Yes, of course."

"Let us help your mother before it's too late, Mister Stryker. Please think about it. If you have any questions, don't hesitate to call."

"I'll think about it."

"I look forward to hearing from you. Have a nice day."

They shook hands, and Sam headed for the elevators. He was proud of himself: he thought his sales pitch to Stryker had been pretty good.

Chapter 18

1

On his way to work, Mark stopped by the Dallas laboratory of Express DNA Testing Service and dropped off the sample.

When he dusted the handle of the knife sent by Chuck, Mark saw that there were fingerprints all over it. He found two full prints on one side and two on the other, and as he looked at them, his heart began to beat faster.

In less than an hour, he would know who had really murdered Helen.

Mark photographed the prints, then lifted them from the handle and placed them on backing cards.

He asked Todd Castor to run the fingerprints through the system. One match was found for the first print.

It's Sam Curtis, Mark thought, looking at the computer screen.

Castor clicked a button, and the match's name and photo appeared on the screen. Mark's heart stopped for a second.

The match's name was Edward Phillips. The man looked like the Edward Phillips convicted of Helen's murder.

When Mark saw the match's latest conviction, his last doubts vanished: it was *that* Edward Phillips.

Phillips had lied to him, and he had been stupid enough to believe this son of a bitch. He was a shitty judge of character, wasn't he?

Thank God I didn't waste a lot of time spying on Sam Curtis.

"Do you want a printout?" Castor asked.

"No. I know this guy," Mark said, frowning with indignation.

I shouldn't jump to conclusions. I still don't know if those brown stains on the blade are Helen's blood.

Yes, he should wait until he saw the DNA test results.

AN EVIL MIND

Maybe Phillips got hold of the knife after the killer threw it away.

The second print belonged to Edward Phillips, too, and so did the third and the fourth.

At five o'clock Joan called Mark and asked if he had found any fingerprints on the knife.

"No, I didn't," Mark replied. "He must have wiped it."

He would tell her the truth tomorrow, after he got the DNA test results.

"Phillips wrote you another letter," Joan said.

"Open it and read it to me, please."

Joan tore open the envelope, took out the letter, and read it to Mark: "Dear Mark, I hope this finds you well. Have you read Sam's text messages? Have there been any new cases similar to Helen's? Did they catch Leonard's killer? I look forward to hearing from you." Then she asked, "Who's Leonard?"

"He was Phillips's lawyer."

"He was murdered?"

"Yes."

"Have there been any new cases similar to Helen's?"

"Not that I know of."

On the way home, Mark thought: You have to be an idiot to throw away a murder weapon without wiping off your fingerprints. Edward Phillips didn't strike him as an idiot.

2

Detective Aguero had planned to talk to Edward Phillips's parents on Tuesday, October 24, but delayed his visit for a day because he had to interrogate two suspects in another case he was working on. He left Austin at two o'clock and arrived at the Phillipses' house at five minutes past five. After killing the engine, Aguero grabbed his phone and opened his email.

There were no new messages from the Allan B. Polunsky Unit.

Twelve days had passed since their meeting, and Edward Phillips still hadn't warned his partner. The only person he had contacted in that period was Detective Mark Hinton.

Aguero took out his notebook and found Jeff Phillips's license plate number. It matched the license plate number on the black Cadillac CTS parked in front of the Phillipses' house.

Aguero got out of the car and rang the doorbell. Jeff Phillips answered the door. Aguero showed his badge and said, "I'm Detective Aguero. I'm with the Austin Police Department. Are you Jeff Phillips?"

"Yes."

"Do you mind if I ask you a few questions?"

"Can I see your badge again?"

"Sure."

Aguero held his badge out. Jeff studied it and then said, "Please come in."

In the living room, Jeff said, "I'm all ears."

"Did you go out of town on August twenty-third?"

"August twenty-third." Jeff thought for a moment and then said, "No, I didn't."

He looked calm and friendly, his posture easy, his hands resting on the arms of his chair. It was hard to tell if he was lying.

"Where were you from eight p.m. to midnight on August twenty-third?"

"What day of the week was that?"

"Wednesday."

"I was probably home."

"You don't remember where you were that night?"

He should find out if any of Jeff Phillips's or Emily Phillips's credit card transactions had taken place in Austin on August twenty-third.

"It was such a long time ago. But I'm pretty sure I was home. I don't go out on weekday nights."

"Are you married?"

"Yes."

"Is your wife home?"

"No. She's out shopping."

"The black Cadillac parked in front of your house—is it yours?"

"Yes. Why are you asking me these questions? Do you think I did something wrong?"

Aguero leaned back in his chair and said, "Last December, your son, Edward Phillips, murdered a fifteen-year-old girl named Helen Hinton. Two months ago, a young woman named Laura Sumner was killed in the same manner as Helen Hinton. We believe these murders are connected."

Helen Hinton's murder was still the only one that might be connected to Laura Sumner's: so far none of the agencies Aguero had sent inquiries to had reported a case similar to Sumner's.

Jeff's placid look gave way to a serious expression. Frowning, he said, "I see. Where did the second murder take place?"

"Austin."

"What did you say the victim's name was?"

"Laura Sumner."

"Poor woman. So she was killed in August?"

"Yes, on August twenty-third. Do you have any information about this murder?"

Jeff shook his head. "No, I don't. I wish I could help you, but I don't know anything about this murder."

"Did Edward confess to you that he killed Helen Hinton?"

"No."

"Did you ever ask him if he did it?"

"Yes. He said he was innocent."

"Do you believe him?"

"I want to believe him, but... He was found guilty. There's proof that he killed that girl." Jeff stroked his chin. "You know, sometimes I wonder where we went wrong with Ed. Maybe we weren't strict enough with him when he was a child. As far as I remember, we never physically punished Ed." Jeff paused. "Maybe we failed to instill the right values in him." He sighed. "I really hope it wasn't our fault."

"Did your son have any close friends?"

"I suppose he did, but I don't know who they were."

"Is Edward your only child?"

"Yes?"

Aguero heard the front door open and close.

"What do you do for a living?"

Emily Phillips walked into the room. She wore jeans and a long-sleeved blouse, and had a shopping bag in her hand.

"Hi." She smiled at Aguero.

"Honey, this is Detective Aguero," Jeff said.

"Good evening, ma'am," Aguero said.

"Good evening, Detective."

"This is my wife, Emily," Jeff said to Aguero.

Emily smiled at Aguero again. "I'll be upstairs." She left the room.

"I teach sociology at the University of Texas at Dallas," Jeff said.

"Can I have your cellphone number?"

"Sure."

Jeff told Aguero his cellphone number.

"Do you mind asking Mrs. Phillips to come here?" Aguero said.

"No problem."

Jeff brought his wife to the living room and asked Aguero if he had any more questions for him.

"No, I don't," Aguero replied. "Thanks for your time, Mister Phillips."

AN EVIL MIND

"You're welcome."

After Jeff walked out of the room, Aguero showed Emily his badge and said, "I'm Detective Aguero with the Austin Police Department. Can I ask you a few questions?"

"Yes, of course," Emily said.

She was about five feet seven and seemed to be in good physical shape. She was strong enough to have killed Helen Hinton and Laura Sumner.

"Did you go out of town on August twenty-third?"

"No, I didn't."

"Do you remember where you were from eight p.m. to midnight on August twenty-third?"

"Was it a weekday?"

"Yes."

"I was home. What happened on August twenty-third?"

"A young woman was murdered in Austin. Her name was Laura Sumner. I believe your son might know who killed her."

"How can Ed know that? He's been in prison since last December."

"I know that. Did you ever ask Edward if he killed Helen Hinton?"

"Yes, I did."

"What did he say?"

"He said he didn't do it."

"Do you think he's innocent?"

"Yes, I think he's innocent."

"Would you like to save his life?"

"Yes, of course."

Emily sat up straighter in her chair, her eyes lit up.

"As I said, I believe Edward might know who killed Laura Sumner. If he helps us catch the perpetrator, we'll get the governor to commute his death sentence to life imprisonment. I need you to help me persuade him to cooperate with us."

"Ed doesn't want to cooperate?"

"No, he doesn't."

"Why?"

"I don't know."

"Do you want me to talk to him?"

"Yes."

"What prison is Ed in?"

"The Allan B. Polunsky Unit. It's in Livingston."

"Okay, I'll talk to him."

"I wrote the prison's phone number on the back." Aguero gave Emily his card. "I believe Laura Sumner was murdered by someone Edward knows very well. Did your son have any close friends?"

"Yes, he did. His best friend's name was Chris, I forget his last name."

"Do you have his contact information?"

"No."

"Did your son live alone?"

"Yes."

"Did Edward have a girlfriend?"

"Yes, he did. Her name was Anna."

"Do you have her contact information?"

"No."

"Can you give me your cellphone number?"

After Emily told him her number, Mark stood up and said, "Well, thanks for your time, Mrs. Phillips. Please call me after you talk to Edward."

AN EVIL MIND

Chapter 19

1

Gordon Stryker called Sam the next day around ten in the morning, while he was sitting in a coffee shop in Arlington. Stryker asked if Sam could come to his office tomorrow morning to discuss Sam's proposal.

"Sure." Sam grinned, his heart hammering in his chest.

Ten million dollars was now almost within his reach.

"What time?" he asked.

"How about ten o'clock?"

"Ten is fine."

2

A few minutes after Gordon Stryker phoned Sam Curtis, Seth Elsworthy, a technician at the Express DNA Testing Service lab, handed Mark the DNA test report. According to the document, the sample submitted by Mark was human blood. Mark took Helen's DNA report from his jacket pocket, gave it to Elsworthy, and said, "Can you tell me if both of these samples came from the same person?"

Elsworthy studied the reports for about two minutes, his eyes shifting between the documents every two seconds, and then said, "Yes, they came from the same person. The profiles match perfectly. All markers are identical."

"What are the chances that these samples came from two different people?"

"One in a billion."

So the knife sent by Chuck was really the knife used to kill Helen.

And Edward Phillips's story was really a lie.

If it was Phillips who had murdered Helen, then who had killed Laura Sumner?

Either Laura Sumner's murder was unrelated to Helen's, or she had been killed by one of Phillips's friends.

Mark called the Allan B. Polunsky Unit and scheduled a visit with Phillips. This was going to be the last time he ever spoke to him. He decided to turn the knife over to Detective Blanco on Monday.

3

On Thursday, Aguero requested a search warrant for Jeff Phillips's and his wife's credit card and bank records for last August. He also applied for a warrant for geolocation records for Jeff's cellphones (because Jeff might have more than one cellphone number, the warrant covered all cellphone numbers registered to him). The good thing about cellphone tracking was that a phone's location was recorded by the network—usually several times a minute—as long as it was switched on and getting a signal.

4

"A police detective came to my house yesterday," Jeff said.

"What did he want?" Sam asked.

They were in Sam's living room, drinking beer.

"He's investigating Laura Sumner's murder. He asked me if I left Dallas on August twenty-third."

Laura Sumner. That was the name of the girl Sam had killed in Austin last August.

"What did you tell him?"

"I said I didn't."

"The name of the girl I killed in Austin was Laura Sumner."

"Yep."

"When did we go to Austin? August twenty-third?"

"Yes."

"Did he explain why he asked *you* this question?"

"He thinks that Laura Sumner's murder is connected to the murder of Helen Hinton."

"I see."

"He probably thinks that Edward had a partner and that the partner killed Laura Sumner."

"And he thought it might be you."

He thought *it might be you.*

What he should have said was "He *thinks* it might be you." Sam hoped the detective had crossed Jeff's name off the suspect list but doubted it had happened.

"He asked Emily where she was on August twenty-third," Jeff said.

"Jesus, is she a suspect, too?"

"I guess so."

"They might want to search your house. Make sure you have nothing illegal there."

"Illegal… I'll bring the guns here."

Jeff was talking about the two unregistered pistols he had at home.

"Okay."

"I'm glad we installed those cameras."

"Do you think this detective talked to Edward?"

"I bet he did. I wonder if Edward told him I killed that girl in Austin."

Could Edward have told the detective that Jeff had murdered Laura Sumner? Of course he could. Not because he thought Jeff was Sam's partner—he had no reason to think so—but because he wanted to hurt Sam.

Why hadn't Edward told the detective that Sam was his partner?

Perhaps he thought the detective wouldn't believe him.

"I'm glad we buried Edgar," Jeff said.

Sam nodded slowly. "Yeah."

Chapter 20

1

"Thanks for visiting me," Phillips said.

"No problem," Mark replied.

"Did you get my letter?"

"Yes, I did."

Phillips ran his right hand through his hair. When his eyes fell on the barbwire tattoo on Phillips's wrist, Mark remembered that Curtis had a similar tattoo on his wrist.

"Curtis has the same tattoo as you," Mark said.

"You mean this?" Phillips raised his right hand.

"Yes. When did you get it?"

"A year ago. Have you read the text messages Sam and my dad sent each other?"

"No, I haven't."

Sam Curtis's cellphone company had sent the text messages to Mark on Wednesday, but he hadn't bothered to read them yet.

"Are you going to?"

Mark's heart was thumping hard in his chest. He wanted to scream at Phillips, to bang the receiver against the glass separating them.

"Yes."

"Have there been any new cases similar to Helen's?"

"No."

"Have you followed Sam since last Saturday?"

"No."

"You still don't believe me, do you?"

"No, I don't."

"Did they catch Leonard's killer?"

"No."

"You sound… irritated. Is something wrong?"

"Everything's fine."

"Good. I got a new lawyer. I met him yesterday."

"I received the knife I told you about the other day."

Phillips's calm expression did not change.

"Did it have Helen's blood on it?" Phillips asked.

"Yes. Also, there were fingerprints on the handle. You want to know who they belong to?"

"Who is it?"

"You. These fingerprints are yours, Edward."

Mark wished he could have said 'motherfucker' instead of 'Edward.'

Would his visit be terminated if he called Phillips a motherfucker?

Phillips raised his eyebrows in surprise and removed the phone from his ear. Mark sensed that his surprise was feigned. They stared at each other in silence for a long moment, and finally Mark said, "How do you explain it?"

"It's not the knife your daughter was killed with."

"There's Helen's blood on the blade. I did a DNA test. It's her blood." Mark clenched his teeth, feeling anger heating his skin.

"It can't be that knife because I didn't kill Helen."

"Are you deaf? There's my daughter's blood on the blade. You killed her, you son of a bitch!"

Phillips shook his head. "I didn't kill Helen."

"Do you think I'm an idiot? Well, I guess I am an idiot, because I believed you. What was this charade all about? Did you get bored?" Mark squeezed the phone hard and closed his right hand into a fist.

"I didn't kill your daughter, Mark." Phillips sighed deeply. "I can explain this, but you're not going to believe me."

"Try me."

"Leonard didn't believe me, and he was my lawyer."

"I'll believe you if you can prove what you say."

"Let me think about it."

"Did you kill Helen?"

"No."

"Cut the crap, Edward. I know you killed her. Your fingerprints are on the murder weapon. There are no other prints on it."

Why wouldn't this bastard admit that he had killed Helen? Why the hell was he so stubborn?

"I didn't kill your daughter. Sam Curtis sent you that knife. He's trying to frame me."

"Is that your explanation?"

"No."

"So that knife was sent by Sam Curtis?"

"Yes."

"Was that knife used to kill my daughter?"

"Maybe."

"Why did he keep the knife? To frame you?"

"I don't know."

"How did your fingerprints get on the knife?"

"I can explain it, but you won't believe me."

Mark shook his head in exasperation. "I've had enough of this bullshit. You fooled me, Edward. Congratulations. But guess what? The joke's on you. You'll be dead in a few years. Enjoy your stay in hell."

He slammed the receiver on the hook.

2

Could Phillips have left fingerprints on the handle of the knife before or during the trial?

This would have required assistance from a guard.

Sam Curtis might have bribed a guard.

Mark was convinced that Phillips's prints had gotten on the knife when he used it to murder Helen, but for some reason his mind was thinking up alternative theories, and he was unable to stop it. He felt as though his mind was a debate club, where two teams argued for opposite positions.

Maybe Curtis had killed Helen with a knife he had stolen from Edward Phillips's house?

Or maybe Curtis had collected some of Helen's blood after killing her and then sprinkled it on the knife (which he had stolen from Phillips's house)?

Why didn't Phillips say he'd found the knife after Helen was killed? Because he didn't want to lie?

Phillips had said his lawyer hadn't believed his explanation. Leonard Barlow might have written Phillips's explanation down in his notebook. Would Alice Barlow let him go through her husband's notebooks? Mark doubted it, but he thought it was worth a try.

Chapter 21

1

On Monday morning, Mark called Detective Nelson Coogan and asked him for an update on the Leonard Barlow case. Mark thought Alice Barlow would be more cooperative if he gave her some inside information about her husband's case. Coogan said that no arrest had been made yet and that they still had no suspect.

As he climbed the porch steps of Alice Barlow's house, Mark asked himself what he was doing here.

There were Edward Phillips's prints on the murder weapon and Helen's belt buckle. Phillips's jeans and boots had Helen's blood on them. It had been proved beyond doubt that Phillips had killed Helen. He ought to accept it and move on instead of trying to refute the evidence against Phillips.

What the hell is wrong with me?

Alice Barlow looked pale and weary. She recognized Mark as soon as she saw him.

"What can I do for you?" she asked.

"I'd like to ask you for a favor. Leonard defended the man who killed my daughter. That man was sentenced to death. I was wondering if you would let me read Leonard's notes about this case."

If she says no, I'll get up and go home.

"I'm very sorry about your daughter. What was her name?"

"Helen. She was fifteen."

"When did it happen?"

"Last December."

"What's the man's name?"

"Edward Phillips."

"Why do you want to read Leo's notes?"

Should he tell her the truth?

AN EVIL MIND

"I think Edward Phillips might be innocent, and I believe that your husband might have found evidence exonerating him."

"You think Edward Phillips might be innocent? I find it hard to believe."

"Well, that's what I think."

"Leo was working on Edward Phillips's appeal. How do I know you're not gathering information for the DA's office?"

"It's not the kind of thing the DA's office would do."

"What makes you think Leo found evidence exonerating Edward Phillips?"

She was not going to let him look at Barlow's notes. It was time to get up and go home.

"I have an idea. Can you go through your husband's notes for me? What I want to know is how Phillips explained his fingerprints on the murder weapon."

"They never found the murder weapon."

"Did Leonard talk to you about the Phillips case?"

"Yes."

"They found the murder weapon a few days ago. It has Phillips's fingerprints on it."

"Where did they find it?"

"It was sent to the police by mail."

He should go home. The investigation was over. Phillips was guilty.

"So the murder weapon has Phillips's fingerprints on it, but you still think he might be innocent?"

"Phillips told me he was being framed."

"You talked to Phillips?"

"Yes, I did."

"Is that all he told you?"

"He said he knew who killed my daughter."

"Did he strike you as insane?"

"No."

"Did he say anything weird?"

"No."

"Did he ever mention body switching?"

"Body switching? No. So what do you think about my idea?"

After a silence, Alice said, "You don't need to read Leo's notes. I know what Phillips told him." She paused. "He said that he wasn't Edward Phillips."

"What does that mean?"

"He told Leo that Edward Phillips had switched bodies with him last January."

"Switched bodies?"

"Yes. Have you seen Freaky Friday?"

Switched bodies. Had Phillips lost his mind?

"Did he tell your husband who he really was?"

"Yes. Leo mentioned his real name to me, but I don't remember it."

"Is it Sam Curtis?"

Alice thought for a moment, then shrugged. "It could be Sam Curtis."

"Did he say he used to share a cell with Phillips?"

"Yes, he did."

"Did he explain how Phillips had switched bodies with him?"

"He said it was black magic."

Of course it was black magic. What else could it have been?

"This is crazy," Mark said.

"He said he could prove that Phillips swapped bodies with him."

"Did he prove it?"

"Leo told him that the jury wouldn't believe him no matter how much proof there was."

Mark stared at the floor for a few seconds and then said, "You're not pulling my leg, are you?"

Alice smiled. "No. Why would I do that?"

"What did Leonard think about Phillips's story?"
"He thought it was nonsense."

2

Why had Phillips told Barlow this ridiculous story?

Phillips wasn't crazy, that was for sure. If he was, Barlow would have tried an insanity defense.

Why didn't he tell me about the body swap?
Because he knew I'd laugh in his face.

He had said he could prove that Phillips had switched bodies with him. It had to be bullshit. Why? Because body switching was impossible.

Ridiculous as it was, Mark was intrigued by Edward Phillips's body-swap story. The next morning he realized that he wanted to hear Phillips's proof. He was motivated by curiosity, and he thought it was as good a reason as any. On Wednesday, Mark scheduled a visit with Phillips.

3

Sam was watching a rerun of Family Guy when his disposable phone rang. It was Gordon Stryker.

"Hello, Mister Stryker," Sam said cheerfully. "How are you doing?"

They had met in Stryker's office on October 27 and talked for forty-five minutes. Stryker asked a dozen questions and then said that he wanted his mother to try the procedure.

"Do you have two hours? I'd like you to explain the procedure to her," he said.

"Sure, no problem," Sam replied.

He reminded Stryker that the procedure cost ten million dollars, and Stryker said that he remembered that. They got in Stryker's Mercedes and went to Stryker's house in Preston Hollow. After Sam explained the procedure to Charlotte Stryker, Gordon told his mother that she should try it.

"Yes, it sounds great," Charlotte said. "Let's do it."

Sam had said that he would schedule her for November 3.

"Good evening, Jake," Stryker said. "I'm calling to tell you that I have to cancel the deal."

Sam's heart sank.

"Why? What happened?"

Had this motherfucker gotten cold feet? Or was Stryker trying to make him lower the price?

"My mother passed away last night."

"Oh my God! I'm very sorry."

Sam grimaced. Three days. All this old bitch had had to do was stay alive for three more days.

"Goodbye, Jake."

Sam put his cellphone on the couch and shouted, "Shit! Shit! Shit!"

The next day he searched the website of The Dallas Morning News for Charlotte Stryker's obituary and found it. Gordon had told the truth, his mother had really kicked the bucket.

AN EVIL MIND

Chapter 22

1

"I didn't think I'd ever see you again," Edward Phillips said. "Are you still mad at me?"

"Did you tell Leonard Barlow that Edward Phillips switched bodies with you?" Mark asked.

There was a moment of silence, then Phillips nodded. "Yes, I did."

"Why did you tell him that?"

"Because it's true."

"It's true? Phillips actually switched bodies with you?"

"Yes. I used to... I used to reside in Sam Curtis's body. Edward Phillips took my body because he knew he had no chance of acquittal."

"You can't be serious."

"I know it sounds unbelievable, but it's true. Edward Phillips stole my body."

A thought flashed through Mark's mind: This story is too crazy to be a lie.

"So you're Sam Curtis?"

"Yes. You asked me why Jeff Phillips hung out with Sam Curtis. Now you know."

"When did he swap bodies with you?"

"January eleventh."

"How do you think he did it?"

"He probably used some kind of black magic."

"Black magic?"

"Do you know how to switch bodies without magic?"

"No."

"Neither do I. It had to be something supernatural."

"Something like a spell?"

"Yes. I believe Phillips killed your daughter and Laura Sumner because the ritual requires him to make a human sacrifice."

"You mean the body switch ritual?"

Phillips nodded.

"What did he do just before he swapped bodies with you?"

The knife. He still hadn't handed the knife over to Detective Blanco. Was it because he thought that Phillips might be innocent?

No, I just forgot.

"I didn't see anything. He did it while I was asleep. There was a full moon on the night we switched bodies. I don't know whether it's a coincidence or not."

Phillips wouldn't have mentioned this fact if he thought it was a coincidence, would he?

"Barlow didn't believe you, did he?"

"No, he didn't. Do you believe me?"

"Can you prove that Phillips swapped bodies with you?"

Would he believe Phillips if his proof was convincing and irrefutable?

Being a rational man, Mark did not believe in any kind of magic. However, he would believe Phillips's body-switch story if the proof presented by him was *truly* convincing and irrefutable. It would be irrational not to.

"I can prove that I'm Sam Curtis."

"Go ahead, I'm listening."

"I know things only Sam Curtis would know."

"What are they?"

"The gun in the vent. I was the only one who knew where it was."

"You mean the gun used to rob that convenience store in Garland?"

"Yes."

That was not convincing proof. He might have heard about the pistol from Sam Curtis.

"What else do you know?"

"My email address is samcurtisx@gmail.com. The password is tigger123. I'm the only person who knows it. Try it when you get home. You'll see that it's the correct password."

"How do I know it's Sam Curtis's email address?"

"Ask my parents. They'll confirm it's my email address."

"All right, I'll ask them. And I'll try the password." Mark took out his notebook and pen. "Can you repeat the email address and password?"

Phillips repeated his email address and password, and Mark jotted them down.

Could Curtis have told Phillips his email password? Mark didn't think so. People rarely shared their email passwords with others.

"What are your parents' names?" Mark asked.

"My father's name is Brian Curtis. And my mother's name is Caroline Dolman."

He had to verify that these people were really Phillips's parents.

"Are they divorced?"

"Yes, they are."

"Where do they live?"

"My father lives in Dallas, and my mother in San Antonio."

"What are their addresses?"

Phillips told Mark his parents' addresses and then said, "I know my Social Security number."

"Okay, give it to me."

Phillips told Mark his Social Security number.

"Sixteen years ago my mother cheated on my father with a guy named Aaron Townsend," Phillips said. "Ask my dad about it when you meet him."

"Okay."

"When I was fifteen, I broke my dad's video camera. I dropped it from the roof of our house. I had a Border Collie named Bruno. I got him when I was eleven. He died when I was twenty-two. I could give you my ATM PIN code, but I'm sure Phillips has changed it."

"Did you have an eBay account?"

"Yes. The username is rogue999, and the password is Sherlock123, with an uppercase S."

After Mark wrote down the username and password, Phillips asked, "If everything I said checks out, will you help me bring Edward Phillips to justice?"

"I don't know. I'll have to think about it. Why did you rob that store in Garland?"

"I needed money."

"Did you commit any other robberies?"

"No, I didn't."

"Did you ever kill anyone?"

"No."

Was he really going to check out what Phillips had said?

Why not? What if Phillips was telling the truth?

He had to do it for Helen.

"Who do you think Phillips told about the body switch?" Mark asked.

"His father. You saw them together in a bar, didn't you?"

"What about his mother?"

"He probably told her, too."

"His girlfriend?"

"If I were him, I wouldn't tell my girlfriend about this."

"Did you have a girlfriend at the time of your arrest?"

"Yes. Her name's Sandra Chandler."

"Do you think Phillips broke up with her?"

"Yes. Don't ask his parents about the body switch, please."

"Okay. Did you tell anyone about this besides Barlow?"

"No."

Mark put his notebook in his pocket and said, "Do you have anything else to tell me?"

AN EVIL MIND

Phillips hesitated. "Have you given that knife to the police?"

"No, not yet."

"Thank you, Mark."

"Goodbye." Mark hung up the phone.

2

At 1:17 p.m. Mark switched on his laptop, opened the web browser, and went to gmail.com. He typed samcurtisx into the Username field and tigger123 into the Password field and hit Enter. The inbox appeared on the screen. The password worked.

Mark opened the Sent Mail folder and saw that the latest email had been sent on December 15 of last year, the day before Sam Curtis's DWI arrest.

The last read email had been received at 12:13 p.m. on December 16 of last year.

It appeared that this email account hadn't been used since the day of Sam Curtis's DWI arrest.

Mark went to eBay.com and tried the username and password he had gotten from Phillips. The username and password were valid. The account belonged to Sam Curtis. Its registered email address was samcurtisx@gmail.com. Mark checked the purchase history and discovered that the last purchase (it was a pair of earbuds) had been made on November 21 of last year.

Chapter 23

1

On October 27, Aguero received responses from all the cellphone companies from which he had requested geolocation records. It turned out that the cellphone number Jeff Phillips had given him was Jeff's only number. The geolocation records showed that between eight p.m. and midnight on August 23, the estimated time of Laura Sumner's death, Jeff's phone had been in Carrollton. It had been connected to one cell tower the whole time; the tower was located near Jeff's house, which led Aguero to the conclusion that Jeff had left his phone at home that night.

Jeff's credit card records showed that his Visa card had been used at a Burger King restaurant in Austin at 6:07 p.m. on August 23. However, this transaction alone did not prove beyond doubt that Jeff Phillips had been in Austin on August 23. The purchase might have been made by someone Jeff had allowed to use his Visa card. Or Jeff might have lost the card on or before August 23, and the person who had found it had used it at the Burger King.

People rarely—perhaps almost never—went out of town without their cellphones, if they owned one. Why had Jeff Phillips left his phone at home when he went to Austin on August 23?

To prevent the police from finding out his whereabouts on that day?

He had done it intentionally, that was for sure.

On November 3, Aguero called the Allan B. Polunsky Unit and asked if anyone had visited Edward Phillips since October 25. He was surprised to learn that neither Emily Phillips nor her husband had visited Edward Phillips.

Was Emily Phillips too busy to visit Edward? She had seemed enthusiastic about helping her son when Aguero talked to her.

Had she changed her mind? Maybe she had found out that Jeff was Edward's partner?

On November 4, Aguero went to Carrollton to talk to Jeff Phillips.

2

"When we first met, I asked you if you went out of town on August twenty-third. You said that you didn't. Is that correct, Jeff?" Aguero said.

"Yes, that's correct," Jeff Phillips replied.

"Are you sure you didn't go out of town on August twenty-third?"

"Yes, I'm sure."

"Did you let anyone use your credit cards last August?"

"No."

"Did you lose your Visa card last August?"

"No."

"Do you have it on you?"

"Yes. Why?"

Aguero reached into his pocket and took out a printout of Jeff Phillips's Visa transactions. "According to your credit card records, you made a purchase at a Burger King in Austin on August twenty-third. That means you were in Austin on that day, doesn't it?"

He unfolded the printout and handed it to Jeff. He had highlighted the transaction in question with a yellow marker to make it easy to find. Jeff stared at the document for a long moment, then shifted in his chair and said, "I suppose I forgot I was in Austin in August. I thought I went there in September."

"What were you doing in Austin?"

Jeff returned the printout to Aguero and said, "I went there to meet someone."

"Who?"

"A woman," Jeff said with an embarrassed smile. "Please don't tell my wife."

"Is she your mistress?"

"No. It was a one-night stand."

"What's her name?"

"She said her name was Kim. She didn't tell me her last name."

"What's her phone number?"

"I don't know. She never gave it to me."

"Did you and Kim go to a hotel?"

"No, we went to her place."

"What's her address?"

"I don't remember it."

"Did you communicate with Kim after this encounter?

"No."

"Where did you meet her?"

"In a bar."

"What's the bar's name?"

"I don't remember it. It was somewhere downtown."

Aguero's sixth sense told him the one-night stand story was a lie, but he couldn't think of a way to prove it.

The guy could think on his feet, you had to give him that.

Jeff didn't look annoyed or nervous. Perhaps he believed that cops found people who showed emotion during questioning suspicious.

"So you went to Austin only to pick up a woman for a one-night stand? There were no other reasons?"

"There were no other reasons. I hate being a cheater, you know. And I would appreciate it if you didn't tell my wife about this."

"Why did you go all the way to Austin to find a woman? There are women in bars here in the Dallas area."

"I don't pick up women in the local bars because I'm afraid one of Emily's friends will catch me in the act."

"When did you leave Austin?"

"About half an hour after I had sex with Kim."

"Do you remember what time it was when you left Austin?"

"Around one a.m."

"Did you arrive in Austin the day you met Kim?"

"Yes. I believe I arrived around five in the afternoon."

Aguero considered asking Jeff if he had taken his cellphone with him to Austin, and decided against it: Jeff would simply say that he had forgotten his phone at home.

"Where were you the night your son killed Helen Hinton?"

"I was in a bar in Dallas."

"What's the name of the bar?"

"Cuckoo's Nest."

"Did you see your son that night?"

"No."

"What time did you arrive at Cuckoo's Nest and what time did you leave?"

"I think I was there from nine to midnight."

"Were you alone?"

"Yes."

"Did you pay with a credit card?"

"I paid with cash."

Jeff didn't have an alibi for the night of Helen Hinton's murder. He didn't have an alibi for the night of Laura Sumner's murder, either.

"How many cellphones do you have?"

"One."

"What time is your wife coming home?"

Jeff looked at his watch. "She should be home in two hours."

3

When Aguero got behind the wheel of his car, he called Emily Phillips and asked her if she had talked to her son.

"Oh, I'm so sorry," Emily said. "No, I haven't talked to him yet. I've been very busy. His prison is so far from Carrollton. I'm sorry."

She promised to talk to Edward Phillips soon.

Chapter 24

1

"Do you have children?" Mark asked.

"Yes." Brian Curtis nodded.

According to his birth certificate, Sam Curtis's parents' were Brian James Curtis and Caroline Rose Burke. Caroline had remarried two years after divorcing Sam's father and taken her new husband's last name, Dolman. Both Brian and Caroline still lived at the addresses provided by Edward Phillips.

Brian Curtis was a thickset man with a sizable bald spot. He wore gray sweatpants, a black T-shirt, and brown leather slippers. He spoke with an accent that sounded Australian.

"What are their names?" Mark said.

"Sam and Debra."

"How old is Sam?"

"Thirty."

"And Debra?"

"Twenty five."

"Can you tell me your son's email address?"

"Let me look." Brian grabbed his cellphone. About fifteen seconds later he said, "It's samcurtis99z@yahoo.com."

"What about samcurtisx@gmail.com?"

"That's his old email address. He doesn't use it anymore. Is he in trouble?"

"No, he's not in any trouble. I'm just trying to verify some information. Can you show me one of the emails Sam sent you from his old email address?"

"Sure."

Brian searched his inbox for half a minute and then handed his phone to Mark. "Here you go."

The message found by Brian had been sent from samcurtisx@gmail.com on December 2 of last year; its subject line was "Check this out." It contained a link to an online video.

"Can I forward it to my email?" Mark asked.

"Yeah, sure."

Mark forwarded the message to his personal email, and then said, "Did Sam have a dog when he was in middle school?"

"Yes. A Border Collie."

"What was its name?"

"Bruno."

"Did Sam break your video camera when he was fifteen?"

Looking puzzled, Brian said, "Yes, he did. That thing cost fifteen hundred dollars."

"How did he break it?"

"He dropped it from the roof of our house."

Edward Phillips (or rather Sam Curtis) must hate his parents, Mark thought. If Brian and Caroline had posted their son's bail before January 11, Edward Phillips wouldn't have stolen his body.

"Sam spent four weeks in jail last winter because he couldn't post bail," Mark said. "Did he ask you to help him with bail?"

"Yes, he did."

"Did you say no?"

"I told him that a few weeks in jail would teach him not to drink and drive. I suppose I was right, because he hasn't made that mistake again."

"Did Sam ask his mother for help?"

"Yes. I asked Caroline not to help him."

Mark wished he could tell Brian that because of his tough love his son had ended up on death row.

"Was it you who paid Sam's bail in January?"

"No. It was one of his friends."

It must have been Jeff Phillips.

"Do you have any pictures of you with Sam?"

Mark had little doubt that the man sitting in front of him was Sam Curtis's dad: his middle name was James and his place and date of birth matched the place and date of birth in the

AN EVIL MIND

father section of Sam Curtis's birth certificate. He wanted to see photos of Brian with Sam to be completely sure.

"Yes, I do."

"Can I see them?"

"Sure. Let's go to the study."

In the study, Brian turned on his laptop, opened the Pictures folder, and then clicked on a subfolder named Sam.

"I'd like to see the most recent photo," Mark said.

"Okay." Brian clicked on the first thumbnail in the top row.

It was a picture of Brian and Sam sitting at a restaurant table. Both men were smiling.

"It was taken about four years ago," Brian said.

Mark looked at the photo for a long moment and then said, "I need to ask you a personal question, Brian. If you don't want to answer it, just say so."

"Okay."

"Did Sam's mother ever cheat on you?"

Brian pushed the laptop aside. "I guess you have good reason to ask this question. And I'll answer it. Yes, Caroline did cheat on me."

"Did she cheat on you with a man named Aaron?"

"Yes, he was one of her lovers. I should have beaten the crap out of him." Brian smiled. "How do you know about him?"

"A friend of Caroline's told me. What was his last name?"

"Townsend."

"How often do you talk to Sam?"

"Not very often. I haven't talked to him since March. He changed his number and didn't give me the new one."

"Do you know where he lives?"

"No, I don't."

A short dark-haired woman in her late forties stepped into the room. She kissed Brian on the cheek and said, "Oh, we have a guest." She smiled at Mark.

"This is Mark. He's a Dallas police detective."

"Police detective?" the woman said.

"Please meet my wife, Melanie," Brian said to Mark.

"Nice to meet you, Melanie," Mark said.

"I'll leave you two alone." Melanie smiled again, and walked out of the study.

"You know, I'm not upset that Sam doesn't call me," Brian said. "To me, it's a sign that he finally turned his life around." Brian paused. "You see, he used to ask Caroline and me for money every month. He doesn't do it anymore. Evidently, he found a well-paying job."

"Does Sam call Caroline?"

Brian shook his head. "No, he doesn't." He clasped his hands in his lap. "I know Sam's mad at us, maybe even hates us, but I'm sure we made the right decision. Jail changed him for the better. Have you met Sam?"

"Yes."

"How's he doing?"

"I don't know how he's doing now. I met him last November. But I'm sure he's fine. Does he keep in touch with his sister?"

"Debra's Melanie's daughter. Sam's met her only a couple of times."

Sam Curtis had stopped communicating with his family. It was quite a drastic change, wasn't it?

"I need you to do me a favor, Brian. Please don't tell anyone about our conversation, including Sam and Caroline."

"Okay. So Sam's not in trouble, right?"

"He's not in trouble."

2

Let's review the facts.

Sam Curtis actually had a Border Collie named Bruno.

Sam Curtis actually dropped his father's video camera from the roof of his house.

AN EVIL MIND

Sam Curtis's mother actually *cheated on her husband with Aaron Townsend.*

Phillips knows Sam's email and eBay passwords. He knew where Sam kept the gun.

This morning Mark had obtained Sam Curtis's Social Security number and found that it matched the number he had gotten from Phillips.

Every piece of information given by Edward Phillips had proved correct, and there were a significant number of them.

Could someone other than Sam Curtis know all this?

It would take a lot of effort to gather this information. Why would Phillips do it? He had nothing to gain by tricking his victim's father into believing that he was Sam Curtis. And he had to know that no judge and no governor in America would believe a body-switch story, no matter how much proof was presented.

The logical conclusion was that Phillips hadn't acquired this information by making inquiries and hacking Sam Curtis's email.

Sam had abandoned the email and eBay accounts he had used before his DWI arrest. He had stopped talking to his parents and started hanging out with Jeff Phillips. These facts supported Phillips's claim.

He's telling the truth, Mark thought. Edward Phillips did swap bodies with him.

If Edward Phillips loved his girlfriend very much, he might have told her about the body switch.

Phillips had had no female visitors except for his mother while he was in the Dallas County Jail, which meant that his visitor records didn't contain his girlfriend's name.

Detective Blanco might know Phillips's girlfriend's name.

Mark looked at his watch. It was eight-fifty.

It wasn't too late to call Blanco.

Mark dialed Blanco's number. The phone rang twice and then Blanco answered.

"Hi, Mark. What's up?"

"Hi, Rob. I'm calling about Edward Phillips's girlfriend. Do you happen to know her name?"

"I didn't know he had a girlfriend."

"I see. Goodbye, Rob."

Chris Novak. He used to be Phillips's close friend. He should know Phillips's girlfriend's name (assuming Phillips had had a girlfriend). He might even have her phone number.

There was one more thing he could ask Novak about: Edward Phillips's interest in black magic.

It wasn't too late to pay Chris Novak a visit. His place was only twenty minutes away.

Mark found Novak's address and entered it into the GPS.

3

Christopher Novak was home.

"We met a few weeks ago," Mark said after introducing himself.

"Oh yeah, I remember you." Novak nodded.

In the living room, Novak asked, "To what do I owe this pleasure?"

"I'd like to ask you a few questions about your friend Edward Phillips."

"He's not my friend anymore."

"Right. Your *former* friend Edward Phillips. Did Edward have a girlfriend before he went to prison?"

"Yes. Her name was Anna."

"Do you have her number?"

"I think I have it in my phone." Novak picked up his cell from the coffee table and about fifteen seconds later told Mark Anna's number.

"Do you still keep in touch with Anna?" Mark asked.

"No, I don't."

"Do you know her last name?"

"No."

"Do you know where she lives?"

"No."

"Was Edward interested in black magic?"

"Black magic? I don't know. Maybe a little. He likes movies about ghosts and that kind of stuff. I like them, too."

"Did he have books on black magic?"

"No. I didn't see any books on black magic at his place."

"Did his father have books on black magic?"

"I don't know."

"Have you ever been to Edward's parents' place?"

"Yes, I have, but I never paid any attention to their books."

"Did Edward ever talk about magic rituals?"

Novak smiled. "Rituals? Well, we went to a few witchcraft websites, just for fun. We tried a couple of love spells, but they didn't work." Novak giggled. "We tried like ten money spells, but they didn't work, either."

Did Phillips find the body switch ritual on the Internet?

"We played with a Ouija board a few times, but nothing happened. Do you believe in witchcraft and ghosts?"

"Yes, I do."

"Really?"

"Yes. Did Edward ever talk about Satanism?"

"Satanism? No. You think he's a Satanist?"

"I think it's possible."

Mark took out Sam Curtis's picture and showed it to Novak. "Have you ever met this man?"

Novak looked at the photo for a long moment and said, "No, I've never met him."

Novak didn't seem to have recognized Sam Curtis. Evidently, Curtis hadn't told him about the body swap.

"Do you keep in touch with Edward's parents?"

"No, I don't."

Chapter 25

1

On Tuesday morning Mark read the text messages Sam Curtis and Jeff Phillips had sent each other from August 22 to 24.

On August 22, at 4:32 p.m., Jeff Phillips texted Sam Curtis: "Wanna go to Ninja Sushi?"

At 4:51 p.m., Curtis replied: "OK. What time?"

At 4:58 p.m., Phillips texted: "6:30."

At 5:01 p.m., Curtis replied: "OK."

On August 23, at 12:33 p.m., Curtis texted Phillips: "Call me."

They had sent no messages to each other on August 24.

There was no mention of Austin. Jeff Phillips hadn't called Sam Curtis Son, and Sam Curtis hadn't called Jeff Phillips Dad.

These guys were cautious.

At four o'clock, Mark received a response from Edward Phillips's former girlfriend's cellphone company. The number Mark had gotten from Chris Novak was registered to Anna Wesley. She had to be Phillips's former girlfriend because the number had belonged to her for three years.

Anna Wesley lived in Irving, eleven miles from Sam Curtis's house. Interviewing her was not a good idea: if she knew about the body switch, she might tell Curtis that he was under investigation. Mark decided to inquire if Anna Wesley had received any text messages or calls from Sam Curtis.

At half past five, Detective Aguero called Mark to give him an update on the Laura Sumner case.

"Two weeks ago, I talked to Edward Phillips's father," Aguero said. "His name's Jeff Phillips. I asked him if he went out of town on August twenty-third. As you may remember, Laura Sumner was killed on August twenty-third. Jeff said he didn't go out of town that day. I checked his credit card records and found out that he was in Austin on August twenty-third."

"He lied."

"Yes, he lied. Last Saturday I asked him for an explanation. He said that he went to Austin to get laid."

"Can he prove it?"

"No."

"Do you believe him?"

"No, I don't."

"If Jeff was involved in Laura Sumner's murder, he was probably involved in my daughter's murder, too."

"I agree."

"Did you ask Jeff where he'd been on the night of Helen's murder?"

"Yes, I did. He said he'd been in a bar in Dallas. He has no alibi."

"What's your next move?"

"I want to talk to Edward's friends. I asked Edward's mother to persuade him to help us. I hope she pulls it off. By the way, I saw that you visited Edward three times in the last month. Are you trying to get him to give you his partner's name?"

"Yes."

"Did he tell you anything useful?"

"No, he didn't. He keeps saying he's innocent."

2

When Mark finished his steak, he took three sips of water and then looked at Joan, who sat across from him, eating a salad, her eyes fixed on her plate.

"This steak is amazing," Mark said. "Thank you, honey."

"You're welcome." Joan smiled.

"You know what Edward Phillips told me last Saturday?"

"You went to see Phillips last Saturday?"

"Yes."

Mark wanted to discuss Edward Phillips's fantastical story with someone, and Joan was probably the only person he could talk to about switched bodies and black magic without worrying about his reputation.

"What did he tell you?"

"He said he wasn't Edward Phillips. He said Edward Phillips switched bodies with him last January, while he was in the county jail."

I still haven't told her about Phillips's prints on the knife used to kill Helen.

There was no point in telling Joan about the prints now, was there? What good would it do?

"Edward Phillips switched bodies with him? What does that mean?"

"Remember the movie Freaky Friday?"

"Is that the one with Jamie Lee Curtis?"

"Yes."

"He actually said that?"

"Yes, he did."

"Is he trying to play crazy?"

"No. He can prove it."

Joan raised her eyebrows. "Did he give you the proof?"

"Yes, he did. He said he used to be Sam Curtis. He gave me Sam Curtis's email password and Social Security number, I checked them, and they turned out to be correct. He knows Sam Curtis's eBay password, he knows the name of the dog Sam Curtis had when he was a child, and he knows the name of the guy Sam Curtis's mother cheated with sixteen years ago."

"That's his proof?"

"I think it's solid."

"Don't tell me you believe him."

"How does he know all this?"

"Maybe they're friends."

"They're not friends."

"Have you seen this Sam Curtis guy?"

"Yes."

"You said Phillips knew the name of the man Sam Curtis's mother cheated with. How did you verify that?"

"I asked Sam's father about it."

"How did Phillips switch bodies with him?"

"He thinks Phillips used black magic."

Joan shook her head. "I don't care what he knows. Body switching is impossible."

"Why would he make this up?"

"Maybe he wants you to help him overturn his conviction."

"He knows I can't help him with that."

"Did he ask you for anything?"

"No, he didn't."

"Do you believe him?"

"I haven't made up my mind yet."

"Do you believe in black magic?"

"I believe that Satan exists. Maybe Satan helped Phillips swap bodies with Sam Curtis."

"Come on, Mark. You can't be serious."

"Let's agree to disagree."

Mark glanced at his watch. It was 8:21 p.m.

If he weren't exhausted, he would spy on Sam Curtis tonight.

I'll spy on him tomorrow, Mark thought.

Chapter 26

1

Sam took two bottles of beer from the refrigerator and returned to the living room. He handed one of the bottles to Jeff, dropped onto the couch, and put a spicy tuna roll in his mouth. Jeff sat in a chair with a plate of sushi in his lap, his feet on the ottoman.

"That detective I told you about the other day came again yesterday," Jeff said.

"Why?"

"He checked my credit card records. When we were in Austin, we stopped at Burger King, remember?"

Sam nodded. If memory served, he had ordered a Double Whopper meal.

"I used my credit card to pay for the food. He asked me what I was doing in Austin."

Now the cops knew that Jeff had been in Austin on August twenty-third. Did that mean Jeff was in trouble?

Sam didn't think so. The police would never find proof that Jeff was involved in Laura Sumner's murder: such proof simply did not exist.

"What did you tell him?" Sam asked.

Jeff recounted the one-night stand story that he had given to Detective Aguero.

It was true that Jeff could think on his feet, but he hadn't used this ability to concoct his salacious tale: he had come up with it the morning after Detective Aguero's first visit. He was sitting on the toilet in his bathroom, reading the back of the toothpaste tube, when he suddenly remembered that he had used his credit card at a Burger King in Austin on August twenty-third. It took him half an hour to think up the one-night stand story and answers to the likely questions Aguero might have about it. What Jeff had told the detective was partly true: he did pick up women in bars every once in a while.

"Good job," Sam said. "Do you think he believed you?"

"Cops believe no one but other cops."

Sam's disposable phone rang. It was Leticia.

"It's Leticia," he said to Jeff, and then tapped the Answer button.

"Hi, Leticia. How is it going?"

"I'm fine. Can you talk?"

"Yes, I can."

"I've got another one for you. His name's Paul Pruitt. He has an inoperable brain tumor. His father is Eric Pruitt, the president of Pruitt Private Capital."

Sam grabbed a pen and notepad and wrote down the names of the patient and his father. "How old is Paul?"

"Twenty-one."

"Where does he live?"

"Dallas. I have his father's phone number."

Leticia told Sam Eric Pruitt's number and Paul Pruitt's address and number.

"Are you home?" Sam asked.

"Yes."

"I'll bring you the money around nine."

"Okay."

"Bye." Sam hung up and said to Jeff, "Good news, Dad. We have another prospect."

They looked up Eric Pruitt and his company on the Internet and discovered that his net worth was estimated to be between one hundred and three hundred million dollars. The main office of Pruitt Private Capital was located in downtown Dallas.

They drank to success, and then Jeff said, "I wonder if that Hinton woman turned the knife over to the cops."

It was Sam's idea to send the knife he had used to murder Helen Hinton to Joan Hinton so she would give it to the police. The reason for relinquishing the knife was simple: Sam wanted to ruin Edward Phillips's chances of winning the appeal and thus ensure that he stayed behind bars until he died. By the way, his desire for Edward's appeal to fail was why he had killed Leonard Barlow (public defenders were worse than private attorneys at preparing and arguing appeals, and Sam doubted that Edward would be able to find another private lawyer who would agree to work for him pro bono).

Sam had begun to worry about Edward's conviction being overturned on appeal last September, after he watched a documentary about exonerated death row inmates. He was surprised that it hadn't required a superhuman effort to get the people featured in the documentary released; the task was challenging, for sure, but it was very doable. This made him realize there was a small but real chance that Edward would get his freedom back, and Sam knew that as soon as he left prison, Edward would start looking for the man who had stolen his body to exact revenge. Although he thought Edward was not going to succeed in killing him, he had figured it was best to avoid this problem altogether. He would have wasted Edward in the county jail if he could have escaped the consequences.

Speaking of the swap, it was a good trade. Sam liked his new body: his new face was rather handsome, and his new penis was half an inch longer than the old one.

"I'm sure she did," Sam said.

"I hope she didn't mess up the fingerprints."

Why hadn't he gotten rid of the knife right after slaying Helen Hinton?

After leaving the building where the killing had taken place, Sam (his name had been Edward Phillips then as he had still been in his old body) had given the knife to Jeff so he would dispose of it (he had put it in a plastic bag before going outside), and when Jeff came home, he had locked it in the safe in his study, intending to get rid of it the next night. Shortly after he learned of Sam's arrest, it occurred to Jeff that his son could avoid going to prison for Helen Hinton's murder by switching bodies with his cellmate. There was no longer a need to ditch the knife, and he decided to keep it as a souvenir, which just went to show that he was a little crazy.

"There's been no mention of the knife in the papers," Jeff said.

"Maybe nobody cares about this case anymore."

Jeff ate a salmon roll and said, "Do you think Edward told Aguero about the body switch?"

Sam shook his head. "If he did, he's an idiot. Would you believe him if you were Aguero?"

"No." Jeff took a sip from his bottle. "I wonder if he told anyone about it."

"He might have told his cellmate."

2

The next day, Sam called Eric Pruitt's office and made an appointment for Wednesday morning.

He arrived at the headquarters of Pruitt Private Capital fifteen minutes before the scheduled time, wearing a suit and a tie. At 10:03 a.m. Pruitt's secretary, a black woman in her forties with big earrings, told Sam that Pruitt was ready to see him.

After they shook hands, Pruitt said, "You have ten minutes, Jake."

Eric Pruitt was forty-nine years old. He had deep-set brown eyes, an aquiline nose, and thin lips.

"My company would like to help your son, Paul, get rid of his cancer," Sam said. "We've developed a procedure that can permanently cure anaplastic astrocytoma."

Anaplastic astrocytoma was the scientific name of Paul Pruitt's tumor.

Pruitt looked at Sam for a long moment, and then said, "What's your company's name?"

"New Horizons. It's an experimental, highly effective procedure. It doesn't involve surgery, drugs, or radiation. So far the success rate's been one hundred percent. This is a totally risk-free offer. If we don't deliver, you don't pay."

"No drugs and no radiation? Is it a homeopathic treatment?"

"No. We will transfer Paul's consciousness to another body. A healthy body."

"Transfer his consciousness to another body? How are you going to do that?"

"As you may know, consciousness arises from the electrical activity of nerve cells. We found a way to record human consciousness and then place it in another brain."

"Where are you going to get the healthy body?"

"We have a pool of people who are willing to do a body swap for a fee. It's going to be a white man between eighteen and twenty-five."

Although Sam didn't think Pruitt was racist, he was sure the millionaire would prefer his son's new body to be the same race as the old one.

"How many patients have you treated?" Pruitt asked.

"Ten."

"Can I talk to them?"

"No. Our clients' names are confidential. I'm sorry."

Judging by the skeptical look in his eyes, Pruitt did not trust him, and Sam expected the millionaire to think it was a scam until he got proof that his precious son's consciousness had actually been moved to a different body.

"How much is the procedure?"

"Twenty million."

The twenty-million-dollar price wasn't set in stone. Sam was willing to negotiate.

"Did you say twenty million?"

"Yes. You don't have to pay anything upfront. You pay only if the procedure is successful."

Pruitt sat back in his chair. "Can I see your facility?"

"Sure. I can show it to you today."

New Horizons' office didn't look like a high-tech scientific facility, but Sam thought that terminally ill folks and their parents and children wouldn't care about that. Desperate people were eager to be fooled.

"Where is it located?"

"Dallas."

Pruitt thought for a long time and then said, "This is an interesting proposal, Jake. Let me sleep on it."

Sam nodded. "Here's my card." He laid his card on the desk in front of Pruitt. "If you have any questions, give me a call."

Chapter 27

1

Mark spied on Sam Curtis from eight p.m. to midnight on Wednesday. He saw nothing suspicious. Curtis came home at half past eight, and Mark waited three and a half hours for him to leave the house, but he never did.

Was Curtis going to kill again?

Curtis had killed Laura Sumner because the body swap ritual required human sacrifice. Obviously, Curtis or Jeff Phillips planned to switch bodies. Both of them were still in the bodies they had been in before Laura's murder, so they didn't need to make another sacrifice. They might kill again after one of them got a new body.

What was Mark going to do next?

His objective was to punish the man who had murdered his daughter. Since that man's soul currently occupied Sam Curtis's body, his objective was to punish Sam Curtis. The easiest and quickest way to do it was to kill him. Did Mark need a confession? It would be nice if Curtis confessed to swapping bodies and murdering Helen but not necessary. If Curtis told him that Jeff Phillips was his accomplice, Mark would waste Jeff, too.

Putting Curtis in prison wasn't a good option because he would switch bodies with his cellmate while in jail awaiting trial.

Should he help Edward Phillips gain his freedom? At the present time, Edward Phillips was an innocent man, who'd had nothing to do with Helen's murder. He had robbed a convenience store, but he didn't deserve to be executed or remain in prison for the rest of his life. Mark had to do his best to set him free. After all, if it hadn't been for Phillips, he wouldn't have known that his daughter's killer was on the loose.

He could hire a good appeals attorney for Phillips. The problem was, the case was going to cost tens of thousands of dollars. He would have to find a way to raise the money.

Could the swap be reversed? Mark searched the Internet for a body switch ritual involving human sacrifice but found nothing useful.

Anna Wesley's cellphone company informed Mark that she had never received any calls or messages from Sam Curtis. Evidently, Curtis had chosen to dump his girlfriend. Mark reviewed the text messages Curtis had sent to Sandra Chandler and found that he had broken up with her shortly after his release from the Dallas County Jail.

On Friday, as Mark browsed websites dedicated to black magic, he recalled the murder of Walter Kindred, who had been killed the same way as Helen and Laura (he had read about it in late October, when he was looking for cases similar to his daughter's). Had Kindred's murder been part of a body switch ritual?

The man convicted of killing Walter Kindred knew the answer to that question. Mark realized that he wanted to talk to him. The fact that the guy was in Massachusetts, eighteen hundred miles from Dallas, didn't discourage Mark. He decided to visit Kindred's killer next Thursday.

2

Edward Phillips's face lit up when he saw Mark. He sat down, picked up the phone, and said, "How are you doing?"

"I'm fine," Mark replied.

What was going on in Phillips's head? He must be constantly on edge, angry, and anguished, with no alcohol or drugs or cigarettes to dull the pain.

Did Phillips have nightmares every night?

I may be the only person who can give him hope, Mark thought.

"I did some digging and came to the conclusion that you're telling the truth," he said.

"Thank you, Mark. You made my year." Phillips smiled. "Did you talk to my parents?"

"I talked to your father."

"How's he doing?"

"He's fine. Is he from Australia?"

"Yes, he is. Can you check on my mom, please? Just give her a call."

"Sure. Have you thought about telling your parents about the body switch?"

"They're not going to believe me. Do you know how often Phillips visits my dad?"

"Your father said that he hadn't talked to him since March."

"That's good."

"I checked Jeff Phillips's credit card records and found out that he was in Austin the day Laura Sumner was killed. I suspect he helped his son murder Laura."

"You're probably right."

"I also suspect Jeff helped his son kill Helen."

"Are you going to follow Edward every day?"

"I'll try."

"Whatever you do, don't kill him. After you arrest him, please make sure they put him in solitary confinement."

If Phillips thought that Mark could arrange for Curtis to be held in solitary confinement until he was transferred to the state prison system, he was badly mistaken. In county jails, well-behaved adults without mental health issues were not supposed to be kept in segregation for long periods of time. His lawyer would get Curtis released into the general population within a month of his arrest.

"You think he'll confess to killing Helen?"

"I hope he will. You'll have to tell the police that he killed Helen and Laura Sumner."

"I will."

"Remember I told you there was a full moon on the night he switched bodies with me? I'm beginning to think it wasn't a coincidence. It's possible that the ritual works only on full-moon nights. You see, if Edward could switch bodies whenever he wanted, he would have done it the day we first met. Why did he wait twenty-five days?"

That was a good point.

If Curtis could swap bodies only on full-moon nights, he'd need to be placed in solitary confinement just once a month.

"When did he switch bodies with you?" Mark asked.

"January eleventh."

"Maybe the ritual works only on the eleventh day of the month."

"That's possible, too. Please follow Edward on the next full-moon night. If he switches bodies, you should find out who he switched bodies with. The next full moon is on December second."

"Okay."

"Today is eleventh. Please follow him tonight, too."

Mark nodded. "Okay."

"Have you told Detective Aguero about the body switch?"

"No."

"Don't tell him. Don't tell anyone."

"I've already told my wife."

"What did she say?"

"She thinks it's bullshit."

"Does Aguero have any new leads?"

"He knows that Jeff Phillips was in Austin the day Laura Sumner was killed, and he suspects that Jeff was involved in her murder."

"Does Jeff know he's a suspect?"

"I don't know."

"He might get a new body. Keep an eye on him."

Maybe he should follow Jeff Phillips tonight instead of Curtis?

"How is your appeal going?" Mark asked.

"My lawyer's working on the brief."

"When is he going to file it?"

"Next month."

"How are you holding up?"

"Not very well." Phillips paused. "I think it's partly my fault. If I hadn't gotten behind the wheel that night, I wouldn't have been arrested and I wouldn't have met Edward Phillips. I think about this every day." He sighed. "Every day. My lawyer advised me to plead guilty. He said I'd get a suspended sentence. Edward told me that I shouldn't listen to him because he was a public defender. Edward said he knew a good lawyer, who would help me for free. And I believed him. If I'd done what my lawyer told me to do, I'd be home now. God, I was such an idiot."

"Don't think about what you could have done. It's going to drive you crazy."

"Easier said than done."

Phillips lowered his head and wiped his eyes.

"Did Barlow tell you about Walter Kindred?"

"No. Who is he?"

"He lived in Massachusetts. He was killed the same way as Helen."

"When?"

"October of last year. I'm going to visit his killer in prison next Thursday."

Phillips thought for a long moment and then said, "If he knows how to perform the ritual, ask him how to reverse the switch."

"That's why I want to talk to him."

"Thank you, Mark. I appreciate everything you're doing for me."

"No problem."

"Ask him where he learned how to perform the ritual."
"Okay."
"Did you find any information about the ritual on the Internet?"
"No, I didn't."
Looking over Mark's shoulder, Phillips said dreamily, "It would be great if there was a way to get my body back."

3

When Mark got home, he called Edward Phillips's mother and she told him that she was doing fine. He spied on Sam Curtis from seven to twelve that night. When he arrived at Curtis's house, he saw Jeff Phillips's Cadillac parked in front of it. At eight o'clock Curtis and Jeff Phillips got in Curtis's car and went to Pistons Bar and Grill, where they stayed until eleven-forty. In the bar, Mark watched them from a distance, being careful not to attract their attention. When they returned to Curtis's house, Jeff got in his Cadillac and drove home (Mark followed him to his place, waited twenty minutes, and then left).

Chapter 28

1

Eric Pruitt called Sam two days after their first meeting and said that he had a couple of questions for him.

"Can you meet me today?" Pruitt asked.

"I can meet you in two hours," Sam said. He wasn't busy and could get to Pruitt Private Capital's headquarters in less than an hour, but if he did that, Pruitt might think he had a lot of free time on his hands, and that wasn't the image Sam wanted to project.

"Sounds good."

Sam walked into Pruitt's office one hour and fifty minutes later. They sat down on the leather sofa, and Pruitt said that he was very interested in the consciousness transfer procedure.

"How do you record consciousness?" Pruitt asked. "And how do you put it in another brain?"

"I'm afraid I can't tell you that. It's a trade secret."

"You said you'd put my son's consciousness in a different body. How will I know that the consciousness in that body belongs to my son?"

"That's a very good question. We thought over this problem and came up with a solution. Are there things that only you and your son know?"

"I suppose so."

"After the procedure, you're going to quiz him on those things. You'll know it's your son's consciousness in that body if he gives you correct answers. Am I right?"

Pruitt made no reply. He was probably trying to figure out if there was a flaw in the method suggested by Sam that would allow a fake Paul Pruitt to be passed off as the real one.

"If I were you, I'd think up a password and give it to Paul," Sam said. "Ask him to memorize it, and don't share it with anyone else."

"Can his mind get scrambled during the procedure?"

"No. Your son's mind is guaranteed to remain intact."

"I don't have to pay anything upfront, right?"

"That's right. You'll pay us after verifying that Paul's consciousness has been successfully transferred to a new body."

"How do you want me to pay you?"

"We prefer wire transfers."

"All right. And the price is twenty million?"

"Yes."

Sam's heart began to pound harder. He had a feeling Pruitt had decided to try the procedure.

"I did some research and found no mention of your company on the Internet," Pruitt said.

"We prefer to stay under the radar. Very few people can afford our service, so we don't do any marketing."

"Do you have a website?"

"No."

"I found no mention of a technology that allows to transfer consciousness from one body to another. Science says that it's still impossible to transfer consciousness."

Sam smiled. "We keep our technology secret, and we have no plans to let the public know about it."

"Why?"

"Let me ask you this. Suppose scientists discover a serum that allows people to live forever or several hundred years. Do you think they'll tell the press about it?"

"Yes, I think they will."

"You're wrong. You can't let people live forever. The earth can barely sustain the population it has now. Can you imagine what will happen if people stopped dying from old age? The global economy will collapse, countries will fight for resources, the world will be in chaos. And if they tell the public that only the elite will be permitted to live forever, there will be rebellions. So, when an immortality serum is discovered, only a select few will be told about it. Our technology is in the same league as the immortality serum."

"You could win a Novel prize for this."

"We don't care for fame or recognition."

"Are you going to drill holes in Paul's skull?"

"No. The procedure doesn't involve surgery and is completely safe."

"How long is the recovery period?"

"One hour."

"Will the consciousness of the original owner of the body stay in that body?"

"No. We'll transfer it to Paul's old body."

"Are you going to tell him that my son has inoperable brain cancer?"

"Yes, we are."

"And you think he'll agree to trade bodies with Paul?"

"Yes. We're going to pay him a million dollars for that."

Pruitt's cellphone rang. Pruitt stood up, picked up his phone from his desk, looked at the screen, and then tapped the Decline button.

"I'd like to see your facility," he said. "When can I do it?"

"How about tomorrow?"

"Tomorrow's fine. Can we do it at noon?"

"Sure."

Sam gave Pruitt New Horizons' address.

2

Sam and Jeff had been in the office of their fake company for two and a half hours when Eric Pruitt came at a quarter past noon. Sam introduced Jeff as a technician named Peter Grayson.

After taking a tour of the office, which consisted of two rooms—one was three hundred square feet and the other two hundred—Pruitt sat in a chair in the larger room and said, "Where's your main office?"

"This is our main and only office. We're a very lean company."

"Do you perform the procedure here?"

"Yes. There." Sam pointed to the door to the smaller room. "I know this place isn't as fancy as those research labs you see on TV, but I promise you we will save your son's life. We don't need expensive furniture to transfer his consciousness to a new healthy body."

Pruitt didn't walk out of the office, which meant that he still thought New Horizons might be able to help his son.

"Can I watch the procedure?"

Sam shook his head. "No. But you can wait in this room while we perform it."

"How long does the procedure take?"

"About two hours."

Pruitt turned to Jeff, who was sitting to his right, stared at him for a few seconds and then tilted his head back.

"How long does Paul have to live?" Sam asked.

"One year."

The ritual worked only on full moon nights, and the next full moon was on the night of December 2. Sam needed Paul Pruitt to remain alive for twenty-one more days, and although doctors' predictions weren't completely reliable, it was safe to say Paul had more than three weeks to live.

"I'm sorry to hear that."

Pruitt turned to Sam and asked, "How long has your company been doing this?"

"A little over a year."

It was a risk-free proposition, so why the hell was Pruitt hesitating? It wasn't as if his son had any other options.

Perhaps Pruitt wasn't desperate.

"Are you sure I can't talk to your previous customers?"

"Yes, I'm sure. I'm sorry, Mister Pruitt." Sam smiled. "So what do you say? Would you like us to help your son?"

"I need to think about it."

"All right. If you have any questions, don't hesitate to call me."

Sam hoped Pruitt wasn't going to take several months to make the decision.

3

On the way home Sam thought about his grand plan.

By trading an old body for a young one, he could live forever. The thought of being immortal made him shiver with excitement. Eternal life was the holy grail of holy grails, every human being in history had dreamed of achieving it, major religions were based on the promise of it.

Was he the first person ever to use this ritual to live forever? He doubted it. There were probably a number of people who had been hopping from body to body for centuries or even millennia.

Sam believed a man was in his prime between the ages of eighteen and forty-five, so he was going to get a new body about every twenty-seven years.

He wondered why it hadn't occurred to Gordon Stryker that he could use the consciousness transfer technology to live forever. Was Eric Pruitt smart enough to think of that? He would charge Pruitt at least twenty-five percent of his net worth to transfer his mind to a young body.

Sam wanted not only to live forever but also to live in luxury (immortality was much more fun when you were rich), and the ritual was going to help him attain this goal, too. He and Jeff planned to make thirty million dollars a year providing consciousness transfer services to wealthy people.

He thought it would be nice to swap bodies with a movie star or Prince Charles of the United Kingdom. The downside of being Prince Charles was that the guy was too old, and Sam didn't want to live in an old body. The downside of taking over the body of a movie star was that you had to be able to act, and Sam didn't consider himself a good actor.

AN EVIL MIND

His favorite idea was to switch bodies with a billionaire, transfer all of the billionaire's assets to his father, and then move into the body of an eighteen-year-old guy. There were plenty of potential targets: almost six hundred billionaires lived in the United States and Canada. The problem was that billionaires had bodyguards, who might kill him while he tried to kidnap their client. However, Sam believed he would eventually be able to carry out this plan. When he became a multimillionaire, he might be able to stay overnight at a billionaire's house or to get a billionaire to stay overnight at his place.

Chapter 29

1

Walter Kindred had been murdered in Newton, a Boston suburb, on October 10 of last year. He was nineteen years old at the time of his death. His killer's name was Douglas Fleming. Fleming was arrested on October 12. At the time, he was a resident of Waltham, a city ten miles west of Boston. At his trial, he had been found guilty of murder in the first degree and then sentenced to life imprisonment without possibility of parole.

Fleming was serving his sentence at the Souza-Baranowski Correctional Center, a maximum security prison in Lancaster, about forty miles from Boston. He was twenty-nine years old.

Mark arrived in Boston at eight-fifteen p.m. on Wednesday, November 15. He had told Joan he was going to Boston to visit a friend. After he checked into the hotel, Mark walked around the block for an hour thinking about Douglas Fleming.

If Walter Kindred's murder had been part of a body switch ritual, would Fleming tell him how the ritual worked and how to reverse the switch? Because Mark thought that Fleming would be reluctant to share information with a cop, he was going to pose as a writer working on a book about a serial killer. Mark believed he had a good chance of getting Fleming to tell him what he wanted to know.

Did Edward Phillips—the Edward Phillips whose soul occupied Sam Curtis's body—and Douglas Fleming know each other? Had Phillips learned about the ritual from Fleming? Had it been the other way around?

What if Fleming had switched bodies with his cellmate before the trial and was on the loose? If that was the case, Mark would have to hope Fleming hadn't made another switch after getting out of jail.

AN EVIL MIND

2

Mark set out for the Souza-Baranowski Correctional Center at eleven o'clock in the morning. About half an hour after he left the hotel, it began to rain. Soon it was pouring so hard the windshield wipers could barely keep up. The cold dampness seeping into the car was refreshing, the steady drumming of raindrops on the roof soothing. As thunder cracked in the distance, Mark remembered that when they drove through a heavy rain, Helen used to say she felt as if she were in a submarine. At the thought of Helen, tears came to his eyes, and he wiped them away with the heel of his hand.

He turned up the heater and then tuned the radio to a sports station.

If it had rained that night, Helen would have stayed home and would still be alive.

Mark pulled into the parking lot of the Souza-Baranowski Correctional Center at ten past noon, fifty minutes before the first visiting period began. After killing the engine, he sat for a while, looking at the sprawling building behind the fence, and then got out of the car. His hair was soaked by the time he reached the prison entrance.

In the visiting room, Mark was instructed to keep both of his feet on the floor and both of his hands in front of him during the visit. He was told he was allowed to give the inmate a brief welcoming and departing hug and a kiss. Mark waited ten minutes before Douglas Fleming came into the room. A guard told Fleming where his visitor was sitting, and he walked over to Mark.

"How are you doing, Douglas?" Mark said without getting up.

Fleming was about five ten and slim. A five o'clock shadow darkened his square, dimpled chin. He looked ten years older than his age, probably thanks to the stress of being in prison and knowing that he would remain behind bars for the rest of his life. Staring at Mark with great curiosity, Fleming took the seat to his right and said, "Who are you? I don't know you."

He's lucky Massachusetts abolished the death penalty, Mark thought. He'll die in prison, but he'll die an old man.

"My name is Mark Hinton. I'm a writer."

Fleming smiled, revealing yellow teeth. "A writer? What brings you here, Mister Writer?"

"I want to talk to you about Walter Kindred."

"Are you writing a book about me?"

"I'm writing a book, but it's not about you."

Mark brushed his hair back; it was still wet.

"What is it about?"

"It's about a serial killer. The story is told from his point of view."

"So you came here to find out what makes serial killers tick?"

"Yes, that's exactly why I'm here."

"But I'm not a serial killer. I've only killed one person."

Mark was surprised Fleming hadn't told him he was innocent.

"That's true, but I'd really like to know more about you, nevertheless."

"All right. Let's talk."

"You have a logical mind, Douglas. I like that."

"Where are you from?"

"Dallas."

"I've never been to Dallas. Is it a beautiful city?"

"Yes, it is."

"Are you a famous writer?"

"No. Not yet. This book could be the one that will make me famous."

"Are you going to acknowledge my help in your book?"

"Sure."

"Good. Send me the book when it comes out."

"Okay."

"So what do you want to know?"

"Why did you kill Walter Kindred?"

"I snapped. I bumped into him on the street, he called me an asshole, I snapped and killed him."

"Why did you snap? I get called an asshole all the time, and it doesn't bother me, at least not enough to kill someone."

"I was in a bad place mentally then. Walter calling me an asshole was, as they say, the straw that broke the camel's back."

Fleming sounded as if he believed what he was saying.

Maybe he was telling the truth? Maybe he was just another psycho with a very short fuse?

"Were you depressed?" Mark asked.

"Yeah."

"What were you depressed about?"

"Life in general. I was broke, I hated my job, I had no girlfriend. I think most people are depressed about life, they just don't want to admit it. You can't be happy if you're not a millionaire. Or a billionaire."

"There are plenty of rich people who are depressed."

Fleming sneered. "You know what my dad says about people like that? They're too well off for their own good."

"Where did you get the knife you used to kill Walter?"

"I killed him with the knife I carried for protection."

"Why did you need protection? Did you live in a dangerous neighborhood?"

"No, I wouldn't say it was dangerous. The thing is, there are a lot of crazies out there, and you never know when you'll run into one. Look what happened to Walter. If he'd had a knife on him that night, he might be alive today." Fleming grinned.

"What kind of knife was it?"

"A kitchen knife."

"Did you stab Walter in the chest before or after you ripped open his stomach?"

"Before. Does the guy in your book kill with a knife?"

"Yes. Why did you cut open his stomach? I'm sure stabbing him in the chest would have been enough to kill him."

"I was very angry." Fleming smiled. "A few years ago, I read about a woman who stabbed her ex-boyfriend twenty-seven times, then slit his throat, and then shot him. Talk about overkill."

"Did you try an insanity defense?"

"No. I wasn't insane, I just lost my temper."

"Did you take any drugs the day you killed Walter?"

"No. I don't do drugs. They're bad for your health. Is your serial killer a sex maniac?"

"No."

"Why does he kill?"

"He just likes to do it."

"Does he kill both women and men?"

"He kills only men."

"Do they catch him in the end?"

"Yes."

"Does he die?"

"No, he doesn't."

Mark crossed his legs, and a moment later a guard came up to him and told him to keep both of his feet on the floor. Mark quickly complied.

"Did your father abuse you?" he asked Fleming.

"No. My dad's a cool guy. He yelled at me sometimes, but he never abused me."

"Were you bullied when you were a kid?"

"No. They tried, but I kicked their asses."

"Were you a bully?"

"No, I wasn't."

"Did you torture animals when you were a child?"

"No. I loved animals. And I still do."

"Are you religious?"

"I believe in God, but I'm not a fanatic. I've never read the Bible."

"Have you ever been interested in black magic?"

Fleming's lips curved in a small smile. "That's a... an odd question."

"It's for the book."

"Is the guy in your book into black magic?"

"Yes."

"Well... I think black magic is cool."

"Did you ever study it?"

"No, I didn't."

"Have you ever played with a Ouija board?"

"No."

"I'm going to ask you another odd question. And I want you to be completely honest with me, Douglas. I want you to tell me the truth no matter how crazy it sounds."

"Okay, go ahead."

"Did anyone switch bodies with you?"

He's going to think I'm a kook.

"Switch bodies? What do you mean?" Fleming's mouth was smiling, but his eyes were serious, probing.

"Did anyone trade bodies with you? Did you have this body before you were arrested for killing Walter Kindred?"

His smile evaporated, and Fleming said, "That's a strange question. Are you joking?"

"In my book, the main character swaps bodies with other people by means of black magic. The ritual he uses requires human sacrifice."

"Sounds interesting, but what does that have to do with your question?"

"When I read the description of Walter Kindred's wounds, I wondered if it was a ritual killing."

"Oh, I see. That's why you asked me about black magic."

"So was it a ritual killing?"

Fleming shook his head. "No, it wasn't."

"Please tell me the truth, Douglas."

"It wasn't a ritual killing. I simply snapped."

"Okay."

"Do you really think there's a black magic ritual that lets you switch bodies with other people?"

"Yes. I heard about it from a friend."

"Is he an expert in black magic?"

"Yes, he is."

"Did he tell how it's done?"

"No. He doesn't know how it's done."

"No one switched bodies with me," Fleming said, looking away from Mark.

"I want you to teach me how to do it, Douglas."

"Do what?"

"Switch bodies with other people."

Fleming smiled. "I'm sorry, man. I can't help you. I don't know how to switch bodies with other people."

"Edward Phillips told me that you do."

"Who's Edward Phillips?"

"You know who he is."

"I've never heard this name before. Do you have any more questions, Mister Writer?"

"That's all for now. Are you allowed to make phone calls?"

"Yeah."

"Let me give you my phone number. In case you change your mind."

"Okay."

Mark told Fleming his cell number and then repeated it twice.

"It was nice talking to you, Douglas." Mark stood up, and shook Fleming's hand. "Goodbye."

"Take care, man."

3

He had no way of knowing whether or not Fleming had lied about his reason for killing Walter Kindred, and he had no way of making Fleming tell the truth, so all he could do was move on. He was going to stay in Boston until Sunday because he wanted to do some sightseeing. Considering that he got to see one of the most interesting cities in the country, this trip wasn't a waste of time.

It was still raining when Mark came out of the Souza-Baranowski Correctional Center. He covered his head with his jacket and ran to his car. He got back to the hotel at three o'clock. As he rode the elevator up to his floor, a thought occurred to him: if Jeff Phillips and Sam Curtis intend to switch bodies on the same day, they'll need to make one more human sacrifice.

Mark was changing his socks when his phone rang. It was Detective Aguero.

Chapter 30

1

Carlos Aguero looked up the Cuckoo's Nest bar on Google Maps and found that there really was a bar named Cuckoo's Nest in Dallas; it was located thirteen miles from where Helen Hinton had been murdered.

On November 9, Aguero requested geolocation records for Jeff Phillips's phone for December 11 and 12 of last year: he wanted to see where Jeff's phone had been on the night of Helen Hinton's murder. He also requested geolocation records for Edward Phillips's cellphone for the same period.

If it turned out that Edward's and Jeff's phones had been connected at the same time to the same cell tower near the place where Helen Hinton had been killed on the night of December 11 of last year, Jeff would be in trouble, because that would suggest Jeff had been with his son when he murdered Helen.

When he reviewed the geolocation records, Aguero was disappointed to learn that from 7:23 p.m. on December 11 to 8:16 a.m. on December 12 Jeff Phillips's phone had been connected to a cell tower near his house. During that period, Edward Phillips's phone had been connected a cell tower near his place.

The fact that Edward Phillips had left his cell at home on the night he had murdered Helen Hinton indicated that he knew the police could use geolocation records to trace the movements of his cellphone, and Aguero had no doubt he had shared that knowledge with his father.

Jeff Phillips probably had an anonymous burner phone, which he used when he wanted to keep his movements secret.

On November 15, Aguero called Emily Phillips and asked if she had talked to her son yet.

"No, I haven't," Emily replied. "I'm sorry, Detective. I've been very busy. I'll talk to him by the end of the month."

AN EVIL MIND

It was clear to Aguero that Emily had no desire to talk to her son. Earlier, he had discovered that she had never visited Edward Phillips at the Allan B. Polunsky Unit.

The next day Aguero called Mark Hinton and asked if he was still trying to persuade Edward Phillips to tell him his partner's name.

"Yes, I am," Mark said.

"Have you made any progress?"

"No."

"Did he admit he had a partner?"

"No. Did you find any evidence that his father was involved in Laura Sumner's or my daughter's murder?"

"No, I didn't."

Aguero told Mark where Jeff Phillips's cellphone had been on the nights of December 11 and August 23, and then said, "He's a very careful guy. I think he has a burner phone."

2

Mark's phone rang again two hours after Aguero's call. He did not recognize the number.

"Hello."

"Hi. Is this Mark Hinton?"

"Yes."

"This is Douglas Fleming."

"Hello, Douglas."

Mark swung his legs off the bed and sat up.

"Are you still in Massachusetts?"

"Yes."

"Great. I have good news for you, Mark. I decided to tell you the whole truth."

"About what?"

"About the murder. You're right. It was a ritual killing."

"What was the purpose of the ritual?"

"I don't want to talk about it on the phone. Let's meet. Can you come here on Saturday?"

"Yes."

He couldn't meet Fleming on Friday because the visiting days for Fleming's housing block were Tuesday, Thursday, and Saturday.

"Can you do me a favor?"

"What is it?"

"I'd appreciate it if you put five hundred dollars in my inmate account."

Five hundred bucks. He could afford that.

"All right," Mark replied.

"They only accept checks and money orders. There's a special mailbox in the administration building lobby. It's marked Inmate Accounts. Put your check in that mailbox."

Mark stood up and walked to the window. The lights of the city shone brightly. The rain had stopped. He could finally go sightseeing.

"Got it."

"Thank you. Put my inmate ID number on the check."

Fleming told Mark his inmate ID number, and he wrote it down.

"See you on Saturday," Fleming said. "Goodbye."

"Goodbye."

Mark tossed the phone on the bed. Then he got dressed and went to explore downtown Boston.

He returned to the hotel at half past eleven. After checking his email, he spent an hour studying the text messages that Jeff Phillips and Sam Curtis had sent and received from July 1 to November 10. Mark searched the messages for "kill," "murder," "stab," "knife," "sacrifice," "ritual," "Helen Hinton," "Laura Sumner," "full moon," and "Douglas Fleming," and got no hits. Then he did a search for "dad," "father," and "son," and found no matches.

3

AN EVIL MIND

The next day, Mark visited South Boston, East Boston, and Charlestown. While in Charlestown, he purchased a money order for five hundred dollars. He spent two hours in downtown Boston before heading back to the hotel.

On Saturday, Mark arrived at the Souza-Baranowski Correctional Center at a quarter past noon. He considered depositing the money order in the mailbox before meeting with Fleming, then thought better of it. He needed to make sure that Fleming wasn't trying to swindle him.

When Fleming entered the visiting room, Mark waved to him and he waved back. He sat next to Mark and said, "How's it going, man?"

"I'm fine."

"I'm sorry I lied to you on Thursday."

"It's okay."

"Did you deposit the check in the mailbox?"

"Yes."

"Thank you."

"You said Walter Kindred's murder was a ritual killing. What was the purpose of the ritual?"

"It's a body switch ritual, and it requires human sacrifice. Walter was the sacrifice."

"How is this ritual performed?"

"First you make a human sacrifice. You have to stab each breast once and then cut open the stomach. The sacrifice can be any age and any gender. It doesn't have to be a virgin. You have to do the body switch within six months of making the sacrifice."

"What if you don't do the switch within six months?"

"You have to make another sacrifice. To switch bodies, you need to press your head to the head of the person you want to switch bodies with, and say the incantation three times. Your head must remain pressed to the other person's head until you finish saying the incantation. The incantation works only on full moon nights."

"Do you remember the incantation?"

"No. It's hard to remember because it sounds like gibberish."

"What language is it in?"

"Some ancient language. I don't know what it's called."

"Do you remember any words from the incantation?"

"I think the first word is naiz, and that's all I remember."

"Can the switch be reversed?"

"I suppose it can. You just have to perform the ritual again."

"And you have to make another sacrifice?"

"Of course."

"Who told you about this ritual?"

"A guy on a paranormal forum. His name's Brent."

"An Internet forum?"

"Yes. It's called Paranormal Mysteries. Brent told me he'd found a body switch ritual in some old book, and asked if I wanted to try it. I said yes, and he emailed me the instructions."

"When did he send you the instructions?"

"About three weeks before I killed Walter."

Had Brent told Fleming about the ritual to see if it worked?

"Do you remember the name of the book where Brent found the ritual?"

"No. It's a French book. Very old."

"Did you ever meet Brent in person?"

Fleming shook his head. "No."

"Do you know his phone number?"

"No."

"Do you remember his email address?"

"No, I don't."

"Did you delete his emails?"

"Yeah, I deleted all of them."

"Did Brent tell you where he lived?"

"He said he lived in San Diego." Fleming paused. "I don't think Brent is his real name."

AN EVIL MIND

"What's the forum's address?"

"It's very easy to find. Just google "paranormal mysteries forum." Brent's username is rogueghost. Are you going to contact him?"

"Yes. The human sacrifice—who is it made to?"

"Satan, I suppose. I'm sure God is against human sacrifice." Fleming smiled.

"Why didn't you switch bodies with a cellmate while you were in the county jail?"

"I couldn't. I made a mistake. I was supposed to declare that Walter was a sacrifice right after I killed him, but I forgot to do it." Fleming smiled sourly. "My whole plan went to shit because of one little mistake."

"What was your plan?"

Fleming laced his hands together and said, "I wanted to switch bodies with a billionaire. These guys must be the happiest people on earth." He looked at Mark. "If you could switch bodies with anyone, who would it be?"

"Samuel L. Jackson."

"Good choice. He's cool. I really liked him in Pulp Fiction. Have you seen Pulp Fiction?"

"Yes."

"Are you really a writer?"

"Yes."

"Can you send me one of your books?"

"Sure. I'll send it when I get home."

"Do you know if anyone else was killed the same way I killed Walter?"

"I haven't looked into that."

"Well, if I were you, I'd look into that. I'm sure Brent already tried the ritual himself."

"I'll look into that."

"Let me know if you find someone who pulled it off."

"Okay."

"If Brent tells you the incantation, are you going to perform the ritual?" Fleming said in a low voice.

"No. Do your relatives and friends visit you?"

"My mom visits me every two months. She lives in Syracuse. My friends don't visit me, but they answer my letters. By the way, do you want to be my pen pal?"

"Sure."

4

Mark dropped the money order in the mailbox before he left the Souza-Baranowski Correctional Center. When he returned to the hotel, he signed up to the Paranormal Mysteries forum and sent Brent a private message saying, "Hey, how's it going?"

None of Brent's forum posts mentioned a body swap ritual. His latest post had been made on October 5 of last year.

Mark got no reply from Brent that day.

Chapter 31

1

Sam was on pins and needles, waiting for Eric Pruitt's call. Fortunately, Pruitt didn't take months to make the decision: he called on November 18, one week after visiting New Horizons' office.

"I want to do the procedure," Pruitt said.

"Very good." Sam grinned. "I'll schedule your son's procedure for December second."

"Can we do it next week?"

"No."

"Why?"

"It's going to take some time to find the guy who will swap bodies with your son."

"Okay. December second is fine. By the way, how will I know that this guy is healthy?"

"I can give you a sample of his blood two days before the procedure."

"I want to watch you draw his blood."

Sam grimaced.

If he didn't agree to let Pruitt watch, Pruitt would most likely back out of the deal.

"All right," Sam said. "I'll give you a call on November thirtieth. Have you told your son about the procedure?"

"Yes. You said it would be a white man between eighteen and twenty-five."

"That's right."

"Is there any paperwork I have to sign?"

"No. It's a verbal contract."

"Okay. Thank you, Jake. Have a nice day." Pruitt hung up.

Sam jumped up from the couch and raised his arms triumphantly, shouting, "Yesss!"

It would be risky to let Pruitt know where they held the guy who was going to switch bodies with his son, so they would have to draw the blood sample somewhere else. Sam's and Jeff's houses were out of the question.

How about Pruitt's house? Sam didn't like this idea. He preferred neutral territory.

A hotel room was an acceptable place. It would have to be something respectable; Holiday Inn, for example, or Sheraton.

Sam called Jeff and told him that Pruitt wanted to do the procedure. Jeff suggested celebrating the good news at the Sparrow bar in North Dallas.

AN EVIL MIND

Chapter 32

1

On Sunday, Mark called Chris Novak and asked if he had seen any old books in Jeff Phillips's house. Novak said Jeff had a whole shelf of old books, some of which were over two hundred years old.

Two days later, as he looked at the knife used to kill Helen (now he was sure that it had been sent by Sam Curtis), an idea came to Mark. He could manufacture evidence incriminating Jeff Phillips by getting him to leave his prints on the handle of the knife. Then he could plant the knife in Jeff's house. If Jeff was convicted of Helen's murder, Edward would be exonerated.

On Saturday, Mark went to the Allan B. Polunsky Unit to visit Edward Phillips. He told Phillips why Douglas Fleming killed Walter Kindred and then said, "You were right. The ritual works only on full moon nights."

"Who told Fleming about the ritual?"

"Some guy on an Internet forum. I think it was the Phillipses."

"Did he tell you the name of the forum?"

"Paranormal Mysteries. I sent a message to the guy who told Fleming about the ritual. He hasn't replied yet."

"Can the switch be reversed?"

"Fleming doesn't know."

Phillips frowned.

"I don't want to die." Phillips cleared his throat. "I don't want to die, Mark."

"Your appeal hasn't been denied yet."

"Suppose I get a new trial. It'll take a miracle for me to get acquitted."

If he's released on bail, he can simply flee the country before the new trial begins.

"I have an idea. If we prove that Jeff Phillips killed Helen, you'll be exonerated."

"How are you going to prove that Jeff Phillips killed Helen?"

"I haven't figured that part out yet. I know he has no alibi for the night of Helen's murder."

Phillips stared at Mark for a long moment, and then said, "Do you believe God has a plan for everyone?"

"I don't know."

"Is my being executed for a crime I didn't commit part of God's plan? Was your daughter's murder part of His plan?"

Ever since Helen's murder, Mark had been wanting to ask his pastor if his daughter's death was part of God's plan. He had never done it because he was afraid he wouldn't like the answer.

"What do you think?" he asked.

Phillips rubbed his chin and said, "There was a guy by the name of Ken Waters. He spent eighteen years in prison for a murder he didn't commit. They made a movie about him. Hilary Swank was in it; she played his sister. His sister was an amazing woman. She put herself through law school just to help him get out of prison. Half a year after he was released, Ken fell from a wall and fractured his skull. He died two weeks later." Phillips paused. "If he hadn't been released from prison, he wouldn't have fallen from that wall and might still be alive today."

"It's a sad story."

"Sometimes I wonder if God put me through this to save me from a fatal accident."

"Just hang in there, okay? I'll do my best to get you out of here."

"Thank you, Mark. Did you check on my mom?"

"Yes. She's doing fine."

"Thank you. Do you know what kind of car Jeff drives?"

"Cadillac CTS."

"Do you know when he bought it?"

AN EVIL MIND

"No."

"I want to know what kind of car he had on December eleventh of last year. Could you find that out for me?"

"Yes."

"Thank you."

On Monday, Mark wrote Phillips a letter, in which he informed him that Jeff had bought his Cadillac two years ago.

Chapter 33

1

"Do you have any plans for the weekend?" Sam asked. It was 8:13 p.m. He was running on a treadmill in a gym called Energy Fitness, which he had joined a month ago.

"I'm going to the movies with my cousin," said Luke Gannon, who was on the treadmill next to Sam. Luke was twenty-one years old. He was white and was in great physical shape. He didn't use drugs, which was one of the reasons Sam had chosen him to trade bodies with Eric Pruitt's son.

"What are you going to see?"

"Some horror movie." Luke got off the treadmill, wiped his forehead with the back of his hand, and said, "I'm going home."

"Me, too." Sam stepped off the treadmill. "Let me give you a ride."

Luke lived about a mile from the gym and usually walked here. In the month they had known each other Sam had given him three rides home.

"Okay," Luke said.

As they went to the locker room, Sam sent Jeff a message saying, "Be ready."

When they walked out of the gym, Sam said, "It's cold tonight."

"Yeah."

They got in Sam's car, and as soon as Luke shut the door, Jeff, who was hiding in the backseat, clapped a chloroform-soaked rag over his face. Sam grabbed Luke's arms to prevent him from using them. When Luke passed out, Sam took the phone from Luke's pocket and removed the battery from it.

"Did anyone see him get in your car?" Jeff asked as they pulled out of the parking lot.

"No."

AN EVIL MIND

Jeff put the rag in the duffel bag and injected Luke with one hundred and fifty milligrams of chlorpromazine.

Twenty minutes later they arrived at the Vagabond Motel, which was located in Dallas, three miles from New Horizons' office. They parked in front of the room Sam had rented (he had paid cash to avoid the paper trail) and got out of the car. There was no one in the parking lot or in the hallway. They carried Luke into the room and laid him on a bed. Sam checked his watch. It was 8:42 p.m. He sat on the other bed, picked up the phone from the nightstand, and unplugged it.

Jeff brought in the duffel bag and took a coil of rope, a hunting knife, a pair of handcuffs, and a roll of duct tape out of it. He handed the rope to Sam, then cuffed Luke's wrists and taped his mouth shut.

As Sam bound Luke's feet, a woman began to moan loudly in the room next door. Grinning, Sam looked at Jeff and said, "Someone's fucking."

"Yeah." Jeff chuckled. He pulled the gun, a Glock 17, out of the bag and put it in his jacket pocket. "When are you going to call Pruitt?"

"Now."

Sam went outside, got in the car, and dialed Eric Pruitt's number. He didn't want to talk to Pruitt in the room because he feared that Luke could hear.

Pruitt answered after three rings.

"Good evening, Mister Pruitt. This is Jake Ford. I'm sorry to call so late."

"It's all right."

"We found a person willing to trade bodies with your son. I can give you a sample of his blood tomorrow morning. What time are you free?"

"Let's meet at ten a.m. Are you going to bring him to my office?"

"We're going to meet at his hotel room. He's staying at the Sheraton in downtown Dallas."

Sam didn't think Pruitt would mind meeting at the Sheraton because the hotel was less than two miles from his office.

"Okay. Let's meet there at ten. What's his room number?"

"Eleven fourteen. How is Paul doing?"

"He's okay."

"I'm glad to hear that. See you tomorrow at ten. Goodbye."

"Goodbye."

When Sam returned to the room, he hung a Do Not Disturb sign on the door.

"Did you talk to him?" Jeff asked.

"Yes. We're meeting tomorrow morning at ten."

The woman was still moaning in the room next door. Sam felt his penis harden.

"At the Sheraton?"

"Yes." Sam switched on the heater. "When is he going to wake up?"

"In an hour."

"I'm going to Burger King. Do you want me to get you something?"

"Get me two chicken sandwiches." Jeff turned on the TV.

"Okay."

2

Sam drove to the Burger King three blocks from the Vagabond Motel and bought two Whoppers, two bacon cheeseburgers, two chicken sandwiches, a garden side salad, and a Diet Coke. When he got back to the motel, he discovered that Jeff had latched the door.

"It's me, Jake," Sam announced.

"Okay." Jeff went to the door and let him in.

They sat down at the table, facing Luke.

"You know what they say about carrots?" Jeff said, plucking a carrot from the salad. "Everyone who's ever eaten a carrot has died or will die."

He chuckled.

As he unwrapped a chicken sandwich, Jeff asked, "Who's going to watch over him at night?"

"Can you do it?" Sam bit into his cheeseburger.

"Yeah."

"Wake me up at six-thirty."

"Who's going to wipe his ass after he takes a shit?" Jeff smiled.

"We'll flip a coin."

They laughed.

Jeff ate both chicken sandwiches and Sam one cheeseburger.

Luke woke at ten o'clock. He sat up and looked around, confusion on his face. When he reached to remove the duct tape from his mouth, Jeff, who was sitting on the other bed, pointed his gun at him and said, "Hey, pal. Don't touch it."

Pale with fear, Luke looked at Sam.

"Luke, you've been kidnapped," Sam said. "But don't worry. Everything will be fine. Do as we tell you, and you won't get hurt." He picked the hunting knife up from the table. "I'm going to take that tape off. If you scream, I'll cut your throat." Sam waved the knife. "Do you understand?"

Luke nodded.

Sam peeled the tape off Luke's mouth, wadded it up, and threw it in the bag.

"Are you hungry?" he said. "I bought you a hamburger."

"No." Luke shook his head. "What do you want from me?"

"We want your parents to pay us a hundred grand."

"They don't have that kind of money. They're not rich. They're regular people."

"Your mother said they'd find the money."

"You talked to my mother?"

"Yeah. We gave your parents five days to come up with the money."

"What if they don't find it?"

Sam smiled. "Relax, Luke. We're not going to kill you. Do you promise not to tell anyone who kidnapped you?"

Luke nodded vigorously. "Yes, I promise."

"Excellent. I believe you. Are you going to do as we tell you?"

"Yes."

"Your best course of action is to do nothing. Do not take chances, okay?"

"Okay. Can I have something to drink?"

"Sure." Sam opened a bottle of water and gave it to Luke.

Luke drank some water and then said, "Why did you choose me? I don't look rich."

"You don't look dirt poor, either."

"It's going to take my parents more than five days to find a hundred grand."

"We're willing to wait. And we're willing to lower the ransom. We'd settle for seventy grand."

"How many times have you done this before?"

"Two."

"Did you kill any of those people?"

"No. Do you have any more questions?"

"You're not going to kill me, right?"

"We're not going to kill you, I promise."

Sam taped Luke's mouth and then, at Jeff's suggestion, cuffed his hands behind his back.

An hour later Sam ate the other cheeseburger. He asked Luke again if he was hungry. Luke shook his head.

Sam went to bed at midnight. He didn't turn off the lights: Jeff said the light would help him stay awake.

"Wake me up when you feel sleepy," he told Jeff.

3

Sam was awakened by a beeping sound. When he rolled onto his back, Jeff slapped his thigh and said, "Wake up!"

Sam sat up, rubbed his eyes, and looked at Luke. Luke lay on his side, asleep. Sam glanced at his watch. It was 6:30 a.m.

"When did he fall asleep?" he asked.

"Around four hours ago." Jeff yawned.

The Whoppers Sam had bought for Luke were still in the bag.

Sam went to the rental van, which sat in the motel parking lot, took out the folding wheelchair, and returned to the room. After Jeff gave Luke an injection of chlorpromazine, they lifted Luke from the bed and put him in the wheelchair. Then Sam removed the handcuffs and cut the rope binding Luke's feet. To prevent Luke's face from being caught on the Sheraton's security cameras, Sam placed large sunglasses on Luke's face and a baseball cap on his head.

"Let's cuff him to the wheelchair," Jeff said.

"Okay."

Sam cuffed Luke's right hand to the wheelchair armrest, covered the handcuffs with his jacket, and said, "Luke, if you scream, I'll stab you to death."

They got Luke into the van and headed for the Sheraton, with Sam driving.

Luke remained silent and motionless all the way to their hotel room. Sam carefully watched Luke's face while in the lobby and the eleventh-floor hallway.

"Did he go to the bathroom?" Sam asked when Jeff lay down on the bed.

"Yeah." Jeff closed his eyes. "He pissed in a cup."

"Did you uncuff him?"

"No."

"Did you hold his dick?"

"No."

Sam took the bag with blood supplies out of the duffel and put it on the table. His stomach was churning. What if Pruitt changed his mind? What if he got in a terrible car accident this morning? What if he died in that accident?

He wasn't worried about the blood test. He was pretty sure the test wouldn't reveal anything that would make Pruitt demand a different body: ninety-five percent of twenty-one-year-old men were in fairly good health.

At nine-thirty Sam injected Luke with one hundred milligrams of chlorpromazine. Then he put on his suit and tie, removed the handcuffs, and woke up Jeff. They took the jacket off Luke and laid him on the bed. Sam put the wheelchair in the closet. At a quarter to ten Eric Pruitt called and told Sam that he was on his way to the Sheraton. Sam breathed a sigh of relief. Ten minutes later there was a knock on the door. It was Pruitt.

"Is that him?" Pruitt asked, pointing at Luke.

"Yes," Sam replied.

"Is he asleep?"

"Yes."

Sam washed his hands and then sat down in the chair next to the bed. The blood collection supplies lay on the nightstand, which he had covered with a towel.

"Can you wake him up?" Pruitt stood beside Sam.

"Let him sleep. Sleep relaxes the brain, which will help the transfer process." Sam put on latex gloves.

"What's his name?"

"Luke." Sam tied a tourniquet around Luke's right arm. "He's as healthy as a horse. He goes to the gym three times a week."

"How old is he?"

"Twenty-one." Sam found a vein in Luke's forearm and tapped it with his fingers.

"Is he an American?"

"Yes."

"Can I take his picture?"

AN EVIL MIND

Sam wiped Luke's forearm with an alcohol swab. He looked as if he was experienced in drawing venous blood, although he'd practiced the procedure only twice before, on Jeff, using the instructions he'd found on the Internet.

"Sure."

He's afraid we'll switch Luke with someone sick, Sam thought as he attached a needle to the syringe.

Pruitt pulled out his phone and snapped Luke's picture. Then he went to the foot of the bed, lifted Luke's pant legs, and said to Jeff, "Can you take off his socks, please?"

Would you like to check his dick and balls, too? Sam thought.

Jeff stripped off Luke's socks, and Pruitt bent down and examined Luke's feet. He seemed to be pleased with what he saw.

"Take the sample to the lab right away, please," Sam said, drawing blood into the syringe.

"Okay."

"If we don't do it this Saturday, you'll have to wait another month."

As Sam transferred the blood to a blood collection tube, Pruitt asked, "Can I talk to Luke today or tomorrow?"

"Yes. If he agrees to talk to you."

Why did Pruitt want to talk to Luke? Did he suspect they were forcing Luke to trade bodies with his son?

If Pruitt loved his son, he shouldn't care how they had gotten Luke to swap bodies with Paul.

Sam put the collection tube in a zipper bag and handed the bag to Pruitt. "Bring your son to our office this Saturday at eight p.m. Please don't be late." He stood up.

"Eight p.m. Okay." Pruitt looked at the collection tube for a moment and then pocketed it.

"Have a nice day, Eric."

"Have a nice day, Mister Pruitt," Jeff said.

Pruitt shook Sam's hand and left the room.

Chapter 34

1

"Do you remember me?" Aguero asked.

Edward Phillips nodded. "Yeah, I remember you."

It was December 1. Seven weeks had passed since he made Phillips an offer, and Aguero was hoping he had changed his mind.

"I'm Detective Carlos Aguero with the Austin Police Department. I'm investigating the murder of Laura Sumner."

"I remember that."

"My offer still stands. Do you know who killed Laura Sumner?"

Phillips shook his head. "No, I don't."

"If you help us catch Laura Sumner's killer, the governor will commute your death sentence. Do you understand that?"

"Yes. I don't know who killed her."

Aguero felt a prickle of disappointment. He had driven two hundred miles for nothing. "Did you have a partner?"

"What do you mean?"

"Did anyone help you kill Helen Hinton?"

"I didn't kill that girl."

Aguero stared at his notepad for a moment, and then said, "I talked to your mother. She wants you to cooperate with us. She wants you to help us find Laura's killer."

Phillips said nothing.

"Your mother loves you very much, Edward. She doesn't want you to die."

"I love her, too."

"Why are you protecting this person?"

"I'm not protecting anyone."

Perhaps he would change his mind after all his appeals failed.

"Laura was killed by someone you know. Tell us his name."

AN EVIL MIND

"I don't know who killed Laura."

"Your death's going to break your mother's heart. There's nothing worse for a mother than to bury her child."

"I miss my mom. Can you ask the warden to let me call her? I haven't heard her voice in a year."

"Sure. I'll do my best."

His boss should be able to persuade the Warden of the Allan B. Polunsky Unit to let Edward Phillips give his mother a call.

"Do you have her cellphone number? Phillips asked.

"Yes. Let me write it down for you." Aguero pulled out his phone, found Emily Phillips's number, and wrote it on his pad. Then he ripped out the page with the number and gave it to Phillips.

"Do you miss your dad?" Aguero asked.

After a brief hesitation, Phillips said, "Yes, I do."

Aguero made a mental note of Phillips's hesitation, but he didn't want to read too much into it.

"Have you gotten used to this place?"

"I don't think you can get used to this place."

"Let me help you get out of here, Edward. Tell me who killed Laura Sumner."

"Can you get the governor to pardon me?"

"We'll try."

"You think I had a partner."

"Yes."

"For the sake of argument, let's say you're right. Let's say my partner killed Laura Sumner. Will you ask the governor to commute my sentence if he's acquitted? Guilty people go free all the time, you know."

"This is Texas. If there's evidence, he's going to be convicted." Aguero leaned forward. "What's his name?"

"I didn't say I had a partner."

Aguero closed his pad. "Think about your mother, Edward. Don't break her heart."

TIM KIZER

AN EVIL MIND

Chapter 35

1

"Do you think he believes we're paying Luke a million bucks to switch bodies with his son?" Jeff said, opening a bottle of Diet Coke.

Sam shrugged. "I don't know." He looked at Luke, who was sleeping peacefully on the sofa.

They had arrived at New Horizons' office at half past six in the evening. Luke's face was concealed from the building's security cameras by the same sunglasses and baseball cap he'd worn at the Sheraton two days ago.

Luke had been a good boy: he had never called for help or tried to escape. Since neither of them wanted to wipe his ass, they let Luke defecate without handcuffs. On Thursday, to make their lie believable, Sam took a picture of Luke holding Thursday's issue of USA Today. They told Luke they'd email the photo to his parents to prove he was alive. After taking the picture, Sam drove five miles from the Vagabond Motel, parked the car, and switched on Luke's phone. He discovered that Luke's mother had called him four times and sent him three text messages since the abduction. Sam sent Luke's mother a message saying, "I'm OK. I'm at my friend's place." On Friday night, he sent her another message, which read: "I'm fine. I'm still at my friend's place."

This morning Luke had showered for the first time since Wednesday night and put on new underwear, socks, and T-shirt.

"Tomorrow we'll become millionaires." Jeff smiled.

"As soon as we get the money, I'll buy a Ferrari."

Sam wore a dark suit and tie, and Jeff brown khakis and a blue long-sleeved shirt.

Jeff glanced at his watch. "It's time for another shot."

He got up, grabbed the syringe, and gave Luke an injection of chlorpromazine.

Sam's burner phone rang. It was Eric Pruitt.

"We're on our way," Pruitt said. "We'll be there in fifteen minutes."

"Excellent."

Pruitt brought two people with him: his son and his assistant Ryan.

"Ryan will wait in the hallway," Pruitt said.

Ryan was clean-shaven, in his late thirties, broad-shouldered, and dressed in a suit and tie. When Sam had first seen him, he had thought he was Pruitt's bodyguard.

Maybe he was Pruitt's assistant-slash-bodyguard?

"He can wait here, if he wants," Sam said.

Ryan accepted the invitation and sat down in a chair in the larger room.

Paul Pruitt was tall and skinny, with a gaunt face and short brown hair. Sam motioned him and Eric Pruitt to follow him into the smaller room.

He led Paul to the sofa and said, "This is Luke. We're going to transfer your consciousness to his brain. Do you like his body?"

"Yeah, he looks good," Paul said, his eyes fixed on Luke.

Sam turned to Eric and asked, "Is Paul allergic to Ambien?"

"No. Are you going to give him Ambien?"

"Yes. The procedure requires that the subject be asleep."

Paul sat down in a chair.

"Did you and your son agree on a password?" Sam said.

"Yes, we did."

"Have you thought up the questions you're going to ask to verify your son's identity?"

"Yes."

"How long is the procedure going to take?" Paul asked.

"About two hours," Sam replied. "Are you nervous?"

"A little."

"There's no need to be nervous. We have a one hundred percent success rate."

Sam picked a bottle of Ambien and a bottle of water up from the desk, handed them to Paul, and said, "This is Ambien. Please take two pills."

Paul put two tablets in his mouth and washed them down with water.

"Now sit back and relax," Sam said. He closed the door and then said to Eric in a low voice, "Just to remind you, Eric, the procedure costs twenty million dollars."

"I remember that."

"Of course. If you verify your son's identity tonight, we'd like you to wire the money tomorrow."

"Tomorrow's Sunday. I'll wire the money on Monday."

When Paul fell asleep, Sam asked Eric to leave the room. He locked the door behind Eric and checked his watch. It was 8:43.

The instructions did not specify the time at which the ritual had to be performed. They just said that it had to done on a full moon night, so Sam figured they were good to go as soon as it got dark. It had been over two hours since night had fallen.

At first he had planned to wait until midnight: he had started the ritual at ten minutes past midnight when he performed it in the Dallas County Jail last January. Then he had decided to do it when it got dark; if he failed, he would try again after midnight.

Sam opened the file drawer and retrieved the surveillance monitor, which received the video signal from the hidden camera in the larger room. Both men sat in chairs. Eric Pruitt was reading a magazine, and Ryan was doing nothing.

"When are we going to do it?" Jeff whispered.

"Now," Sam whispered back, and placed the monitor on the desk.

They lifted Luke from the sofa and laid him on the floor. Luke stirred, let out a low groan, and smacked his lips. His eyes remained shut. Jeff pushed Paul's chair to the sofa, grabbed Paul under the armpits, and with a grunt pulled him up.

"Need help?" Sam asked.

"No, I got this." Jeff put Paul on the floor beside Luke.

Sam turned Paul on his right side and bent his legs at the knees so he wouldn't roll onto his stomach or back. Jeff pushed Luke close to Paul, turned him on his side so he was facing Paul, and then pressed his face against the back of Paul's head. Sam took an adjustable nylon belt out of the bag and bound the young men's heads together with it. To stabilize Luke's position, Jeff put his left arm over Paul's body.

"Look at them. They're spooning." Jeff laughed.

Sam smiled. As he stared at Luke and Paul, he remembered lying behind Sam Curtis on Sam's bed in the Dallas County Jail on the night of January eleventh, breathing in the smells of his hair and sweat, whispering the incantation, with his face pressed to the back of Sam's head and his left arm wrapped around him. If a guard had seen them, he would have thought they were having sex.

Although he was not gay or bisexual, spooning his cellmate had not made Sam feel uncomfortable.

Has Edward been raped yet? Sam wondered. Edward wasn't a muscleman, so there must be plenty of inmates in his unit who were strong enough to force him into submission.

Did rape take place in death row prisons?

Sam looked at the surveillance monitor. Eric Pruitt was still reading the magazine, and Ryan was gazing at the ceiling.

From his pants pocket, Sam pulled the piece of paper on which he had written the incantation, and unfolded it.

"Let's do it," he said.

Jeff stepped a few feet away from Luke and Paul and folded his arms across his chest.

"Naiz orod imat semas tauni mopela tus," Sam read aloud.

The incantation had to be said by Sam because it worked only if it was said by the person who had performed the sacrifice.

"Naiz orod imat semas tauni mopela tus."

Sam's heart was pounding as hard as it had when he performed the ritual in the Dallas County Jail.

"Naiz orod imat semas tauni mopela tus."

In his imagination, Sam saw lightning streak the sky and heard thunder roar.

Sam removed the belt from Luke's and Paul's heads and put it in the bag. Then they sat Luke and Paul down on the sofa.

"Let's wake him up," Jeff suggested.

"Okay." Sam shook Luke's shoulder. "Wake up! Wake up!"

No reaction.

Sam shook him for about fifteen seconds before giving up. He figured Luke still had a significant amount of chlorpromazine in his system.

He tried to wake Luke up again half an hour later. After Sam shook his shoulder a few times, Luke opened his eyes and looked around. When he saw Paul, he raised his eyebrows and said, "Is it over?"

"What's your name?" Sam asked.

"Paul Pruitt." Luke pointed at Paul. "Is this my body? My old body?"

"When is your birthday?"

"July nineteenth."

Paul Pruitt's birthday was July 19.

"What's your father's name?"

"Eric Pruitt." Luke was staring at his hands with disbelief.

"What illness did you have?"

"Brain tumor. Is the procedure over?"

"Yes, it is." Grinning from ear to ear, Sam turned to Jeff and said, "It worked."

Sam was euphoric. He was glowing with excitement. Everything was going according to plan, and in two days he would be twenty million dollars richer.

Jeff clapped Luke on the shoulder and said, "Congratulations, son."

Luke stood up and looked closely at Paul's face.

"How are you feeling?" Sam asked.

"I'm feeling great," Luke replied.

Sam patted Paul's jeans pockets. "Did you have anything in your pockets?"

"No."

"Would you like to get your clothes back?"

"No. Do you have a mirror?"

"Yes, we do."

Sam opened the file drawer, took out a handheld mirror, and gave it to Luke.

Luke examined his face for half a minute, and then said to Sam, "Thank you, Jake. Thank you very much."

"You're welcome. Come with me."

Sam and Luke walked out of the room, and Sam said to Eric, "The procedure's over. We've successfully transferred your son's consciousness to Luke's brain."

Eric got up from the chair.

"Dad, it worked," Luke said to him with a smile.

Looking fixedly at Luke, Eric asked, "What's the password?"

"Godfather and shenanigans."

"What movie did we watch last night?"

"Inception and Skyfall."

Eric's serious expression softened.

"Is that correct?" Sam asked.

"Yes." Eric nodded. To Luke, he said, "Tell me the joke you told me this morning."

"What's the difference between a bull and a cow? A bull smiles when you milk it."

"What's the name of the girl that gave you your first blowjob?"

"Julia Burns."

"What's the name of your cousin in Seattle?"
"Adam Browning."
"I put something in my pants pocket before we left the house. What was it?"
"A Japanese coin. Fifty yen. It's me, Dad. Are you going to ask me all the questions we prepared?"
"Yes. Who did we meet in Vegas last May?"
"Robert Downey Junior."
"What happened in Hawaii last August?"
"I lost my phone."
"What's the name of your uncle in Houston?"
"James Pruitt."
"What did you have for breakfast this morning?"
"Scrambled eggs with smoked salmon and a lettuce salad."
"What happened in the great room two weeks ago?"
"I broke a vase."
"Who's Jordan Duggan?"
"He was my classmate. When I was seventeen, he asked if he could suck my dick. I said no." Luke smiled. "Dad, it's me."
"Are his answers correct?" Sam asked Eric.
Eric nodded. "Yes." His eyes filled with tears. He put his arms around Luke, and said, "This is amazing. This is amazing."
"I don't have a tumor anymore." Luke's eyes were swimming with tears.
Eric shook Sam's hand, and said, "Thank you very much."
"You're welcome," Sam replied.
To Luke, Eric said, "I need to talk to Jake. Will you please wait in the hallway?"
Then he asked his assistant to wait in the hallway, and when Ryan and Luke stepped out of the office, he said to Sam, "Can I talk to Luke?"
"Why? Do you still have doubts?"
"I'll feel better if I talk to him."

"What do you want to talk to him about?"

"I'll ask him the questions I asked Paul."

Would Pruitt refuse to pay if they didn't let him speak to Luke?

Sam thought for a moment and then said, holding up five fingers, "Five questions. You can ask him five questions."

"Okay."

"Don't tell him you're the father of the guy he traded bodies with."

"Why?"

"He might try to pretend he's still your son. It's happened before."

They went into the smaller room, and Sam asked Jeff to wake Paul up.

It took Jeff less than a minute to rouse Paul from sleep.

"What's going on?" Paul said when he awoke. He looked at Jeff and then at Eric, who was standing next to Jeff.

"What's your name?" Eric asked.

"Luke," Paul said.

"What's your last name?"

"Gannon." Paul frowned.

"Do you know who I am?"

"No." Paul shook his head.

"Are you satisfied?" Sam asked Eric.

"Have we ever met before?" Eric asked Paul.

"No." Paul shifted his gaze to Sam.

"Good night, Luke." Eric headed for the door, and Sam followed him.

When they walked out of the room, Sam explained to Eric what needed to be done next. Then he gave Eric the bank account number that the twenty million was to be wired to. Eric asked Sam to come to his house on Monday at one p.m.

"I'm going to use my home computer to make the wire transfer," he said. "I want you to verify that all the information is correct before I send the money."

AN EVIL MIND

Chapter 36

1

Had Sam Curtis switched bodies?

It was Sunday, December 3. Last night, Mark had watched Curtis's house from five p.m. to one a.m., with a two-hour break from eight to ten. He had seen no one leave or enter the house, the windows had been dark, and Curtis's car had been nowhere to be found.

Even if Curtis had gotten a new body, he would still have gone home, wouldn't he?

Mark checked his watch. It was 9:14 p.m.

Where the hell was Curtis?

Maybe he's asleep?

Mark got out of his Impala, stretched his back, walked twenty yards down the street, then turned around and went back to his car.

The night was quiet and windless.

He would have to kill Sam Curtis eventually. He simply had no choice: if Curtis was prevented from swapping bodies in a county jail, he would do it later in a state prison. The only prison in Texas where Curtis wouldn't be able to switch bodies was the death row block at the Allan B. Polunsky Unit, where the inmates were held in single cells for twenty-two hours a day. Curtis was not going to be sentenced to death for attempted murder.

Through the gaps in the blinds Mark could see a huge flat-screen TV in the house in front of which he had parked. Mark got in the car, picked up his phone, and sent Joan a message saying, "I'll be home by 11." A minute later, a white Mazda 6 pulled up to the curb in front of Curtis's house. The driver got out, and when Mark saw his face, he let out a sigh of relief: it was Sam Curtis.

2

Emily Phillips was walking across the parking lot of Hamilton Middle School, where she taught math, when Edward called. She didn't recognize the number and wondered if it was the parents of one of her students.

"Hi, Mom, this is Edward."

Emily's heart jumped when she heard Edward's voice.

"Eddie? Oh my God!"

"How are you?"

"I'm fine. How are you?"

"I miss you, Mom."

"I miss you, too, Eddie."

"It's been a long time since I last saw you. Why aren't you visiting me?"

Emily's stomach churned with guilt. "We've been busy. I'm sorry." Lying to her son made her feel even more ashamed. "Why didn't you call?"

"I thought you didn't want to talk to me."

"Eddie, honey, we love you. You can call any time you want." A thick lump formed in Emily's throat, and tears came to her eyes.

"Did Dad... Did Dad tell you not to visit me?"

"No, no, he didn't." Emily wiped the tears away.

"You can tell me the truth, Mom. I won't be upset."

Emily sighed heavily. "You know how your father is. His reputation is very important to him."

"I understand him. Did Dad tell you not to attend my trial?"

"Yes. But I wanted to go. I really did."

"It's okay. I forgive you."

Emily got in her Ford Explorer and put her purse on the passenger seat.

"Are they treating you well?"

"I have nothing to complain about." Edward paused. "I want to see you. Can you come visit me?"

"I'd love to come. Can I visit you on a Saturday?"

"Yes. You can find the visitation schedule on the Internet."

"I'll look it up."

"I miss you so much, Mom. Please come."

The anguish in Edward's voice made Emily's heart twist.

"I will."

"When?"

"By the end of this month, for sure."

"I love you, Mom."

"I love you, too, honey."

"How's Dad?"

"He's fine."

"Don't tell him I called you, please."

"Okay. Oh, I spoke to a police detective from Austin. His name's Carlos Aguero. Have you met him?"

"Yes, I have."

"He said they'd commute your sentence if you helped them solve the murder of a woman named Laura Sumner."

"Let's talk about it when we meet."

"I think you should help them if you can."

"We'll talk about it when me meet, Mom. My time is up. Goodbye, Mom."

"Goodbye, honey. I love you."

Edward hung up.

Emily took a facial tissue from her purse and blotted her eyes.

Her Eddie wanted to see her. He missed her.

Jeff would be mad if she went to see Edward in prison.

In mid-January, Jeff had told her that they should stop visiting Edward in jail. He said that their son was a psycho murderer and that he deserved to be disowned.

"He disgraced our family. From now on, when people talk about us, they'll say, 'By the way, their son stabbed a girl to death,'" Jeff said.

Emily told herself she had to comply because Jeff was her husband and she loved him. But the truth was, if she had really wanted to visit Edward in prison or attend his trial, she would have done it. The reason she heeded Jeff's request was simple: part of her agreed with him.

From time to time Emily wondered if abandoning Edward made her a bad mother. She did not dwell on this subject because she believed that lack of parents' attention was the least of Edward's concerns. The only thing a man on death row wished for was freedom, and she couldn't give it to her son.

She had to visit Edward. Jeff wasn't going to be mad, because she wouldn't tell him that she'd met with their son.

AN EVIL MIND

Chapter 37

1

As he neared the front porch of Eric Pruitt's marvelous mansion, Sam thought: in just a few hours I'll be able to afford a house like this. He would be able to afford it even if he paid income tax on the money received from Pruitt (they were going to give Uncle Sam his cut because messing with the IRS was a foolish and dangerous idea).

Sam was dressed in the same suit he'd worn in New Horizons' office last Saturday.

Eric Pruitt opened the door before Sam could knock on it.

"Please come in."

They shook hands, and Pruitt led Sam to his study.

"Did you take a cab here?" Pruitt asked, pulling his laptop in front of him.

"Yes."

"How's Luke?"

"He's fine."

It was a lie. Luke was dead and buried in the woods twenty miles east of Dallas. Sam had killed him the same way he had killed Helen Hinton, Laura Sumner, and hitchhiker Edgar.

"Thank you for saving my son's life, Jake. I'm extremely grateful to you."

"You're very welcome, Eric. Did your son speak to Luke's parents?"

"Yes, he did. Everything went smoothly." Pruitt started typing on his laptop.

"Does Paul like his new body?"

"Yes, he does. Are you going to tell Luke who he traded bodies with?"

"No."

The door swung open, and Ryan and a tall burly man in a dark suit entered the study. Ryan walked over to Sam, reached inside his suit jacket, and pulled out a pistol.

"Get up," Ryan commanded.

Sam looked from Ryan to Pruitt and then back to Ryan. "Why?"

"Because I said so."

Sam felt a sinking in the pit of his stomach. He didn't like it when people pointed guns at him. It took virtually no effort to kill with a pistol, and it was very easy to shoot someone accidentally.

"Eric, what's going on?" Sam forced a smile.

"He's got a gun," Pruitt said. "If I were you, I'd get up."

Sam rose to his feet.

This motherfucker didn't want to pay the twenty million!

Were they going to kill him?

Sam's skin crawled into gooseflesh.

The burly man patted Sam down thoroughly and then said, "He's clean."

"Eric, you're a respectable businessman, and I expect you to keep your end of the bargain," Sam said.

The burly man drew his gun and pointed it at Sam.

Sam swallowed hard. "Can you lower your guns, please? They make me really uncomfortable."

Pruitt's goons ignored his request.

"Eric, can you tell your guys to lower their guns? I'm not going to run, I promise."

"Everything will be all right, Jake." Pruitt stepped out from behind his desk. "Cuff him."

Ryan took a pair of handcuffs from his pocket and put them on Sam's wrists.

"You're making a big mistake." Sam glared at Pruitt.

"Get his wallet and phone," Pruitt said to Ryan.

Ryan pulled Sam's wallet and disposable phone from his pockets and handed them to Pruitt. Pruitt opened the wallet, looked at it for a moment, and then said, "Let's go."

They went to the garage and got in Pruitt's Mercedes.

Were they taking him to the woods?

"Where are we going?" Sam asked as they drove out of the garage, his palms sweaty, his heart pounding harder than ever.

"You'll see," said Pruitt, who sat behind the wheel.

"Is it about money? If twenty million is too much, we can lower the price."

There was nothing he could do to save himself right now.

It was impossible for him to escape from the car because he was sandwiched between Ryan and the burly man.

"It's not about money."

"Then what is it about?"

"I'll tell you when we get there."

"If anything happens to me, the company will reverse the procedure and Paul's consciousness will go back to his old sick body."

"That's bullshit."

"You don't have to pay us anything. Just let me go."

"It's not about money, Jake."

"We have a lot of powerful friends. If you hurt me, they're going to destroy you."

Pruitt laughed. "Please shut up."

When they entered I-35E northbound, Pruitt ordered Ryan to put a sack on Sam's head, and he did. About half an hour later the car stopped, and Ryan pulled the sack off.

"Get out," he said.

Sam climbed out of the Mercedes and saw that they were in a four-car garage. Two of the other three spaces were empty and one was occupied by a silver Ford Explorer.

They entered the house and went to the great room, where Pruitt and Sam sat down across the table from each other.

"Patrick, check the other rooms and see if there's anyone there," Pruitt said to the burly man.

When Patrick left, Sam asked, "Where are we?"

"One of my properties."

"So why did you kidnap me?"

"First, tell me your real name. Is it Jake Ford or Samuel Curtis?"

"Jake Ford."

"What about the driver's license in your wallet? It has your picture on it and it's in the name of Samuel Curtis."

"Sam Curtis is my alias."

"Why do you need an alias?"

"For security reasons. Why does it matter? We helped your son, didn't we?"

"How many people work in your company?"

"Why do you ask?"

"Just curious."

"Ten people."

"Who invented this technology? You?"

"No."

"Don't lie to me. If you lie, we'll kill you."

"We bought the rights to this technology from the people who developed it."

"How much did you pay them?"

"I don't know."

This motherfucker wanted to steal the consciousness transfer technology!

"What are their names?"

"I don't know. I wasn't involved in this transaction."

"Who owns New Horizons?"

"Do you want to buy the company?"

"Yes."

"Let me talk to my boss. He knows the owners."

"What's your boss's name?"

"John Branson."

Pruitt pulled out Sam's phone, opened the contact list, and then said, "There's no John Branson in your contacts. Are you lying to me, Jake?"

"No, I'm not. It's my personal phone."

"I think there's no John Branson. I think you're the boss of New Horizons."

"I'm just an employee. I talk to prospective clients and help perform the procedure."

"I'm going to send my guys to your company's office, and I want you to tell your people to give them the equipment used to perform the procedure."

Patrick walked into the room, and announced, "There's no one else in the house."

"Very good," Pruitt said.

"You're not going to get away with this, Eric," Sam said.

"I think I am." Pruitt stood up, walked over to Sam, and handed him his phone. "Now call the office and tell your people you sent three guys to pick up the equipment. Put the call on speaker."

"The office is closed today."

Pruitt took the phone back, then pulled out his phone and dialed a number.

"Hi, Lucas," he said. "Go to the office and see if it's closed."

Pruitt sat down, and asked Sam, "Do you have the office keys?"

What was Pruitt going to do when he discovered that there was no consciousness transfer software on those computers?

"Yes," Sam replied.

"Give them to Ryan."

Sam fished his keys from his pocket and handed them to Ryan, who stood beside him.

"The yellow keys," he said.

Pruitt put the phone back to his ear and said, "Yes." A pause. "Okay. You'll have the key in forty minutes." He hung up. "Do you have an alarm system?" he asked Sam.

"No."

"Take the key to Lucas and then come back," Pruitt said to Ryan.

"Should I take the Explorer?" Ryan asked.

"Yes. The keys are in the visor."

Sam glanced at his watch. It was 2:17 p.m. The computers should be delivered here in about two hours.

He had two hours to figure out how to get out of this predicament.

"Why are you doing this?" he asked Pruitt.

"Isn't it obvious?"

"No."

Pruitt said nothing.

"When did you decide to rob us?"

"Yesterday."

I should have switched bodies with Pruitt instead of saving his son's life.

"Are you going to kill me?"

"If you cooperate, you'll live."

2

Ryan came back at a quarter to four. The computers arrived half an hour later. Sam and Jeff had bought six desktops and two servers for their office, and Pruitt's minions had taken all of them.

Sam was held in a guest bedroom on the second floor, guarded by Patrick and Ryan, while Pruitt's men carried the computers into the house and set them up. At ten past five Patrick and Ryan escorted Sam into the dining room, where New Horizons' computers had been installed, and Pruitt said to him, "Now I want you to show me how it's done."

The computers sat on the dining table; the people who had delivered them were gone. After three hours of racking his brain, Sam still had no rescue plan. Sooner or later he would have to admit to Pruitt that they hadn't used computers to transfer Paul's consciousness to Luke's body. Would Pruitt let him go if he told him about the ritual?

Sam circled the table, looking intently at the computers, and then said, "We need a brain-scanning cap."

"What's that?" Pruitt asked.

"It's a device that receives electrical signals from the brain and transmits them to the computer. You put it on the subject's head."

"Where is it?"

"Peter has it."

Pruitt grimaced as if he had bitten into a lemon, and said, "Stop lying, Jake."

"I'm telling you the truth. He's the chief technician. He brings the cap to the office when we perform the procedure."

"Why didn't you tell me this before?" Pruitt scowled.

"I forgot. I was in shock."

"Where does he live?"

"I don't know."

"What's his phone number?"

"I don't know."

"Bullshit."

"It's not bullshit. He's a very secretive guy."

"How do you communicate with him?"

"Through email."

"Is there a procedure scheduled for tonight?"

"No."

Pruitt pointed at the chair at the head of the table. "Sit down."

Sam did as told.

"Do you want to live, Jake?" Pruitt asked.

"Yes, I do."

"In order to get out of this alive, you need to show me how the procedure is performed. If you don't do it, I'll blow your brains out. Now tell me where the brain-scanning cap is."

"Peter's place."

"What does it look like?"

"It looks like a swimming cap. It has electrodes and wires on it."

"And if we search your place in Arlington, we won't find it?"

"No. I don't have it. I want to cooperate with you, Eric. I have no reason not to cooperate."

"Do you live alone?"

"Yes."

"What's Peter's email address?"

Sam gave Pruitt one of his email addresses.

"I want you to log into your email," Pruitt said.

Sam opened the Internet browser and logged into another of his email accounts. Pruitt stood behind him, and asked, "Is this the email you use to communicate with Peter?"

"Yes."

"Get up."

Sam stood up, and Pruitt sat down on the chair.

"Does he live in the Dallas area?" Pruitt clicked the Compose button.

"Yes."

Pruitt typed the email address provided by Sam into the recipient field of the message. "Does he own a gun?"

"No."

When Pruitt finished writing the email, he said to Sam, "Read it."

The message read: "Hi, Peter. Please bring the brain-scanning cap to the office tonight at 9 p.m. We have a new client."

"Does it look right?" Pruitt asked.

"Yeah." Sam nodded.

Pruitt clicked the Send button.

AN EVIL MIND

Chapter 38

1

Pruitt looked at the computer screen, then checked his watch and said, "It's eight o'clock, and Peter still hasn't replied. Why?"

"Maybe he's busy," Sam said.

How much longer could he stall? Would Pruitt agree to wait until tomorrow night?

"Or maybe you gave me the wrong email address."

"Why would I do that?"

"Patrick, hit him in the face." Pruitt touched his cheek.

Patrick nodded, got up, and slammed a fist into Sam's face, almost knocking him off the chair. Pain exploded through Sam's head, bringing tears to his eyes, and he let out a groan. He felt dizzy for a moment.

"What the fuck?" Sam muttered, and sat upright, his left cheek throbbing. He tasted blood in his mouth.

Patrick was grinning.

"Did you give me the wrong email address?" Pruitt asked.

Sam ran his tongue over his teeth to see if any of them were broken or missing. His teeth seemed intact.

"No, I didn't," he said. "It's the right email address. He's probably not home."

"Does he have a cellphone?"

"Yes."

Pruitt placed his hand on the mouse and moved it forward and backward a few times. "If Peter's not at the office at nine, Ryan will shoot you in the foot."

"Come on, Eric! Let's wait until Peter replies."

"No. And if we don't have the brain-scanning cap by midnight, we'll kill you."

"I have a question. Who am I going to do the procedure on?"

"You're not going to perform the procedure. You'll just show how to perform it."

"How will you know that I'm telling the truth?"

Pruitt was silent for a moment and then said, "I'll think about it after we get the cap." He looked at the screen. "Still no reply."

"Are you going to kill me after I show you how to do the procedure?"

"No."

"Will you let me go?"

"Yes. But not right away. A few days later."

Most likely, Pruitt was lying. He had no reason to let Sam go.

At five past nine Pruitt called one of his minions and asked if Peter had arrived at the office. After hanging up, he sighed heavily, glanced at the computer screen, and said, "Peter's not at the office. Ryan's going to shoot you in the foot, Jake. I'm sorry."

Ryan rose to his feet, drew his pistol, and walked over to Sam.

"You want me to do it right here?" Ryan asked Pruitt.

"This is unnecessary," Sam said, his heart fluttering wildly.

"The bullet will damage the floor." Pruitt paused to think. "Let's just cut off his finger." He got up. "We'll do it in the kitchen."

"Eric, I have to tell you something," Sam said.

"Go ahead."

"I lied to you."

"About what?"

"About the procedure. There's no brain-scanning cap. I made it up. And these computers were in the office just for show."

"What do you mean?" Pruitt frowned.

"We didn't use computers to transfer your son's consciousness to Luke's body."

"Then how did you do it?"

"You're not going to believe it."

When Pruitt opened his mouth to reply, a shot thundered, and a moment later Ryan jerked and collapsed to the carpet, a crimson splotch blooming below the breast pocket of his shirt. Before Ryan's body hit the floor, another shot was fired. The bullet entered Patrick's stomach, and a choked groan escaped him. Sam looked toward the archway connecting the dining room to the foyer and saw the shooter.

It was Jeff Phillips.

"Don't kill Pruitt!" Sam shouted, his ears ringing.

He needed Pruitt alive because Pruitt owed them twenty million dollars and he wanted to collect it.

The smell of burnt gunpowder struck Sam's nostrils. Patrick's hand began to move toward the holster, and Jeff pulled the trigger again. Patrick's face exploded, splattering blood and pieces of bone everywhere. Sam felt two drops of blood land on his cheek. He's definitely dead now, Sam thought. As Patrick fell down, Jeff put another bullet in Ryan, this time in the hip.

Had the neighbors heard the gunshots?

Sam jumped up, wheeled around, and saw that Pruitt lay on the floor, staring at Jeff, his face shocked, his body contorted.

The whole shooting must have taken less than five seconds. In just five seconds he had gone from prisoner to captor, and his life was no longer in danger.

Four shots, four hits. Bravo, Dad!

Sam's ears were still ringing.

"Are you okay?" Jeff asked him.

"Yes."

"Did they hurt you?"

"A little."

Jeff pointed his pistol at Pruitt and said, "Hands behind your head. Don't make any sudden moves."

Pruitt put his hands behind his head.

Sam breathed a sigh of relief and wiped Patrick's blood off his cheek with his palm. "Great job, Dad."

Jeff was wearing black leather gloves, which was very prudent of him.

"Is there anyone else in the house?" Jeff asked Pruitt.

"No," Pruitt replied.

"There's no one else here." Sam searched Ryan's pockets for the handcuff key, found it, removed the cuffs, and then picked up Ryan's pistol.

"What did they want from you?" Jeff said as Sam pulled the gun from Patrick's holster.

"He wanted me to show him how to do the procedure." Sam pointed at the table. "These are our computers."

The pools of blood Ryan and Patrick lay in were slowly growing larger. They'll have to replace the carpet, Sam thought.

"They stole our computers?" Jeff said. "I'm very disappointed in you, Mister Pruitt."

Sam gave Patrick's gun to Jeff and told Pruitt to get up.

"Let's talk, guys," Pruitt said. "There's no need for violence."

"Sure."

Pruitt thought he had a chance of getting out of this alive. What an idiot!

His joints creaking, Pruitt rose from the floor. He looked scared and dumbfounded.

"Hands up," Sam commanded. "No sudden moves, okay?"

When Pruitt raised his hands, Sam reached into the millionaire's right pants pocket and withdrew the phone. Then he pulled his burner phone from Pruitt's back pocket. He opened his messages and discovered that Jeff had sent him a text at 1:42 p.m., which read: "What's up?" As he fumbled in Pruitt's left pocket, he said, "Who has the keys to the Mercedes?"

"Ryan."

Sam lifted Pruitt's pant legs and saw that he had no guns or knives strapped to his ankles. Smiling, he transferred the pistol to his left hand and punched Pruitt in the mouth. Pruitt grimaced with pain, baring his bloodied teeth. Sam was about to hit him one more time, and then changed his mind. He didn't want Pruitt to think he was a violent psychopath. People tended to distrust violent psychopaths, and right now he needed Pruitt to trust him. The ass-kicking could wait until he got his money.

Pruitt didn't complain about the assault, perhaps because he knew he deserved to be beaten. He rubbed the underside of his nose with his finger, and Sam said, "Keep your hands in the air."

Sam went to Ryan's corpse, slipped his hand into his left pants pocket, and felt in it. There was nothing there but a phone, which he took out. He found two car keys in the right pocket: one had a BMW logo on it and the other a Mercedes logo. He wiped the keys, which were covered with Ryan's blood, on the carpet, put them in his pocket along with Ryan's phone, and patted the body down for weapons.

"You didn't bring your regular phone with you, did you?" Sam asked Jeff.

"No, I didn't."

"Good."

Sam took Patrick's phone, patted Patrick's body down for weapons, and then handcuffed Pruitt.

"What city are we in?" he asked Jeff.

"Bartonville."

Sam looked around for a telephone. He saw none.

"Where is it?"

"It's near Grapevine Lake."

Grapevine Lake was about twenty miles northwest of Dallas.

Sam went into the great room, unplugged the phone, and returned to the dining room.

"Are there surveillance cameras in this house?" Sam asked Pruitt.

"Yes. But I turned them off last night."

"Where's the recorder?"

"The study, the cabinet to the right of the desk. Jake, I apologize for what we did to you. I'm very sorry. I made a mistake. But I was never going to hurt you."

"You told Ryan to cut off my finger."

"I wasn't going to let him cut off your finger. I just wanted to scare you, that's all. And I was never going to kill you, please keep that in mind."

"Relax, Eric. If you pay us the twenty million you owe us, we'll let you go. We're businessmen, not killers."

"Yes, of course. I'll pay you the money, just don't kill me."

"Jake, I parked my car on the side of the road," Jeff said. "Let me put it in the garage."

"Okay."

Jeff came back ten minutes later.

"What are we going to do with the bodies?" he asked Sam.

The gun his father had used to kill Ryan and Patrick was unregistered, so they didn't have to extract the bullets from the bodies.

When the police found the bodies, they would interrogate Pruitt and he might tell them about Jeff. This meant that the millionaire had to die. (It was only in the movies that you could massacre a bunch of people while rescuing a captive, and be called a hero. In real life you went to prison for it, unless you were a law enforcement agent.)

Had he touched anything in Pruitt's Mercedes?

No, he hadn't.

Had he touched anything in the garage?

No.

The great room?

AN EVIL MIND

Just the phone. He'd have to wipe it.

He had left no fingerprints in the guest bedroom he had been held in.

In the dining room only the computers and the table had his fingerprints on them. They should take the computers with them because the police might be able to figure out that they belonged to New Horizons.

They would kill Pruitt after they got their twenty million dollars. How long would it take Pruitt to arrange the payment? If he had twenty million in his bank account, it should take minutes. If he needed to sell some stocks, it might take a few hours.

Would the cops get suspicious when they discovered that Pruitt had wired twenty million to an offshore bank account shortly before his death? They would if it appeared that Pruitt had been murdered.

They would have to make Pruitt's death look like an accident or suicide.

"Do you have trash bags in this house?" Sam asked Pruitt.

"Yes," Pruitt said.

Pruitt was going to be the prime suspect in the murder of Ryan and Patrick because they had been killed in his house and because he had no alibi. If the cops found the murder weapon in Pruitt's pocket, they would surely pin this crime on him. They would have no trouble thinking up the motive.

He thought Ryan and Patrick were screwing his wife, so he shot them dead.

"After we leave, you'll put the bodies in trash bags and bury them," Sam said.

"Okay."

"Do the guys that brought the computers know that you kidnapped me?"

"No."

"Who else besides you and these two morons knows that you kidnapped me?"

"No one."

"You can't tell the police about Peter or me. Do you understand?"

"Yes, I understand."

"Do you have a computer in this house?"

"Yes. It's in the study."

Sam heard Jeff's stomach rumble angrily.

"Are you hungry, Dad?" he asked.

Jeff smiled. "No. I just ate something that disagrees with me." Jeff rubbed his belly.

"What was it? Milk and cucumbers?" Sam chuckled.

"I think it's the sushi I had for lunch."

Sam pulled out Pruitt's phone and put it on the table. "I want you to call your wife and tell her you're on business in Los Angeles. Tell her you'll be back in a few days."

"Okay."

After Pruitt dialed his wife's number, Sam pressed the Speaker button.

"Hello," a woman's voice said.

"Hi, honey," Pruitt said. "I'm in Los Angeles. I'll be here for a few days."

"What are you doing there?"

"I'm working on a deal."

"Okay."

"I love you, honey. Goodnight."

Pruitt hung up.

"I'll check the house," Sam said to Jeff.

There were seven rooms on the first floor and six on the second floor. Sam covered every light switch and every doorknob with his handkerchief before touching them. In the study, he found the surveillance recorder and saw that it was switched off. When he finished checking the house, he went into the foyer, opened the front door, letting in the cold night air, which smelled of damp earth, and looked down the concrete driveway. He couldn't see the road, not because it was dark but because the road was far from the mansion. The sparse trees scattered around the property loomed like black ghosts.

Sam stepped down the porch and walked about seventy feet from the house to get a better view of the surroundings. Crickets' soothing chirping was the only sound he could hear.

At least a hundred and fifty yards separated Pruitt's mansion from the house on the left and three hundred yards from the one on the right. There was a thick wall of trees about two hundred yards behind Pruitt's mansion, which stretched from one side of the lot to the other. Sam was relieved to find that none of the neighbors could have heard the gunshots, at least not without trespassing on Pruitt's land.

Sam felt fresh and invigorated when he went back inside.

"Now let's talk about our money," Sam said to Pruitt. "I want you to wire the twenty million to our account right now."

Pruitt touched his swollen lower lip and then said, "I don't have it."

"You don't have twenty million?"

"No," Pruitt said with an apologetic smile.

"You mean you don't have it in cash?"

Pruitt shook his head. "My net worth is less than twenty million."

"You were worth three hundred million," Jeff said. "What happened to that money?"

"My companies have been losing money for the last three years. Also, I've made some bad investments."

Sam frowned. "Sell your stocks."

"They're worth only two million dollars."

"How much cash do you have in the bank?"

"About two hundred grand."

"How much are your houses worth?" Jeff asked.

"I have about eight million in equity."

Even at fire-sale prices it would take Pruitt at least two weeks to sell his houses, which was too long.

"Why the fuck did you agree to do this if you didn't have the money?" Sam yelled.

It was a rhetorical question, and Sam knew the answer. Pruitt had intended to screw them over. The son of a bitch had thought he was dealing with pushovers. Well, the joke was on him.

"I'm sorry." Pruitt smiled. "I'm very sorry, Jake."

"Motherfucker." Jeff hit him in the stomach.

Pruitt grunted and doubled over, wincing.

"How long will it take to sell the stocks?" Sam asked.

"It takes the funds three business days to clear," Pruitt said.

Three business days? Jesus Christ!

"So if you sell them now, you'll get the money on Friday?"

"Yes. We can wait here. I won't cause any trouble, I promise."

Sam looked at Jeff. His father shrugged.

"Are you expecting anyone to come here?" Sam asked Pruitt.

"No."

"What about the housekeeper?"

"I suspended the service for three weeks."

"Your wife—can she show up here?"

"No. I told her my friend was staying at this house. I was going to keep you here for a few weeks."

"If she shows up, I'll kill her. Do you care about your wife?"

"Yes."

"Good. By the way, did you tell her about the procedure?"

"Yes, I did."

"Where does your son live?" Jeff asked.

AN EVIL MIND

"He lives with me. But he wants to get his own apartment."

"Let's go to the study," Sam said.

In the study, Jeff turned on the computer and told Pruitt to show them his bank accounts.

"How many accounts do you have?" Jeff asked.

"Four."

"Do you have offshore bank accounts?" Sam asked.

"I have one with a bank in the British Virgin Islands."

"So you have five bank accounts?"

"No, I have four—three in America and one in the British Virgin Islands."

When Pruitt logged into his first American bank account, Sam saw that the total account balance was $40,592.66. There was $62,663.69 in Pruitt's second American bank account. Pruitt had a little over thirty grand in his third American bank account and seventy-two grand in his offshore account. The combined total for all four accounts was over two hundred and five thousand dollars.

"I'd type faster if you took off the handcuffs," Pruitt said.

"We're not in a hurry," Sam said. "Now show us your trading account."

Pruitt opened the login page of his brokerage website, typed in his username and password, and pressed the Enter button.

The value of Pruitt's account's net assets was $2,000,163.53. Looking at the screen, Sam wondered if this was Pruitt's only trading account.

They could torture Pruitt until he told them about his other trading accounts, but Sam had no desire to do it (mainly because he wanted to be done with this as soon as possible). Two million two hundred thousand dollars was enough; it was a fraction of what he had planned to make, but it was nothing to sneeze at. As they say, best is the enemy of good.

They would find another rich guy with a terminally ill kid by the end of the year, Sam was sure of it.

"Sell them all," Sam said.

As he entered sell orders for his stocks, Pruitt said, "Are you guys hungry? There's food in the fridge."

Sam realized that he hadn't eaten since noon, and his stomach growled.

When Pruitt finished placing sell orders, Sam pulled out the piece of paper with the name of their bank and their account number, put it on the desk, and said, "I want you to transfer to this account all the money from your bank accounts. You can leave a grand in each account."

"Okay." Pruitt nodded.

Chapter 39

1

After Pruitt initiated the money transfers, Sam handcuffed his arms around a leg of the coffee table in the great room. At midnight Sam logged into their account at Cayman Commercial Bank to see if the money had arrived.

The account balance hadn't changed.

"How long will it take the money to hit our account?" Sam asked Pruitt.

"A couple of days."

Two days.

Two *business* days. If Pruitt wired the two million dollars received from the sale of his stocks on Friday, they would get the money on Tuesday.

They should stay here at least until Monday night, just in case.

Sam switched off the computer, then went to the window, opened the drapes, and looked out toward the road.

Had the neighbor's surveillance cameras caught his father's car entering Pruitt's driveway? They might have. Were they powerful enough to read the license plate?

Suppose the police found out Jeff had visited Pruitt in Bartonville. What would he tell them when they asked him about the purpose of that visit?

He would say that he had pitched Pruitt an idea and that he hadn't seen Ryan and Patrick.

Sam turned around, and his eyes fell on Patrick's body. They're going to start stinking soon, he thought.

They had to take the corpses out of the dining room.

Sam put on the dishwashing gloves he had found in the kitchen, and said to Jeff, "Let's move the bodies to the library."

"That's a good idea," Jeff replied. To Pruitt, he said, "Don't try anything funny."

As they carried Ryan's body, Sam saw that Jeff had a preoccupied look on his face.

"What are you thinking about, Dad?" Sam asked.

They entered the library and laid the body on the floor by the sofa.

"I'm not sure about this," Jeff said.

"What's not to be sure about?"

They walked out of the room.

"I don't think we should take his money."

"Why?"

"It's too risky. Let's just waste this guy and go find someone else."

"It's not that risky."

"The cops are going to know we got the money. They're going to ask questions."

They picked up Patrick's body—Sam grabbed his legs and Jeff his arms—and headed for the library.

"No one's going to ask any questions, Dad. Besides, he already wired us two hundred grand."

"I'm talking about the two million. Let's take it in cash. No wires. Two million will fit in a suitcase."

"What if he calls for help while he's in the bank?"

"Good point." Jeff yawned.

"If the cops start asking questions, we'll get new bodies."

"Yeah." Jeff smiled. "Great idea."

After wiping off the blood that had dripped onto the floor from the bodies, Sam asked Jeff, "How did you find me?"

Pruitt, who lay on the couch across from them, raised his head from the pillow.

"I put a GPS tracker on this motherfucker's car last Saturday. You see, I didn't trust this guy."

"How long did you wait for me by his house?"

Jeff had given Sam a ride to Pruitt's place and been supposed to take him home after the meeting.

"An hour."

AN EVIL MIND

Sam volunteered to watch over Pruitt tonight. Before Jeff retired to the bedroom, Sam, wearing the dishwashing gloves to avoid leaving fingerprints, went to the garage and took the keys to the Ford Explorer.

2

The next day Sam loaded all of their computers except one into the trunk of Jeff's Cadillac.

On Thursday, December 7, Sam logged into their offshore bank account and saw that all the transfers made by Pruitt had cleared. Now they were two hundred grand richer.

The plan had begun to pay off.

Thanks to the ritual, they would become millionaires in just five days.

The ritual had saved him from execution. The ritual was going to make him wealthy.

It was August 2 of last year that his father had first told him about the ritual. The ritual instructions were written on the piece of paper that was glued to a page in the three-hundred-year-old French book on black magic Jeff had bought at an antique book store in New York. At first they were reluctant to test the ritual themselves. They gave the instructions to a man named Douglas Fleming so he would try the ritual and find out if it worked. Unfortunately, Fleming got caught and was sentenced to life imprisonment. They hadn't heard from him after his arrest, which meant that either Fleming hadn't swapped bodies with a cellmate or the guy he had switched bodies with hadn't been released yet.

The first person they had sacrificed was a fifteen-year-old girl named Jennifer. Sam killed her in Toronto on October 29 of last year. She was cute and slim and had nice breasts. His friends Mickey and Frank Garrison were the first people they had tried the ritual on. Mickey and Frank were twenty-two years old and resided in Fort Worth at the time. Sam had chosen them because they were identical twins (he figured switching bodies was not going to affect their lives). He performed the ritual in his house on the night of November 13, after the Garrisons fell asleep. When Mickey woke up the next morning, he had been astonished to discover that he was wearing Frank's clothes and Frank his and that his cross tattoo had moved from his forearm to Frank's.

Sam told Jeff that the transfers had cleared, and his father high-fived him.

"Are you going let me go as soon as I wire you the two million?" Pruitt asked.

"No. We'll let you go when the money hits our account," Sam said.

"Why?"

"Because we're afraid you'll cancel the transfer. You're not a trustworthy person, Eric."

3

On Friday, Pruitt received the proceeds from the sale of his stocks. As he typed their bank account number into the wire transfer form, Pruitt said, "How do I know you're not going to kill me after I wire the money?"

"I told you we're businessmen, not killers," Sam said. "We'll let you go on Tuesday, I give you my word."

After sending the wire, Pruitt called his wife and told her that he would be back on Tuesday.

The next morning Sam asked Pruitt if he knew any rich people with terminally ill children.

"Yes, I do," Pruitt said.

"Tell me their names."

"You want to offer them your services?"

"Yes."

"I know one guy. His name's Andrew Broder. He runs a hedge fund. He's worth three hundred and fifty million. His son has leukemia."

"What's the name of his fund?" Sam opened the notepad to a blank page.

"Prism Capital."

Sam jotted Broder's name and the name of his fund down on the notepad. "What's his phone number?"

"It's in my cellphone."

Sam took out Pruitt's phone, pressed the Home button, and said, "What's the code?"

"Four, nine, three, eight."

Sam entered the code. He found one Andrew Broder on Pruitt's contact list. He showed the record to Pruitt and asked, "Is this him?"

"Yes."

Sam wrote down Broder's number. "Does he live in Dallas?"

"He lives in Highland Park."

"If he wants to talk to one of our previous clients, will you talk to him?"

Pruitt hesitated, and then said, "Okay. But don't tell him I gave you his name."

"Sure. I can pay you a finder's fee, if you want."

"How much?"

"Five percent. Do you want it?"

"Yeah."

"Do you know any rich people with terminally ill parents?"

"Yes. Gavin Holden. His mother has cancer. He's worth two hundred million. His company's name is Advanced Distribution."

"Does he love his mom?"

"I think he'll pay at least ten million to save her life."

"Ten million. Nice. Is his number in your phone, too?"

"Yes."

Sam found Gavin Holden's number and added it to the list.

"Anyone else?" he asked.

"Nathan Marsh. A hundred and fifty million. His father has cancer. His company's name is MKB Property Holdings."

Pruitt had Nathan Marsh's contact information in his phone.

"How much do you think he'll pay?" Sam asked after writing down Marsh's number.

"I'd say seven million."

"Anyone else?"

"That's it."

"Okay. Thank you, Eric." Sam ripped out the sheet with the phone numbers, folded it, and put it in his pants pocket. "You know what they call cancer? The great equalizer."

4

Sam logged into their account at Cayman Commercial Bank, and when he saw the balance, his heart began to pound with excitement. He had $2,225,450 in his account (of this amount, twenty five thousand dollars had been deposited when Sam opened the account).

Sam drew in a deep breath and exhaled.

They were millionaires! They were fucking millionaires!

He pumped his fist in the air victoriously.

It was time to take care of Pruitt.

He glanced at his watch. 12:31 p.m.

Sam went into the kitchen, put on the latex gloves he'd purchased at the local grocery store, and poured three mugs of coffee. From his pocket, he withdrew a plastic zipper bag, which contained eight crushed Xanax pills and ten crushed Ambien pills, and dumped its contents into Pruitt's mug. He stirred Pruitt's coffee with a spoon for half a minute to make sure that the drugs completely dissolved. Then he put the mugs on a tray, pulled off the gloves, picked up the tray, and went to the great room.

"Coffee's here," he announced as he gave Jeff his mug.

"Did you check your account?" Pruitt asked.

Sam grabbed his mug and set the tray on the coffee table.

"Yes, I did."

"Has the transfer cleared?"

"No. I'll check again in a couple of hours."

"Are you going to let me go? Tell me the truth."

"Yes, we'll let you go."

"Do you remember what you have to do with the bodies?" Jeff asked.

"Yes. Bury them."

Pruitt finished his coffee at one o'clock and fell asleep ten minutes later. They carried him to the master bedroom, where they stripped him naked. The plan was to drown Pruitt in the tub in the master bathroom. The police would conclude that his death was either a suicide or an accident.

Mister Pruitt murdered his associates and then committed suicide out of remorse.

Sam took Jeff's Glock, removed the magazine, and ejected the bullet from the chamber. Then he emptied the magazine, put all the cartridges in his pocket, wiped the magazine with a towel and snapped it back into the pistol. After wiping the gun, Sam wrapped Pruitt's right hand around its grip so Pruitt's fingers would leave prints.

"Put some fingerprints on the barrel," Jeff advised.

Sam nodded, closed Pruitt's hand around the barrel of the Glock for a few seconds, and then put the gun on the nightstand.

Jeff fetched Pruitt's mug, and Sam wiped it and planted Pruitt's fingerprints all over it. He did the same with Ryan's and Patrick's phones. He also planted Pruitt's prints on a plastic baggie that had five Xanax pills in it. He placed the mug and the bag with Xanax on the nightstand.

"Did you touch the coffeemaker without gloves?" Sam asked.

"No."

They put Pruitt in the tub in the master bathroom and turned on the water.

"Did you touch anything here without gloves?" Sam asked.

He should wash the tray and his and Jeff's mugs.

"I wiped everything I touched without gloves."

When the water reached the overflow drain, Sam grabbed Pruitt's arms and Jeff pushed his head underwater. Pruitt struggled for about a minute, jerking his legs and trying to free his arms, and then stopped moving.

AN EVIL MIND

Chapter 40

1

They celebrated at the French Room, a fancy expensive restaurant in the Adolphus Hotel in downtown Dallas. On Thursday, December 14, Jeff and Sam went to the Cayman Islands and opened an account at Alliance Bank, which was across the street from Cayman Commercial Bank. They withdrew two million one hundred fifty thousand dollars from Cayman Commercial Bank and then deposited two million one hundred thousand in their account at Alliance Bank; they took the remaining fifty thousand with them. The next day Jeff signed a lease for a new office (they couldn't use the old one because it had been compromised), and Sam met with Andrew Broder at Prism Capital's headquarters and told him about the consciousness transfer procedure.

On Saturday Emily told Jeff that she had visited their son in prison on December 9.

"Why?" Jeff asked. "I asked you not do it, didn't I?"

"He called and told me he wanted to see me."

Although she disobeyed him, Jeff wasn't mad at his wife. He was in a magnanimous mood, thanks to the money they'd gotten from Eric Pruitt.

"When did he call you?"

"About two weeks ago."

"Why didn't you tell me about it?"

"I didn't think it was important."

Suddenly she looked sad. Very sad. Her eyes misted.

"What did you talk about?"

He was going to get a new, young body in a few months. Should he tell Emily about the body switch or should he move on and find another woman?

He loved Emily, she was his soulmate, but she didn't satisfy him sexually.

Sex was a very important part of his life, so it would be best if he found someone else. Someone young.

"He told me about his life in prison. About his appeal. He said he's innocent."

After he got a new body, they would kill his old one. It was going to break Emily's heart.

Poor Emily. First her son had been sentenced to death, then her husband died.

"There's nothing we can do, honey," Jeff said. "You need to accept it."

Emily wiped her eyes and sighed. "We have to help him."

"We can't help him."

"Let's get him a good appeals lawyer."

"It's going to cost a fortune."

"I don't care how much it costs."

Emily's face twisted, and tears began to seep from the corners of her eyes. Jeff felt a little twinge of guilt.

"How can you be so heartless?" Emily sniffled.

"I'm not heartless. Look, honey, appeals are incredibly difficult to win."

"We have to get Ed a lawyer."

"Let me think about it."

Jeff put his arms around his wife and kissed her lips.

The doorbell rang.

"I'll get it," Jeff said.

He went to the front door and opened it. Standing on the porch was Detective Aguero and four cops.

"I have a warrant to search your house and cars." Aguero handed the warrant to Jeff.

2

"How are you doing, Detective Aguero?" Phillips said.

It was Friday, December 15.

AN EVIL MIND

Aguero pushed the Record button on the voice recorder, picked up his pen, and said, "I'm fine. How are you, Edward?"

"I've been better."

"I'm going to record this conversation."

Phillips nodded.

"I was told you wanted to talk to me."

"I decided to tell you who killed Laura Sumner."

"Go ahead. I'm listening."

"It was my father, Jeff Phillips, who killed Laura Sumner."

"How do you know that?"

"Laura was killed the same way as Helen Hinton. My dad murdered Helen Hinton. I'm sure he killed Laura, too."

"Did you participate in killing Helen Hinton?"

"No, I didn't."

"How do you know that your father killed Helen?"

"I saw him do it. He killed her right in front of me. I tried to stop him, but he wouldn't listen."

Aguero thought for a moment and then said, "Why did he kill Helen in front of you?"

"I don't know."

"Did he explain why he killed the girl?"

"No. I think he murdered those girls because he's crazy."

"How did Jeff lure Helen into the house where she was killed?"

"Here's what happened. My dad came to my place and asked if I wanted to go for a ride. I said yes. He drove to that house, parked the car, and told me to go inside. I went inside, and a few minutes later he came in, carrying Helen. I think she was in the trunk of his car."

"While you were in Jeff's car, did you hear any noise coming from the trunk?"

"No."

Helen had chlorpromazine, a powerful sedative, in her system, and the police believed that it had been injected into her by the killer. Jeff must have given Helen a shot of chlorpromazine before putting her in the trunk.

"What time did Jeff come to your place?"

"Around nine."

"And you went straight to that house?"

"Yes."

"What time did you get there?"

"Probably around nine-twenty. It took us about twenty minutes to get there."

"Did he sexually molest Helen?"

"No. He just pulled out a knife and kill her."

"What happened after Jeff killed Helen?"

"We got in the car, and my dad took me back to my place."

"Was Helen his first victim?"

"I don't know. I asked him how long he'd been doing this, and he said he didn't want to talk about it." Phillips paused. "I don't think she was his first victim."

"Why didn't you tell the police it was your father who murdered Helen?"

"He's my father. I felt I had to protect him."

"Why did you decide to tell me this?"

"I'm afraid he'll kill again, and I don't want that to happen."

"And you don't feel you have to protect your dad anymore?"

"No, I don't. He needs to be locked up."

Phillips's story was wacky, but there was nothing in it that was impossible.

Why had Jeff brought his son to that house?

Maybe he had wanted to make Edward his partner.

His theory turned out to be correct. Now the question was, how was he going to prove that Jeff had murdered Helen and Laura?

Aguero looked at Edward for a long moment and then said, "You're not just trying to save your ass, are you?"

"No, I'm not."

"And you didn't make this up just to get back at your father?"

"No. I'm telling you the truth, Detective."

"Does anyone else know that your father killed Helen and Laura?"

"No."

"Are you willing to testify in court?"

"Yes."

Aguero pressed the Stop button on the voice recorder and said, "Thank you for your help, Edward. Please don't tell anyone that you gave me this information."

"When are you going to interrogate my dad?"

"Soon."

"Can you do me a favor?"

"What is it?"

"After you interrogate my dad, please tell my mom that my dad's a killer and ask her to be careful."

When Aguero came out of the Allan B. Polunsky Unit, he called Mark Hinton.

"I just talked to Edward Phillips," he said. "He told me his father killed your daughter. He was there when it happened."

"Are you going to arrest Jeff?" Mark asked.

"I'll arrest him when I have evidence supporting Phillips's story."

"Let me know when you arrest him."

"Sure. Phillips said he had no part in Helen's murder. He said he tried to stop Jeff."

"Do you believe that?"

"I think it could be true."

"Are you going to search Jeff's house?"

"Yes."

"Search his car, too. There could be Helen's prints in it."

3

After preparing a warrant to search Jeff Phillips's residence, cars, and office at the University of Texas, Aguero called the Senior Warden of the Polunsky Unit and requested that Edward Phillips's conversations with his father be recorded.

Chapter 41

1

His brow furrowed with puzzlement, Jeff Phillips scanned the warrant, then gave it back to Aguero, and said, "Please come in."

The cops entered the house.

"Good afternoon, Detective," Emily said to Aguero when he went into the living room.

"Good afternoon."

"They want to search the house," Jeff said.

"Why?" Emile looked at Aguero with surprise.

"I'll explain later." Aguero turned to Jeff. "Mister Phillips, would you mind coming with me to the station?"

"All right."

Jeff grabbed his jacket and followed the detective outside, to his car, which was double-parked in front of the Phillipses' house. Aguero took Jeff to Carrollton Police Department headquarters, where he advised him of his Miranda rights.

"Would you like to have a lawyer present?" Aguero asked.

"No."

"This interview is being recorded. I'm Detective Carlos Aguero with the Austin Police Department." Aguero opened his notepad. "I talked to your son yesterday. He told me that he saw you murder Helen Hinton. He said you killed her right in front of him."

"What?" Jeff said with a shocked look on his face. "That's impossible. Ed would never have said that."

"Well, he did. He tried to stop you, but you wouldn't listen."

"What exactly did he tell you?"

Aguero recounted Edward Phillips's story, and Jeff said, "He's lying."

"Why would he lie? You're his father."

"I don't know."

"You don't have an alibi for the time of the murder."

"Am I under arrest?"

"No." Aguero shook his head. "Mister Phillips, did you kill Helen Hinton?"

"No, I didn't."

Aguero pulled Helen Hinton's picture from the folder, put it in front of Jeff, and said, "Did you kill this girl?"

"No."

"I'm giving you a chance to tell your side of the story, Jeff."

"I didn't kill this girl."

"Did you help Edward kill Helen Hinton?"

"No, I did not."

Aguero took out Laura Sumner's photo and laid it on the table. "Did you kill Laura Sumner?"

"No. I've never killed anyone in my life." Jeff placed his arms on the table and clasped his hands together.

"Were you with your son when Helen Hinton was murdered?"

"No."

"Did you let Edward use your car the night Helen Hinton was murdered?"

"No, I didn't."

"Would you mind taking a lie detector test?"

"Let me think about it." Jeff looked at his watch. "I want to go home. Can you take me home?"

"If we find Helen Hinton's or Laura Sumner's DNA or prints in your car, you'll be in big trouble, Mister Phillips."

"I've never killed anyone in my life. That's all I have to say. Can you take me home?"

"Sure."

2

AN EVIL MIND

After dropping Jeff off, Aguero called Emily Phillips and told her about Edward's accusations against his father.

"Edward asked me to tell you to be careful," Aguero said. "Be careful with Jeff, Emily. He may be a serial killer."

Chapter 42

1

It was time to kill Sam Curtis. There was no point in delaying.

Murder was a crime and it was his job to uphold the law, but this was a special case. This was the most special case of them all.

On Sunday, December 10, Mark went to Curtis's house, intending to take Curtis to his parents' house at Lake Ray Hubbard, interrogate him there, and then kill him. He was carrying an unregistered SIG Sauer P250 pistol he had purchased from a black market dealer three days earlier. To his disappointment, Curtis didn't come home that night.

On Wednesday night, Sam Curtis was home. When he opened the door, Mark said, "Excuse me, can I talk to John?"

He put his finger on the trigger of his SIG Sauer in his coat pocket.

"I think you got the wrong house," Curtis replied. He didn't seem to recognize Mark.

A young blond woman in tight jeans and a scant top walked up to Curtis, wrapped her arms around his waist from behind, and said, "Who is it?"

"He got the wrong house." Curtis placed his hand on her thigh.

"I'm sorry," Mark said. "I must have the wrong address. Goodnight."

He waited two hours for the woman to leave, and then went home.

Mark was going to try to kidnap Curtis on Friday, but his plans changed when he learned that Edward Phillips had told Detective Aguero his father had killed Helen: he decided to break into Jeff Phillips's house and plant the knife used to murder Helen. He was unable to figure out how to get into the house without tripping the security system, so he abandoned the plan.

Mark made another attempt to capture Sam Curtis on Sunday, December 17. When he got out of the car, a cab pulled up in front of Curtis's house. Mark slipped back behind the wheel, and about fifteen seconds later Curtis came out and got in the cab. Mark followed Curtis to his destination, an elegant Mediterranean mansion on Beverly Drive in Highland Park (later he would find out that the mansion belonged to a man named Andrew Broder).

Curtis spent forty-five minutes in Broder's house and left in a cab. Mark lost the taxi he was in on the Dallas North Tollway.

On December 19, Aguero called to give Mark an update.

The police had searched Jeff Phillips's house for over five hours and found no blood-stained objects and nothing that belonged to Helen Hinton or Laura Sumner.

No traces of blood were found in the Phillipses' cars, and none of the fingerprints in the vehicles matched those of Helen or Laura. The hairs collected from the cars could not be tested for DNA because none of them had a follicle. Jeff's clothes did not have any blood on them.

The examination of the images on the Phillipses' laptops and Jeff's cellphone and university computer revealed no pictures of Helen or Laura. There were no search terms in Jeff's online search history indicating that he had looked for information on how to kill someone or how to destroy evidence of murder (they were able to recover all Jeff's and his wife's Internet history deleted in the last year and a half). The only time Jeff had searched for something that could be considered suspicious was on November 17 of last year when he looked for information on sedatives and sleeping pills.

Aguero said that Jeff Phillips had hidden surveillance cameras in his house, and Mark thanked God that he hadn't broken into Jeff's place last Friday.

TIM KIZER

AN EVIL MIND

Chapter 43

1

Aguero put on a headset and said, "Go ahead."

Edward Phillips picked up the phone and dialed his father's cellphone number. Jeff answered on the third ring.

"Hello, Dad," Edward said.

"Who's this?"

"Edward. How are you?"

"I'm fine," Jeff said in a toneless voice.

"How's Mom?"

"She's fine."

"It's been a long time since we talked."

"Yeah."

After learning that the police had found no evidence against his father during the search of his house, university office, and car, Edward Phillips had asked Aguero to let him call Jeff and try to get him to incriminate himself. Aguero had agreed to his suggestion. Jeff probably knew that prison phone calls were recorded, but it didn't hurt to try.

"Listen, Dad. I decided to tell them the truth. I'm sorry. The cops know it was you who killed Helen Hinton. I'm really sorry, but I had to tell them the truth."

"What are you talking about? Are you insane?"

"The cops know you killed Laura Sumner. You shouldn't have killed those girls, Dad."

"Goodbye, Edward." Jeff hung up.

Aguero took off the headset and put it on the table. "That was short."

"He knows these calls are recorded," Phillips said.

"Yeah."

"Please don't let him get away with it."

"I'll do my best."

2

"Was it Edward?" Sam asked when Jeff pocketed his phone.

"Yes." Jeff grabbed his bottle of beer from the table and crossed his legs.

"What did he want?"

Sam unmuted the TV.

"Nothing."

"Where did he get your number?"

Jeff shrugged. "Maybe Emily gave it to him."

Jeff stood up and went to the bathroom, where he evacuated his bowels. When he returned to the living room, he said, "My dad used to say that a good dump is the next best thing to sex." He laughed.

Sam smiled.

"Is Mom going to visit this motherfucker again?" he said.

"She said she'll go there again this Saturday. By the way, when are we going to tell her about the switch?"

"Never."

"Why?"

"She's not going to believe it."

"You could prove to her that you're Edward."

"Are you going to tell her about the ritual? About the human sacrifices?"

Jeff said nothing.

"Why do you want to tell her about the switch, anyway?"

"Her only son is on death row, and it makes her miserable. I want her to know that that guy in prison isn't her son anymore."

Sam shook his head. "She's not going to believe it. Is she really miserable?"

"Yes."

Emily had been talking about Edward every day since last Saturday, and each time she cried. He supposed that the anguish over Edward's plight had been accumulating in her all these months, and now the spigots were open. It broke Jeff's heart to see her cry.

"Maybe she'll feel better if you buy her a diamond ring."

"She won't. She wants to hire a lawyer for him."

"Let her do it. You'll be gone in two weeks, anyway."

Jeff sighed. "I'm going to miss her."

Did Emily believe Edward's accusations?

Jeff had no idea. When the cops left last Saturday, she had asked him if he had murdered those two girls, and he had said no. He had said Edward had accused him of the murders because he was mad at him for disowning him. She hadn't brought up the subject since, but that didn't mean she'd bought his explanation.

"I'll miss her, too."

"I think we should give her some money."

"I agree. Let's give her five percent of everything we make."

Jeff nodded. "That's a good idea."

Chapter 44

1

Sam Curtis wasn't home on the night of December 21. And he wasn't home on the night of December 23, either.

On Thursday, December 28, thinking that Curtis might be asleep, Mark rang his doorbell. There was no answer; the windows remained dark.

Had Sam Curtis skipped town?

Maybe he's at Jeff Phillips's place?

Mark got in the car and drove to Jeff Phillips's house. Emily Phillips opened the door.

"Good evening. Can I talk to Jeff?" Mark said.

"He's not home. He's in Houston."

There were dark circles around Emily's eyes. She looked as if she hadn't slept well.

"When did he leave?"

"A week ago."

"When is he coming back?"

"Next week."

Maybe Curtis and Jeff Phillips had skipped town together? After all, they were a team.

"I'm sorry to have bothered you," Mark said. "Goodnight."

Were they going to get new bodies? It was a strong possibility.

He needed to find Curtis by the next full moon, which was on the night of January 1.

On Friday, Mark requested geolocation information for Jeff Phillips's and Sam Curtis's phones. He was informed that the phones had been off since December 21. Nobody named Jeff Phillips or Sam Curtis had boarded any planes or trains in the United States in the last ten days. There had been no activity on the two men's credit and bank cards since December 21. On

December 20, Jeff had withdrawn twenty-five thousand dollars from his bank account.

Mark called Detective Aguero and told him that Jeff Phillips seemed to have gone on the run.

"Why would he go on the run?" Aguero said. "We have nothing on him."

He promised Mark to help him find Jeff.

At five o'clock, Mark put out an APB on Sam Curtis and Jeff Phillips.

On Saturday, Mark told Emily Phillips that he was a police detective and asked her when Jeff had last contacted her.

"I haven't heard from him since he left for Houston," Emily said.

"What if something bad happened to him?"

"I'm sure he's fine. He's done this before. Are you still investigating him?"

"No. I just want to ask him a few questions. Do you know what hotel he's staying at?"

"No."

"Did he go to Houston in his car?"

"No. He went there with his friend in his friend's car."

"What's the friend's name?"

"Peter. I don't know his last name."

"Is Jeff's car in the garage?"

"Yes."

Mark asked Emily to show him Jeff's car, and she did.

2

On Sunday night, Mark drilled a hole in Sam Curtis's garage door, looked inside, and saw Curtis's Mazda. He rang Curtis's doorbell. No one answered.

No one answered the door on Monday, January 1, either. The Mazda was still in the garage. Furious, Mark kicked the door a few times and then slammed his fist against it.

This cocksucker was going to get away with it, and Helen would not be avenged.

It was his fault. He should have killed Sam Curtis a month ago.

What would Sam and Jeff do with the people that were going to get their old bodies?

They would kill them so no one would find out who they had switched bodies with.

They would probably kill their old bodies shortly after the swap. Because they wanted the police to think they were dead, they would leave the bodies where they could be easily found.

The bodies would be taken to the morgue.

Suddenly Mark realized he had an opportunity to help Edward Phillips regain his freedom.

What he needed to do was go to the morgue and plant Jeff Phillips's prints on the knife used to kill Helen. The murder weapon with a suspect's prints on it was a powerful piece of evidence. It might be powerful enough to help Edward get a retrial and then win an acquittal.

3

On Tuesday morning, Mark searched the databases of the medical examiner's offices of Dallas, Tarrant, Collin, El Paso, Travis, Harris, McLennan, Hidalgo, and Bexar counties for Jeff Phillips and Sam Curtis and found no matches.

He hoped to God Jeff and Sam hadn't gone out of state to get new bodies.

Mark searched the database of the Dallas County Medical Examiner's Office again at three-thirty and was thrilled to find out that the body of a man named Jeffrey Phillips had been delivered to the county morgue an hour earlier. The man's date of birth was the same as Jeff Phillips's. The place of death was the Sun Motel in Grand Prairie.

Mark drove to the medical examiner's office, flashed his badge to the morgue attendant, and said that he wanted to see Jeffrey Phillips's body. As they walked to the cold room, Mark put on the latex gloves he had brought with him.

When the attendant unzipped the body bag, Mark saw that it was the right Jeff Phillips. He pulled out his phone and said, "I need ten minutes."

"Okay."

The attendant left the room. Mark rubbed some lotion on Jeff's right palm, took the knife out of the plastic bag, and closed Jeff's hand tightly around its handle. Jeff's fingers were stiff as rigor mortis had already set in. There was a long, deep cut caked with blood on his wrist. It appeared they had killed Jeff by slashing his wrists.

Mark put the knife in the plastic bag, then pocketed the bag and wiped Jeff's hand with his handkerchief.

Now he needed to find a way to plant the knife in Jeff Phillips's house.

Mark went to the Sun Motel and asked the front desk clerk when Jeff had checked into his room. The clerk was a stocky man with a buzz cut named Gabriel.

"December twenty-eight," the clerk said.

"Did he stay there alone?"

"I don't know."

"Did he pay cash?"

"Yeah."

"What name did he check in under?"

"John Wells."

Mark showed Gabriel Sam Curtis's photo and asked, "Have you seen this man?"

Gabriel shook his head. "No."

"Does your motel have security cameras?"

"No."

An hour later, Mark read the police reports filed by the first two officers to arrive at the scene of Jeff's death. Jeff's body had been discovered by a maid in Room 118 of the Sun Motel around eleven-thirty this morning. He lay on a bed fully clothed, with his wrists slashed. There was a bloody razor blade on the nightstand. Jeff left no suicide note. No signs of foul play had been found.

Jeff and Sam had made Jeff's death look like suicide so there would be no investigation. Smart move.

The fact that Jeff's death looked like suicide could work in Edward's favor. Edward's lawyer could say that Jeff Phillips had killed himself because he felt remorse for murdering Helen Hinton.

AN EVIL MIND

Chapter 45

1

The next day Mark searched the databases of all medical examiner's offices in Texas for Sam Curtis and found nothing. There was no mention of Sam Curtis in the reports of the Dallas, Fort Worth, Houston, Austin, Plano, Irving, Arlington, El Paso, Corpus Christi, or San Antonio police departments. Mark googled "found dead body Sam Curtis" and got no relevant hits.

Was Sam's body going to pop up later?

Or maybe Sam hadn't gotten a new body? He wasn't a suspect or a person of interest, so he didn't need to get a new body.

Detective Aguero called at two o'clock and told Mark that the Grand Prairie Police Department had found Jeff Phillips.

"He's dead," Aguero said.

"Yes, I heard that. He killed himself."

"Why do you think he did it?"

"I believe he was overwhelmed by guilt. It seems we were right about him."

2

Toxicology tests showed that Jeff had zolpidem (also known as Ambien) in his system. They had put Jeff to sleep and then killed him.

Sam Curtis's cellphone was still off and there was still no activity on his cards on January 4.

At five p.m. on January 4, Aguero called and said, "Are you sitting down?"

"Yes. What happened?"

"You're not going to believe this. I received a video from Jeff Phillips where he confesses to killing your daughter and Laura Sumner."

Mark was so surprised he almost dropped his phone.

"Did you say Jeff Phillips confessed to killing Helen and Laura?" he asked disbelievingly.

"Yes, I did."

"Can I see the video?"

"I'll mail you a copy. I can email you a transcript, if you want."

"Yes, please email it."

Aguero sent the transcript of Jeff's video a few minutes after terminating the call. It read: "Hi, my name is Jeffrey Phillips. I live at 1506 Sandwood Street, Carrollton, Texas. I'm making this video for Detective Carlos Aguero of the Austin Police Department. I want to confess to murdering Helen Hinton and Laura Sumner.

I killed Helen Hinton in Dallas on the night of December 11 of last year. My son, Edward Phillips, had nothing to do with this murder. He tried to stop me from killing Helen. I'm very sorry I caused him so much pain by letting him get convicted of the crime committed by me. Edward, if you're watching this, I'm asking you to forgive me. I'm very very sorry. I also want to apologize to Helen Hinton's family. I'm very sorry I took your daughter's life.

I killed Laura Sumner in Austin on the night of August 23 of this year. I'd like to apologize to Laura's family. I'm very sorry I murdered your daughter.

You probably want to know why I committed these murders. I... I'm a sick man. A very sick man. I have these strange urges I can't control.

Emily, if you're watching this, I'm sorry I let you down.

I'll be gone in a few days, and before I go, I want to tell the world the truth. My son is innocent. He did not kill Helen Hinton. I did. I know I deserve to die for my crimes, and that's what I'm going to do.

Ed, Emily, I'm sorry. I'm very sorry. I love you both very much. Goodbye."

Why had Jeff made his confession video? Did he feel sorry for Edward?

Did he feel sorry for his wife?

3

On Saturday, January 6, Mark met with Edward Phillips and told him about Jeff and Sam's disappearance, Jeff's death, and Jeff's confession video.

"Will they let me go?" Phillips asked, smiling.

"I hope so. What's your lawyer's name?"

"Paul Carlin."

"I'll give him a copy of the video."

"Thank you, Mark."

"I have no doubt Jeff got a new body. Otherwise he wouldn't have made that video."

"What about Sam?"

"His body hasn't been found yet. Maybe he didn't get a new body."

"Maybe they buried his body."

As he glanced around the visiting room, Mark thought about Douglas Fleming. Then he remembered something Fleming had said to him: "I would switch bodies with a billionaire."

When they were at Pistons Bar and Grill, Jeff Phillips had asked if he knew any billionaires.

Perhaps Jeff had traded bodies with a wealthy guy.

Andrew Broder, a hedge fund manager, was a wealthy guy. Sam Curtis had paid him a visit on December 17.

Maybe Jeff, or Sam Curtis, had switched bodies with Broder?

"You know what I think?" Mark said. "I think at least one of them swapped bodies with a rich guy."

Phillips nodded. "Yeah. I think you're right."

Chapter 46

1

Mark checked his watch. 2:13 p.m.

It had been two hours since Mark arrived at Andrew Broder's house, and no one had left or entered the mansion yet.

If Jeff had switched bodies with Broder, Sam Curtis would sooner or later show up at his mansion. He probably lived here; this place was several orders of magnitude better than his old house.

There was a silver Mercedes coupe in Broder's driveway. Mark had run the license plate number and found that the car belonged to a twenty-two-year-old man named Taylor Cowley, who lived in Dallas.

There were very few twenty-two-year-olds who owned ninety-thousand-dollar cars. Where had Taylor Cowley gotten the money to buy the Mercedes? Was he Andrew Broder's son?

Mark googled "Andrew Broder son" and discovered that Andrew Broder's son's name was Logan Broder.

Why would a twenty-two-year-old guy hang out with a man thirty years older than him?

Cowley could be Broder's nephew or illegitimate son.

They could be lovers.

Or maybe Cowley's parents were Broder's friends.

Mark googled "Taylor Cowley Dallas." The fourth search result was a news story about a Dallas man named Taylor Cowley returning home safely on January 3 after being missing for five days. The Taylor Cowley from the news story was twenty-two years old.

The front doors opened, and a young dark-haired man came out of the house. When he got in the Mercedes, Mark started his car. He felt there was a connection between Taylor Cowley and Jeff and Sam, but he couldn't put his finger on it.

The Mercedes pulled out of the driveway and turned right. Mark followed it.

Cowley had gone missing before January 1 and returned home after that day.

Maybe Jeff and Sam had switched bodies with Andrew Broder and Taylor Cowley?

The Mercedes entered US-75 southbound and exited it five minutes later at Live Oak Street. Mark stopped following the car when it went into the parking garage of the Metropolis condominium complex on Liberty Street. Taylor Cowley lived in the Metropolis apartment complex.

Mark drove back to Broder's house and made more inquiries about Taylor Cowley. He discovered that Cowley had changed his address two days ago and that he had bought his Mercedes from Logan Broder for seventy thousand dollars four days ago. Andrew Broder must have forced Logan to give his car to Taylor Cowley.

He needed to talk to Cowley's parents and find out if his behavior had changed after his return.

Sam Curtis still hadn't appeared when Mark went home at five o'clock.

2

Taylor Cowley's mother lived in a three-bedroom house in Fort Worth, and judging by the furniture, she was not well-off enough to lend her son seventy grand to buy a car. Her name was Cindy Cowley. She was a short plump woman with a pleasant face and curly auburn hair.

"I'd like to ask you a few questions about your son, Taylor," Mark said.

Cindy frowned. "Is he okay? Did something happen to him?"

"No. As far as I know, he's fine."

Cindy's face brightened.

"Taylor was missing from December twenty-ninth to January third, wasn't he?"

"Yes, he was."

"Did Taylor tell you where he'd been?"

"Yes. He said he was at his friend's place."

"What was he doing there?"

"He said they hung out."

"Did he tell you the friend's name?"

"No. I asked him for the name a dozen times, but he kept saying it didn't matter."

"Was it a guy or a girl?"

"He said it was a guy."

"Did he explain why he didn't contact you while he stayed at his friend's place?"

"He left his phone at home the day he went missing because it was broken. I asked him why he didn't use his friend's phone, and he said his friend didn't have a phone."

It sounded implausible; everyone had a cellphone these days.

"How did Taylor look when he came back? Did he have any bruises or wounds? Was there blood on his clothes?"

"I didn't see any bruises on his face or arms. And there was no blood on his clothes. By the way, he wore different clothes from those he had on when he went missing."

Maybe Taylor had been on a drug or alcohol—or drug *and* alcohol—binge? That would explain why he hadn't called his mother.

"Did Taylor have a job at the time of his disappearance?"

"Yes."

"Did he go to work while he stayed at his friend's?"

"No, he didn't. He said he quit."

"Why did he quit?"

"He said he found a better job."

"Did he ever disappear for several days before this incident?"

Cindy shook her head. "No. This was the first time. Honestly, I was shocked."

"Did he live with you at the time of his disappearance?"

"Yes, he did. He couldn't afford his own apartment."

"Does he still live with you?"

"No, he got his own place. I guess he's making good money at his new job."

"Do you know where he works?"

"He says he works for a real estate agency in Dallas, but he never told me its name."

"When did he move out?"

"The day he returned home. And he didn't take any of his things with him."

"So he came back, you talked to him, and then he left?"

"Yes."

"Do you know his address?"

"No, he never told me his address. All I know is he lives in an apartment in Dallas."

It was obvious that Taylor didn't want his mother to visit him.

"Does Taylor use drugs?"

"I know he didn't use drugs before he went missing, but I don't know about now."

"Did you notice any personality changes in Taylor after he came back?"

Cindy nodded. "We were very close before he went missing, but not anymore. He never comes to see me, he doesn't call or text and he doesn't answer my calls or texts. And it upsets me very much. He can't find five minutes to call his mother?" She sighed heavily.

"When was the last time you spoke to him?"

"January third."

"Where is Taylor's father?"

Cindy made a sour face at the mention of Taylor's dad, which Mark interpreted as a sign that she disliked him.

"He lives in San Antonio."

"Does Taylor talk to him?"

"I don't think so. They're not close."

"Is his father wealthy?"

"No. He's a mechanical engineer."

So it wasn't Taylor's father who had provided the money to buy the Mercedes.

"What do you do for a living?"

"I'm an accountant. Is Taylor under investigation? Did he do something illegal?"

"No, your son is not under investigation."

"Do you know if he sells drugs?"

"As far as I know, he doesn't. Did Taylor ever mention the name Andrew Broder?"

Cindy thought for a long moment and then said, "No, he didn't. Who is it?"

"He's an entrepreneur. Does Taylor speak any foreign languages?"

"He speaks a little Spanish, and that's it. Do you know Taylor's address?"

"No."

The guy had moved out of his mother's house and quit his job. He used to be poor, and now he owned a luxury car and lived in a luxury condominium complex (the price range for two-bedroom Metropolis condos was from six hundred fifty thousand to two million eight hundred thousand). These were drastic changes, weren't they?

And he didn't want to see or talk to his mother, with whom he used to be very close.

Either Sam or Jeff had swapped bodies with Taylor Cowley, Mark was sure of it now.

He needed to kidnap Cowley and interrogate him until he confessed to body switching.

Could he pull off the kidnapping alone? Cowley didn't have bodyguards, so Mark supposed he could.

He could ambush Cowley in a parking garage and force him into the trunk of his car. Abducting Cowley from his apartment would be a riskier proposition because he might call for help on the way to the car.

TIM KIZER

Chapter 47

1

At nine-thirty p.m. Mark plugged the flash drive sent by Aguero into his laptop and played Jeff's confession video. Joan watched it together with him.

In the video, Jeff sat in a chair at a table in what appeared to be a motel room. Perhaps it was the room where his body had been found. He looked and sounded sincere.

When the video was over, Joan said, "I'm glad he's dead."

As Mark lay in bed that night, he tried to figure out a way to plant the knife used to kill Helen in the Phillipses' house. Around half past midnight an idea came to him, which he decided to try.

He gave a copy of Jeff's confession video to Edward Phillips's lawyer on Tuesday. After work, Mark went to the Phillipses' house and told Emily he had important information for her.

"I'm sorry about your husband," he said when they went into the living room.

"Thank you."

"Did Detective Aguero tell you about the video Jeff had sent him?"

"Yes, he did."

"Have you seen it?"

"Yes."

"You must be in shock."

Emily nodded.

She seemed calm, and Mark wondered if it was just a façade.

"Your son was sentenced to death for one of Jeff's crimes, wasn't he?"

"Yes."

"I hope Jeff's confession will help your son regain his freedom."

"They must release him. He's innocent."

"I gave a copy of Jeff's confession video to Edward's lawyer today."

"Thank you. Do you know Edward?"

"Yes."

"I'm going to get him a new lawyer."

"That's a great idea. Do you mind if I do a quick search of Jeff's study?"

"Why?"

"I think there might be evidence of Jeff's crimes there."

"The police have already searched it. They didn't find anything."

"Did you search the study after Jeff left for Houston?"

"No."

"Maybe Jeff hid the evidence before the search and then brought it back to the study."

"Why would he do that?"

"Because he wanted to help Edward. Let's do it together."

"Just the study?"

"Yes. Look, Emily, Edward will have a much better chance of being released if there's evidence that Jeff murdered that girl."

Emily nodded. "Okay. Let's do it."

There were two walls lined with bookcases and a double-pedestal desk in the study.

"You search the bookcases and I'll search the desk," Mark said, walking to the desk.

"What are we looking for?"

"Something odd, something you've never seen here before. Put these on, please." He pulled a pair of latex gloves from his pocket and gave them to Emily. Then he took out another pair of gloves and put them on.

"Did Jeff speak any foreign languages?" Mark said as he opened the top left drawer.

"Yes, he spoke French and a little Spanish."

Busy searching a bookcase, Emily wasn't looking at him.

Mark opened the bottom right drawer, took the plastic bag with the knife from his jacket pocket, and placed it in the drawer.

"Does Edward speak any foreign languages?" he asked, rifling through the top left drawer.

"He speaks a little French."

Mark shut the top left drawer and opened the one below it.

"I don't see anything odd in here." Emily closed the bookcase doors.

"Search the next one."

Mark shut the middle left drawer, pretended to search the bottom right drawer, and then said, "Emily, come here. I think I found something."

"What is it?" Emily walked up to the desk and looked in the bottom right drawer.

"Have you seen this knife before?" Mark pointed at the knife. "I found it in the back of the drawer."

"No, I haven't. Is it blood?"

Mark picked up the knife and pretended to examine it. "I think it is. It could be the murder weapon."

He put the knife on the desk, took off his gloves, and said, "I'm going to call Detective Aguero."

He called Aguero and told him that he and Emily Phillips had found a possible murder weapon in Jeff's desk.

"Can you ask the Carrollton PD to send someone to pick it up?" he said.

"Okay, I'll give them a call," Aguero said. "Don't go anywhere."

Forty minutes later, Homicide Detective Brady Strout of the Carrollton Police Department came and picked up the knife.

AN EVIL MIND

TIM KIZER

Chapter 48

1

Mark punched in the passcode he had obtained from the building manager's office and, when the gate opened, drove his rental Dodge Charger into the garage. It was seven-fifteen in the morning. He parked in the visitor area, got out of the car, and started looking for Taylor Cowley's Mercedes. He took measures to avoid being identified: he wore sunglasses and a felt hat to hide his face from surveillance cameras, and his car had fake license plates.

He found the Mercedes on the second level, in slot 215. He got in his Charger and moved it to an unoccupied spot five spaces from Cowley's car.

Was it Jeff or Sam who had swapped bodies with Cowley?

Jeff would certainly have loved to be young again, so the odds were good it was him.

It was ten-thirty when Cowley entered the garage. He wore black jeans and a black leather jacket. Mark got out of his car, withdrew his badge, and walked over to Cowley's Mercedes. As Cowley neared his vehicle, Mark held out his badge and said, "Detective Bradbury, Garland PD. Are you Taylor Cowley?"

"Yes," Cowley said warily.

"You're under arrest." He pulled out a pair of handcuffs.

"For what?"

Mark grabbed Cowley's right arm and snapped a cuff on his wrist. "They'll explain the charges at the station." Mark pulled Taylor's arms behind his back and cuffed the other wrist.

"I didn't do anything," Cowley pleaded.

"If you're innocent, you have nothing to worry about."

"Can I call my parents?"

AN EVIL MIND

"You can call from the station." Mark patted Cowley down, took the phone from his jeans pocket, then grasped his arm and led him to his Charger.

"I didn't do anything wrong."

Mark opened the front passenger door and said, "Get in."

He had a Taser in his coat pocket, which he was going to use on Cowley if he resisted or tried to escape from the car.

"What kind of crime do you think I committed?" Cowley got in the Charger. "Is it something serious?"

"No." Mark shut the door.

As he went to the driver's door, he removed the battery from Cowley's phone.

"Relax, son," Mark said when they pulled out of the parking spot. "Just tell the truth, and you'll be fine."

2

Cowley said little on the way to Mark's parents' lake house. To assuage his fears, Mark told him that the crime he was accused of was a misdemeanor, not a felony. When Mark pushed the Open button on the garage door remote, Cowley said, "You said we were going to the police station."

"I need to show you something first."

Mark drove into the garage, pressed the Close button on the remote, and got out of the car.

"Where are we?" Cowley asked.

"Patience, Taylor."

Mark opened the front passenger door. "Get out."

A shadow of fear flitted across Cowley's face.

"What do you want to show me?" he asked. "Whose house is this?"

"There's something in the living room you have to see."

"Take me to the police station."

Mark grabbed Cowley by the arm and pulled him out of the car.

"Go." He pointed toward the door leading into the house. He drew his SIG Sauer to make Cowley more cooperative.

They entered the house and went into the living room.

"Are you really a cop?" Cowley asked in a trembling voice.

"Yes, I am."

"What do you want from me?"

Mark slipped the gun into the holster. "Sit down on the couch."

Cowley did as told, and Mark bound his feet with duct tape.

"I'm going to ask you a few questions," Mark said. "If you don't answer them truthfully, I'll hurt you."

Cowley's forehead was beaded with sweat.

"You're not a cop. Cops don't kidnap people."

"I'm doing this for myself, not the police department."

"Is this your house?"

"What are your parents' names?"

"Cindy and Kevin Cowley."

Mark took a folded sheet of paper from his pocket, unfolded it, and put it in Cowley's lap. Printed on the sheet was a passage from a French fairy tale called The Hunchback and His Two Brothers. The text was in French.

"Tell me what this says."

Cowley lowered his eyes to the sheet. "Once upon a time there was a king who had three sons. Two of whom were fine, handsome young men, and the third one was a hunchback whose name was Alain. His father did not love him, but sent him off to the kitchen with the cooks while his two older brothers ate with him at his own table and went with him everywhere. One day the old king sent for his three sons and said to them—"

"That's enough." Mark grabbed the sheet and put it back in his pocket.

AN EVIL MIND

Apparently, Jeff (or Sam) hadn't yet figured out why he had been kidnapped.

"Jeff, is it you?" Mark smiled. "Or is it Sam?"

"What do you mean?"

"I know everything. I know about the ritual. And I know that one of you switched bodies with Andrew Broder."

"What are you talking about?"

"Come on, Jeff. Stop wasting my time."

"My name's not Jeff. My name's Taylor. You got the wrong guy."

"I know it's you, Jeff. You're not going anywhere until you admit that you're Jeff."

"I'm Taylor."

"No, you're not."

"Yes, I am. Check my driver's license."

"You're not Taylor Cowley. Taylor Cowley doesn't speak French."

Cowley froze. He must have realized he had been tricked.

"You switched bodies with Taylor Cowley and Andrew Broder on January first," Mark said. "Are you Jeff or Sam?"

Cowley sighed, and made no reply.

"If you don't tell me who you are, I'll kill you. Do you want to die?"

Cowley shook his head. "No, I don't," he said hoarsely.

"Then tell me who you are."

Mark took out the Taser and pressed it against Cowley's thigh.

Cowley bit his lip and shifted on the couch. "I'm Logan Broder."

"Andrew Broder's son?"

"Yes."

Why would Logan Broder swap bodies with Taylor Cowley? And why would Sam and Jeff help him do it?

"This is bullshit."

"No, it's not bullshit. I'm Logan Broder."

"Why did you switch bodies with Taylor Cowley?"

"I had leukemia. My dad paid Taylor a million dollars to trade bodies with me. They transferred my consciousness to his body and his consciousness to mine."

The million dollars part must be a lie. No doubt Sam and Jeff had forced Taylor Cowley to switch bodies with Logan Broder.

Mark pulled Jeff Phillips's picture from his pocket and showed it to Cowley. "Is this the man who helped you switch bodies with Taylor?"

"Yes. It was two guys, him and Jake."

Mark took out Sam Curtis's photo. "Is this Jake?"

"Yes. How did you find out about this?"

"What's Jake's last name?"

"I don't know. My dad must know it."

"What's Jake's partner's name?"

"Peter."

"Did your father pay Jake and Peter?"

"Yes. He paid them twenty million dollars."

"Twenty million?"

"Yes."

"How did your father find Jake and Peter?"

"Jake came to my dad and said that he could transfer my consciousness to another body."

Was Logan Broder Sam and Jeff's first client?

"Did he explain how he was going to do it?"

"He has a special machine that can transfer consciousness from one body to another."

Sam Curtis must have decided that Andrew Broder wouldn't believe him if he said he was going to use magic.

"Did the transfer take place on January first?"

"Yes."

"What did Jake and Peter do during the transfer?"

"I didn't see what they did during the procedure. I was asleep. Jake gave me sleeping pills before the procedure."

"Where did the procedure take place?"

"In Jake's company's office. It's somewhere in Dallas."

"Jake has a company?"

"Yes. It's called New Horizons."

"Do you have its phone number?"

"No."

"Do you have Jake's or Peter's number?"

Taylor shook his head. "My dad must have their numbers."

"What happened to Taylor Cowley?"

They must have killed him. They couldn't have let him live because if they did he would have gone to the police.

"I don't know."

"Don't lie to me, Logan. You know what happened to him. Is he dead?"

"I told you I don't know. They said they'd give Taylor a new identity."

Mark googled "Logan Broder found dead" on his phone and got no hits.

"Where did you live before the switch?" he asked.

"I lived in the same building I live now but in a different apartment. Apartment twelve-oh-seven."

"Who lives there now?"

"No one."

"Does your mother know about the body switch?"

"No."

Was Cowley telling the truth?

Mark knew nothing about Logan Broder, so it was going to be difficult to verify that it was Logan who currently occupied Taylor Cowley's body.

"Who else was in the office besides you, Jake, and Peter?" Mark said.

"My dad, my dad's driver, and the guy who was going to trade bodies with another client later that night."

"Do you know this guy's name?"

It must be the man Jeff had switched bodies with.

"No. He was asleep the whole time."

"How old did he look?"

"Early twenties."

"Would you recognize him if you saw him again?"

"I don't think so."

Mark paced the room for a minute, trying to figure out how to verify that Cowley was Logan Broder, and then said, "When did you get your driver's license?"

"Do you mean me or Taylor?"

"You."

"Four years ago. Why?"

"Where did you take the behind-the-wheel test?"

"I took it twice. The first time was in Dallas and the second in Garland."

"How old are you?"

"Twenty."

"Have you gotten any traffic tickets?"

"I got a few speeding tickets, a bunch of parking tickets. I got a ticket for running a red light once."

"When was that?"

"Last March."

"When did you get your latest speeding ticket?"

"Last September."

"I'm going to verify this information, and if it doesn't check out, you'll be in big trouble."

"It will check out."

"Do you go to college?"

"Yes. Well, I did before the procedure."

"What college did you go to?"

"University of Texas at Dallas."

Mark opened the Internet browser, found the portal login page of the University of Texas at Dallas, showed it to Cowley, and said, "Give me your username and password."

Neither Jeff nor Sam could know the username and password for Logan Broder's student account.

Cowley told him his username and password, and Mark entered them.

Logan Broder's student account appeared on the screen.

"Do you believe me now?" Cowley asked.

"Not yet."

Mark called Detective Robert Worster, who worked in the Robbery Unit of the Dallas PD, and asked him to email Logan Broder's DMV driving record to him. He received the record ten minutes later.

Logan Broder had run a red light on March 13 of last year and gotten his latest speeding ticket on September 7 of last year.

The guy was telling the truth; he really was Logan Broder.

"I'm going to let you go." Mark fished the handcuff key out of his pocket. "I want you to keep this meeting between us. If Jake finds out I know who you are, he'll kill you."

"Okay. Please don't tell anyone about the switch."

"I won't."

Mark unlocked and removed the handcuffs.

Should he tell Cindy Cowley what had happened to her son?

Would Cindy believe him?

He didn't think so.

"Don't say anything to your father."

"Okay."

Mark cut the duct tape and stripped it off Cowley's legs.

"Can you take me home?" Cowley asked.

"Yeah."

They went to the garage, and when Mark got in the car, he pounded his fist on the steering wheel and emitted a growl.

He'd thought he'd found Sam and Jeff, and it turned out he'd been wrong.

He might have lost these bastards forever.

"What's wrong?" Cowley asked, looking at him worriedly.

"Nothing."

AN EVIL MIND

Chapter 49

1

Andrew Broder had a tanned, plain-featured face and a receding hairline. He was fifty-three but looked younger. He was a highly educated man: his biography on Prism Capital's website said that he'd earned his BA from the University of Texas at Austin and his MBA from the Wharton School of the University of Pennsylvania. Mark had headed to Prism Capital's headquarters right after he dropped Taylor Cowley off at the Metropolis condominium complex.

"I'd like to ask you a few questions about your son, Logan," Mark said.

"All right," Broder replied.

Did Broder suspect that Taylor Cowley had been forced to swap bodies with his son?

"Do you know where I can find Logan?"

"Why are you looking for him?"

"He's a person of interest in a robbery case."

"When did this robbery take place?"

"Two days ago."

"I don't know where he is."

"When was the last time you saw him?"

"January first."

"When was the last time you spoke to him?"

"January first."

"Do you know where he could be?"

Broder shook his head. "No."

"So you haven't heard from Logan since January first?"

"That's right."

"Are you worried?"

"About what?"

"About Logan. It's been nine days since you last heard from him. He has leukemia, doesn't he?"

Broder leaned forward and said, "Detective, I don't know where Logan is. Do you have any other questions?"

"Yes, I do. Do you know a man named Taylor Cowley?"

"Logan has a friend by that name."

Mark took out Taylor Cowley's photo and laid it on the desk. "Is it him?"

Broder looked at the photo and nodded. "Yes."

"He bought a car from your son for seventy thousand dollars a few days ago. Do you know where he got the money?"

"No, I don't."

"I think he stole it."

Broder said nothing.

"Mister Broder, I know that your son's consciousness was transferred to Taylor Cowley's body."

"I don't know what you're talking about."

"I talked to your son. He told me about New Horizons. He said you paid them twenty million dollars to transfer his consciousness to Taylor Cowley's body."

Broder frowned. "When did you talk to him?"

"This morning."

Broder picked up his cellphone and dialed a number.

Was he calling his lawyer?

Holding the phone to his ear, Broder said, "Can you leave me alone for a minute, Detective?"

Mark stepped out of the room and took a seat in the reception area. About two minutes later, Broder opened the door and asked him to come in.

"Yes, it's true," Broder said. "Logan's consciousness was transferred to Taylor Cowley's body. What do you want from me?"

"I want you to help me find Jake and Peter."

"I don't know where they are."

"When was the last time you spoke to Jake or Peter?"

"January first."

"What are their last names?"

AN EVIL MIND

"Jake's last name is Ford, and I don't remember Peter's last name."

"Did Jake give you his business card?"

"Yes."

"Can I see it?"

"I left it at home."

"Do you have his phone number?"

"Why do you want to find them?"

"They're criminals."

"What did they do?"

"They kidnapped Taylor Cowley."

"Do you have any proof that they kidnapped him?"

"Do you think Taylor switched bodies with your son voluntarily?"

"He did it for money. Jake told me they paid him a million dollars."

"He lied. They forced Taylor to switch bodies with your son."

"I was not aware of that."

Would Andrew Broder have let Logan take Taylor Cowley's body if he had known that Cowley was being forced to trade bodies with his son?

Being a loving father, he probably would.

"Did you talk to Taylor before or after the switch?"

"No."

"I need you to give me Jake's and Peter's phone numbers and their company's address."

Broder picked up his phone, tapped the screen several times, and then told Mark "Jake's" number and New Horizons' address. "Peter didn't give me his number," he said.

"Later I might need you to call Jake and ask him to meet with you," Mark said. "Can you do that?"

"I'll think about it."

"Do you have Jake's email address?"

"Yes."

Broder told him the email address.

"How did you pay them the twenty million?"

"I wired the money to their bank account."

"I need the name of the bank and the account number."

"What do you need this information for?"

"I need it to track down Jake and Peter."

Broder leaned back in his chair and said, "You haven't given me any proof that Jake and Peter kidnapped Taylor Cowley."

"Do you still think that Taylor switched bodies with Logan voluntarily?"

"I think it's possible. A million dollars is a lot of money."

"Mister Broder, I need you to tell me the name of New Horizons' bank and their account number."

"Let me get back to you on this."

"I need this information now."

"I don't have it at hand."

"How long is it going to take you to find it?"

"I don't know for sure."

It was obvious to Mark that Broder had no intention of giving him the details of New Horizons' bank account.

Broder looked at his watch. "I'm sorry, Detective. I have to go. Can we talk some other time?"

"Look, Mister Broder, Jake and Peter murdered Taylor Cowley after the switch. They've killed at least four people, and they will keep killing. We have to stop them as soon as possible. Every day, every hour counts."

"I'm sorry. I have to go."

"I'm not after you, Mister Broder. I'm after New Horizons. Give me their bank account number."

"I said I'll get back to you on this."

"Do you realize you could be charged with obstruction of justice?"

"Let's meet next week."

AN EVIL MIND

Mark pulled out his card and gave it to Broder. "Here's my number. Call me when you change your mind."

"Sure."

"One last thing. Don't tell anyone about this conversation."

Chapter 50

1

He should check Sam's personal bank account first: they might have used one of them to receive payment from Broder. The wire must have been sent on January second or shortly thereafter.

He should obtain a search warrant for Andrew Broder's bank records. The warrant would have to cover Broder's business bank accounts, too, because the money might have been wired from one of them.

If Broder had wired the money from an offshore account, it might be weeks if not months before he found New Horizons' bank account.

On the way to New Horizons' office, Mark realized that none of the cases he was investigating could be used to obtain a search warrant for Andrew Broder's bank records.

Emily Phillips might know New Horizons' bank account number. He should try to get her to tell it to him.

New Horizons' office was located in a nondescript four-story office building in the Lake Highlands area of Dallas. It was closed when Mark arrived. He went to the building manager's office, showed his badge, and asked for the name of the person who had signed New Horizons' lease.

"Just a minute," the clerk said, and disappeared into the manager's office. She came out less than half a minute later, accompanied by her boss, a middle-aged woman with red hair.

The manager looked at Mark's badge and said to the clerk, "It's all right, Alicia, you can give him the name."

Alicia opened New Horizons' file and told Mark that the lease had been signed by Jonathan Medlock. It must be an alias of either Sam or Jeff.

"Do they pay rent by check?" Mark asked.

"No. Money order."

Were Sam and Jeff going to use this office the next time they performed the ritual for money?

It was possible.

The next full moon was on the night of January 30, twenty days from today.

Mark went to Dallas PD headquarters and requested geolocation information for the number Broder had used to contact Sam Curtis. The number was the disposable kind. The cellphone company said that the phone had been off since January 4. Its last recorded location was the city of Downey, California.

Had Sam and Jeff moved to California? If so, it was unlikely they would use their office in Dallas again.

Sam's bank account had received no wire transfers in the last nine days. Mark called Emily Phillips and asked if Jeff had any business bank accounts. She said she didn't know.

2

At two p.m. on Thursday, January 11, as Mark wrote a report on the interview he had conducted earlier, his phone rang.

It was Andrew Broder

"I've given the matter some thought and decided to tell you New Horizons' account number," Broder said.

"Thank you, Mister Broder."

Mark opened a new Word document. "Go ahead."

"You said they murdered Taylor. Did you find his body?"

"No, not yet."

"Then how do you know they killed him?"

"They couldn't have let him live because he saw their faces."

"You said they killed four people. Who are the other three?"

"Jake and Peter kidnapped and forced them to trade bodies with other people. I can't tell you their names."

Mark couldn't tell Broder about the ritual (he was sure Broder would laugh at him if he did), so he had to lie.

"Will my son have to testify in court?"

"No, he won't."

"I want you to give me your word that the government won't call him to testify."

"All right. I give you my word your son won't have to testify."

"I also want you to promise that you won't make public why I paid New Horizons the twenty million."

"Okay. We'll keep this information secret."

"When you find Jake and Peter, don't tell them I helped you."

"I won't."

"The name of the bank is Alliance Bank. It's in the Caymans. The account number is six-two-three-oh-five-six-seven-one-nine-oh-four-two. The Swift Code is ALLBKYKY."

Mark wrote down the information and said, "Can you email me a copy of the wire transfer?"

Broder hesitated, then said, "Okay."

"Thanks for your help, Andrew. Goodbye."

3

Broder had paid the entire twenty million in one transfer, which had been made on January second. The recipient's name was Summit Consulting; its address was 52 North Church Street, Grand Cayman, Cayman Islands.

Because anonymous offshore bank accounts were not allowed anymore, Sam and Jeff had been required to put their names on the application when they opened their account at Cayman Commercial Bank.

Had Sam and Jeff added their new bodies' names to the list of account signatories, individuals authorized to withdraw money from the account and sign checks?

They probably had, but they didn't need to do it because offshore banks allowed their clients to withdraw money via online wire transfers.

Some if not most of the transfers would go to the accounts opened in Sam's and Jeff's new names.

He needed to place the Phillipses' offshore account under surveillance. The Cayman Islands were a foreign country, so he would have to ask the FBI to do it.

Mark faxed a letter to the Dallas FBI office requesting that they place the Phillipses' offshore account under surveillance. In the letter, he wrote that the account belonged to one of the perpetrators of the home invasion that had taken place on November 30 of this year (the robbers had made off with four hundred thousand dollars in cash and jewelry). At seven o'clock, Mark called Broder and told him that the FBI might question him about the money he had paid to New Horizons.

"Don't tell them we talked about New Horizons," Mark said. "Don't mention my name at all."

"All right."

"Don't tell them that your son's consciousness was transferred to Taylor Cowley's body." He paused. "I'm the only cop who knows that."

"What can I tell them?"

"Tell them that New Horizons promised to cure your son and that the treatment didn't work."

"Does anyone else besides us know that we talked about New Horizons?"

"No."

Chapter 51

1

If Broder told Sam and Jeff that one of his friends wanted to use their services, would they agree to meet with that friend?

Most likely, they would.

Would only one of them come or would they come together? He had to assume that they'd come together and that they'd be armed.

Could he handle two armed men alone? It would be nice to have help, but he had no one to turn to for assistance because he was going to kill these bastards not arrest them.

Where should they meet?

His parents' lake house would be a perfect place, but unfortunately it didn't look like a rich man's dwelling. They might sense something was fishy.

What about New Horizons' office in Dallas?

He could interrogate them right in their office and kill them afterwards. He'd wear disguise and use a gun silencer. They should meet on a Saturday, when there were few people in the building.

What if they didn't admit that they were Jeff and Sam?

He didn't really need their admission. Whoever came to the meeting must be Jeff and Sam.

2

"What can I do for you?" Broder said.

"I need you to send Jake Ford an email saying that one of your friends wants to use their services and is willing to pay them twenty million dollars."

Broder shook his head. "I can't do that."

"Why?"

Broder looked toward the window, beyond which the high-rise across the street sparkled in the morning sunlight. "I've already done a lot for you, haven't I?"

"Yes, you have."

"You said they're killers. I'd rather not mess with killers."

"You're not messing with them. I am."

"They'll know I helped you."

"I'll make sure they don't hurt you."

"How?"

"I can't tell you that."

Broder took a sip of coffee from his cup and said, "I can't help you unless I'm sure they're not going to murder me or my family."

Mark couldn't blame Broder for being concerned about his and his family's safety. He'd be worried be, too, if he were in Broder's shoes.

"Okay, I'll tell you. They're not going to hurt you or your family because they won't be alive after I meet them."

Broder started at him for a long moment, and then said, "Are you going to kill them?"

"They won't be alive after I meet them, that's all you need to know, Andrew."

Broder nodded slowly. "All right. I'll do it."

"Tell them that your friend's daughter has cerebral palsy."

"Got it."

Broder turned to his laptop, opened his email, and typed a message, which read: "Dear Jake, a friend of mine would like to use your services. His daughter has cerebral palsy. He'll pay 20 million. I'm looking forward to hearing from you."

After Broder sent the email, Mark said, "Call me when they reply."

"Okay."

"Now I need you to call Jake and leave a message saying the same thing as the email."

Broder took his phone. "All right."

He dialed "Jake's" number. His call went straight to voice mail, and he left a message.

3

At two-thirty in the afternoon, Agent Aaron Ward of the Dallas FBI office called Mark and said that he had a couple of questions about his request for assistance.

"How long do you want this offshore account to be monitored?"

"Until we capture its owner."

"Have these people been involved in any other crimes?"

"Most likely they have."

"Well, that's all for now, Detective. I'll keep you posted."

AN EVIL MIND

Chapter 52

1

Agent Ward called again a week later, on January 19. He told Mark that there were two signatories on the Phillipses' account: Samuel Curtis and Jeffrey Phillips.

"They deposited a little over two million dollars on December fourteenth. On January fourth they received twenty million dollars from Andrew Broder. Do you have any idea what Broder paid them that money for?"

"No, I don't. I'd appreciate it if you didn't question Mister Broder until we got Curtis."

"What about Phillips?"

"Jeff Phillips is dead."

They had deposited a little over two million in December. They must have made that money using the ritual.

"Have they transferred any money from this account to an American bank?" Mark asked.

"No."

"Have they made any withdrawals in the last three weeks?"

"No."

2

Mark took a fake moustache from the box (it was similar to the moustache worn by Tom Selleck in Magnum, P.I. and was made of human hair) and pressed it to his upper lip, looking in the mirror. He was recognizable, but he didn't think that Sam Curtis, who'd seen him only twice, would be able to recognize him.

It was 8:32 p.m. on Sunday, January 21.

Sam Curtis still hadn't replied to Broder, and his burner phone was still off.

Mark put the moustache in the box and sat back, his swivel chair creaking under him.

The next full moon was nine days away. The sun would set around seven in the evening on January 30. He was going to arrive at New Horizons' office at six-thirty p.m.

As Mark opened the top desk drawer, his phone rang. It was Broder.

"Jake has replied to my email," Broder said. "He wants to know when my friend can meet him."

"Tell Jake your friend wants to meet him this Saturday at one p.m. in their office in Dallas."

"Okay. What's my friend's name?"

"George… Westman. George Westman."

"Got it."

"Thank you very much, Andrew."

When Mark hung up, he breathed a sigh of relief.

He got them. He got these bastards.

In six days Helen would be avenged.

Forty-five minutes later, Broder called again and said that "Jake" had agreed to meet "his friend" this Saturday at one p.m. in New Horizons' office in Dallas.

"He's asking for your phone number," Broder said.

Mark gave Broder the number of the disposable phone he'd bought eight days earlier.

AN EVIL MIND

Chapter 53

1

Mark opened the glove box of his rental Mercedes S550 and retrieved the SIG Sauer, which had a silencer on it. He checked the magazine, it was full, put the pistol in his coat pocket, and then looked at himself in the rearview mirror. His moustache was still in place. He slipped on his sunglasses, grabbed his felt hat, and got out of the car.

It was a quarter to one in the afternoon. There were less than a dozen cars in the parking lot; Mark wondered which one of them belonged to Sam and Jeff.

The wind blew around him, flapping his coat, as he walked to the office building. Mark wore his best suit and dress shoes; he'd left his cheap Seiko watch in the car.

Sam Curtis, or maybe it was Jeff Phillips, had phoned him two days ago to confirm the meeting. Half an hour ago, Mark had called Sam and told him that he was on his way.

Mark entered the building, got in the elevator, and rode up to the third floor.

The hallway was as quiet as a tomb. Mark reached New Horizons' office, drew a deep breath, then opened the door and went in.

There were two people in the room: Sam Curtis and a dark-haired man in his mid-twenties. Mark fought the urge to pull out his gun from and shoot Curtis on the spot.

He was glad he didn't have to interrogate anyone to find out which one of the two was Sam Curtis.

The other guy must be Jeff Phillips.

"My name's George Westman," Mark said. "I'm here to see Jake Ford."

"I'm Jake Ford." Sam stood up and shook Mark's hand. "How are you doing, Mister Westman?"

"I'm fine." Mark took off his leather gloves and pocketed them. "How are you?"

Sam put a hand on his partner's back and said, "This is our technician David Fletcher."

"Nice to meet you, Mister Westman." Fletcher shook Mark's hand.

Sam opened the door on the left side of the room. "Please come in."

He must shoot them right now. He didn't need to verify that David Fletcher was Jeff Phillips: the guy *had to* be Jeff Phillips.

He remembered the phrase Tuco said in The Good, the Bad and the Ugly when he shot the one-armed man who came to kill him while he was sitting in a bubble bath: "When you have to shoot, shoot. Don't talk."

They entered the second room. Mark and Sam sat down on the sofa, and Fletcher took a seat behind a desk.

Although Mark was about to kill two people, he felt very calm.

"I'm pleased to tell you that we can help your daughter, Mister Westman," Sam said.

"I'm glad to hear that." Mark reached into his coat pocket, pulled out the pistol, and got up. "Put your hands behind your head, both of you."

Sam frowned. "What's going on?"

Fletcher's right hand disappeared under the desk and emerged moments later holding a pistol. Mark pointed his SIG Sauer at Fletcher and squeezed the trigger twice. The shots were no louder than a handclap. The bullets hit Fletcher in the chest. He dropped the gun, his body went limp, and his head fell forward.

"What the fuck?" Sam shouted, his face twisted in horror. "Why the fuck did you do that?"

"Shut up!"

Sam clasped his hands behind his head. "Don't kill me, man," he whined. "What do you want? Please don't kill me."

AN EVIL MIND

"Do you remember a girl named Helen? You murdered her about a year ago."

"What are you talking about?"

"She was my daughter."

"I didn't murder anyone. Please listen to me."

"Burn in hell, Edward."

"I didn't—"

Before Sam could finish, Mark shot him in the head. Blood splattered on the sofa and the wall behind it. It was a beautiful sight. The bastard who'd murdered his daughter was dead. The fog of pain, anger, and frustration that he'd been living in for the last few months had cleared.

Mark put on his gloves, collected Sam's and Jeff's phones and wallets (Jeff's driver's license was in the name of Jeremy Farney), and left the office.

2

The murders of Sam Curtis and Jeremy Farney were never solved.

In February, Mark learned that Jeff Phillips's name had been removed from the list of signatories of the Phillipses' offshore bank account and Jeremy Farney's name had been added to it.

On February 20, Joan Hinton learned that she was pregnant. She gave birth to a boy on November 7.

On July 10, the Texas Court of Criminal Appeals overturned Edward Phillips's conviction. The Dallas County District Attorney decided not to retry him.

The twenty-two million dollars in the offshore account was inherited by the parents of Sam Curtis and Jeremy Farney.

Mark Hinton and Edward Phillips remain friends to this day.

Edward still has nightmares about the death row block.

THE END

TIM KIZER

A sample chapter from

THE VANISHED

On May 6, five-year-old Annie Miller goes missing in a park. On May 7, her father, David Miller, fails a lie detector test. On May 9, during a hypnosis session, David confesses to murdering his daughter and gives the police the location of the knife he used to kill her. The knife has traces of Annie's blood and David's fingerprints all over it.

Two weeks later, a man named Ben calls David and tells him Annie's alive. Ben is willing to let the girl go, but first David has to do something for him—something that would land David in prison for the rest of his life.

Chapter 1

1

"Annie!" David Miller took off his sunglasses and looked up and down the drive aisle.

He was in a great mood, but that was about to change. Today was the day he would report his daughter missing. And in seventy-two hours he would confess to killing her.

"Annie!"

Annie wasn't in the second aisle, either.

He crossed the parking lot and stepped onto the grass, his eyes sweeping the park. "Annie! Annie!" he shouted at the top of his lungs.

His daughter was nowhere in sight. A stab of fear pierced him.

Where was she?

Perhaps she had wandered off after a stray cat or a butterfly or a squirrel.

THE VANISHED

In the back of his mind, a voice whispered: Annie's been kidnapped, and you'll never see her again.

David supposed it was normal. He was not in a panic. He was sure most, if not all, parents had thoughts like these when they lost sight of their young children in a public place.

Absorbed in thought, he walked over to the path running parallel to the parking lot.

How long had Annie been out of his sight before he got out of the car?

She had stepped out of the car when he switched off the engine. After he pulled the key from the ignition, he checked his cellphone for messages. Then he opened the door, dropped the phone on the floor, picked it up, and got out of the car.

About twenty seconds. How far could she have gone in twenty seconds? Fifteen, maybe twenty yards.

He had spent about twenty seconds checking the parking lot aisles, so she could be as far as forty yards from his car.

David wiped the sweat from his brow with his hand. His anxiety grew by the second.

She was probably not too far away. She couldn't hear him because she was having a convulsive seizure. What if she had been bitten by a snake? Were there poisonous snakes in Ardmore Park?

To find a child one had to think like a child. Where would he go if he were Annie?

The playground. That was her favorite place in the park.

David rushed to the playground and searched it thoroughly, checking every structure and looking into every slide tube. When he was finished, his head throbbed with panic.

Standing at the edge of the playground, he yelled his daughter's name twice.

She's been kidnapped. She's been kidnapped. She's been kidnapped.

The dreadful thought raced through his mind over and over.

David ran over to the pavilion and walked through it from end to end, scanning the tables and the floor. Annie wasn't there. Calling his daughter's name, he circled the pavilion.

No Annie.

His stomach churned with sickness.

David went to the pond, which was near the pavilion, and didn't find Annie there, either. As he stood wondering where Annie could be, he saw a woman in pink leggings and a white T-shirt twenty yards away, who was strolling along the path, watching her Maltese playing on the grass. Cursing himself for not doing it earlier, David pulled his wallet from his jeans pocket, extracted Annie's photo from it, and approached the woman.

"Excuse me, have you seen this girl?" David showed Annie's picture to the woman. "She's wearing a white dress with strawberries on it. Red strawberries."

The woman studied the photo for a few seconds, and said, "No, I haven't seen her. What happened? Is she your daughter?"

David nodded. "Yes. I… I can't find her."

"Oh my God! I'm sorry. I hope you find her."

"Thank you."

David slowly turned full circle, surveying the park.

He would have been so happy to spot a white dress with strawberries on it. He would have been ecstatic.

Maybe she was playing hide-and-seek with him?

It was possible. Annie liked to play hide-and-seek. She had never played hide-and-seek with him in Ardmore Park before, but there was a first time for everything.

He had searched the playground. He had searched the pavilion.

He hadn't checked the restrooms.

David ran to the restrooms and called Annie's name, standing at the entrance to the women's room. Then he asked if there was anyone inside. Having received no response, David went into the room and checked the stalls. No one. He hurried outside and looked behind the building.

Annie was not hiding behind the restrooms.

David showed Annie's photo to four more people—two young women, a middle-aged man, and a boy in his late teens—but none of them had seen his daughter.

As he stood on the walkway, a young unshaven man with long unkempt hair waved to him and said, "Hey, man. I saw that girl."

Dressed in well-worn sneakers, ragged jeans, and a dirty faded sweatshirt, the guy seemed to be going through a rough patch.

"Was she wearing a white dress with strawberries?" David asked as he approached the man.

"Yeah. Four—five years old, brown hair."

"Was it her?" David showed the man Annie's picture.

The man nodded. "Yeah."

"Where did you see her?"

"Here. She was with some chick."

David and his wife had warned Annie not to talk to strangers or get in their cars, but young children were bad at following rules.

Had the woman promised Annie candy?

"Where did they go?"

The man shrugged. "I don't know." He held out his hand. "I'm Eddie."

David shook his hand. "When did you see them?"

"A few minutes ago."

He might have made it all up.

Why would he do that?

Because he has nothing better to do.

"Which direction were they going?" David asked.

"This way." Eddie pointed toward the volleyball court, which was located on the south side of the park.

David peered toward the volleyball court and saw no little children near it.

"Did you see the woman's face?" he asked.

"No. Well, kinda. She had huge sunglasses on."

She wore huge sunglasses so that no one would be able to identify her.

"Thank you," David said.

"No problem, man."

David closed his eyes and pinched the bridge of his nose.

It was time to admit the terrible truth: Annie had been abducted.

He broke into a sweat; his heart dropped into his stomach.

No, she just got lost.

First she had gotten lost, and then she had been kidnapped.

David sprinted to the parking lot. Chances were the kidnapper had already left, but he had to check anyway. He crisscrossed the parking lot several times, shouting Annie's name and looking into cars. Annie was nowhere to be found.

Intending to call his wife, David withdrew his cellphone from his pocket and pressed the Home button. His hand was trembling.

Was it a good idea to tell Carol now that he'd lost Annie?

No, not now. There was still a small chance his daughter would turn up in the next hour or so. He would tell Carol when he got home.

David put the phone back in his pocket. Then he searched the parking lot for surveillance cameras and was disappointed to find none. He hoped he'd seen no cameras because they were inconspicuous and not because they weren't there.

Before he headed home, David combed the wooded part of the park for twenty minutes. The search proved fruitless.

THE VANISHED

2

When he arrived home, David went to his study, switched on his laptop, and printed three pictures of Annie, all of which had been taken in the last month. His heart cramped as he looked at his daughter's photos. As he copied the electronic files of the pictures to a flash drive, he heard Carol's voice: "Where's Annie?"

David turned his face to his wife, who was standing in the doorway, then rose and stepped out from behind his desk. His temples throbbed with pain. "Annie..." His right eye twitched. "She's gone missing."

Carol frowned. "What? Did you say Annie's gone missing?"

She started toward him.

"Yes. I lost her in Ardmore Park."

"Oh. Oh my God! How did you lose her?"

"I'm not sure how it happened. I think someone abducted her." David took her hand in his.

"Oh Jesus! Did you look for her?"

"Yes, I did." His eye twitched again. "I looked everywhere."

Suddenly David remembered telling Carol about the death of their son, Brian, two years ago, and a lump rose in his throat. He had done it over the phone, so he hadn't seen her face when she heard the terrible news.

He felt as if he was going to faint.

"Have you called the police?" Carol's voice was trembling.

"I'm going to the police station now."

They went to the Plano Police Department together. During the initial interview, which took place after he filed a missing child report, David asked the interviewing officer when the police were going to contact the FBI. The officer, whose name was Victor Alvarado, said they would notify the Dallas FBI office shortly. After the interview, Alvarado told David that the Plano PD was going to send a K-9 unit to Ardmore Park to conduct a search. David wanted to say it would be a waste of time because Annie was not in the park, but decided against it. They went to the Millers' house, where Alvarado collected a pair of Annie's sneakers. The officer asked David not to remove anything from Annie's room for the next several days.

When David and Alvarado arrived at Ardmore Park, the K-9 unit was already there. David spotted four police officers canvassing the wooded area. After he showed the K-9 handlers where he had parked when he last visited Ardmore Park, David joined Carol. She had come half an hour earlier and had to leave their car on the street because the parking lot was cordoned off by police cruisers. Her eyes were red and puffy from crying, her mascara smeared all over her face. As they watched the police dogs move around the parking lot, sniffing the air and the ground, David said to Carol, "They're wasting their time. Annie's not here."

Carol said nothing.

Twenty minutes after the search commenced, David began to wonder if the dogs, which had been in the parking lot the whole time, were unable to track Annie's scent. A minute later Alvarado came up to him and asked, "When was the last time your daughter wore those sneakers?"

"Yesterday," David replied.

Alvarado looked at Carol and then back at David. "It appears that she never left the parking lot."

If Annie had never left the parking lot, why hadn't he seen her there?

THE VANISHED

She must have been hiding behind a car. Or maybe she'd been snatched before he started looking for her.

At a quarter past seven the search was called off, and David and Carol went home. As he drove, David thought about how hard it was going to be to find Annie. They had no leads or clues except for the useless—and questionable—information provided by that Eddie fellow.

It would be hard but not impossible. Criminals make mistakes all the time. Annie's abductor was going to slip up at some point. Maybe he or she already had.

David realized that Annie might be dead. Most kidnapped children who were killed were dead within three hours of the abduction, and it was over four hours since Annie's disappearance. Was the kidnapper going to kill Annie?

If his daughter had really been snatched a few seconds after she got out of the car, her abduction had to have been a planned rather than a random act. The kidnapper must have followed him and Annie from their house to the park. David supposed that most planned kidnappings were committed for the sake of ransom. If it was a ransom kidnapping, the perpetrator would try to keep Annie alive at least until his demands were satisfied. And there was a good chance David would get Annie back after he paid the ransom.

THE END OF THE SAMPLE

The Vanished is available now on Amazon.

Manufactured by Amazon.ca
Bolton, ON

42721877R00168